Keely stood in the doorway, covered only by a large white towel.

Then she let the towel drop.

Sweet Lord in heaven. Noah clutched the bathrobe he'd brought her and tried to remember how to breathe. God, he wanted her. And he knew it wouldn't take much to get Keely aroused. He could tell by her shallow breathing, by the way her nipples darkened and puckered, inviting him to linger. Not long ago he'd touched, but he hadn't tasted.

Now he could. Now he could kneel before her and kiss the soft skin of her belly. He could explore lower, parting her auburn curls with his tongue. And he could seek his own release from the hard, grinding pressure building relentlessly within him.

"Noah. The robe?" Keely asked softly.

He glanced at the robe he held, and then at her. His body trembled with the urge to have her, and his mouth grew moist with wanting.

She reached over and took the robe from him. "This is just a sneak pre~~view~~." S~~he~~ sleeves, she tea~~sed~~ all weekend...."

Dear Reader,

This month marks the launch of a supersexy new series—
Harlequin Blaze. If you like love stories with a strong sexual
edge, then this is the line for you! The books are fun and
flirtatious, the heroes are hot and outrageous. Blaze is a
series for the woman who wants *more* in her reading
pleasure....

Leading off the launch is bestselling author
Vicki Lewis Thompson, who brings us a heroine to
remember in the aptly titled #1 *Notorious.* Then popular
Jo Leigh delivers a blazing story in #2 *Going for It,* about
a sex therapist who ought to take her own advice. One of
today's hottest writers, Stephanie Bond, spins a humorous
tale of sexual adventure in #3 *Two Sexy!* Rounding out
the month is talented Julie Elizabeth Leto with the romp
#4 *Exposed,* which exposes the sexy side of San Francisco
and is the first of the SEXY CITY NIGHTS miniseries.

Look for four Blaze books every month at your favorite
bookstore. And check us out online at eHarlequin.com
and tryblaze.com.

Enjoy!

Birgit Davis-Todd
Senior Editor & Editorial Coordinator
Harlequin Blaze

NOTORIOUS
Vicki Lewis Thompson

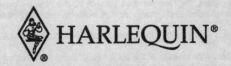

HARLEQUIN®

TORONTO • NEW YORK • LONDON
AMSTERDAM • PARIS • SYDNEY • HAMBURG
STOCKHOLM • ATHENS • TOKYO • MILAN • MADRID
PRAGUE • WARSAW • BUDAPEST • AUCKLAND

For my editor Brenda Chin, fellow trailblazer.

ISBN 0-373-79005-8

NOTORIOUS

A NOTE FROM THE AUTHOR...

The times are definitely changing, and the book you hold in your hand is a prime example. I remember my excitement when I sold my first Harlequin Temptation novel some fifty-plus books ago, because Temptation was part of a revolution in romance fiction. When we, as women, began to claim our own sexuality, many of us wanted a more sensual read. As the song goes, "Girls Just Want To Have Fun."

Well, you haven't seen anything yet! In response to the overwhelming demand from readers wanting books that reflected the needs and lifestyles of women today, Harlequin brings you its newest series—Blaze! And as excited as I was to sell my first Temptation title, I'm even more thrilled to be a part of this new line. I had a great time writing this book, pushing the envelope, pulling out all the stops. Best of all, I imagined you there cheering me on, yelling, "You go, girl." You see, we're all in this revolution together. So read on and let's have some fun.

Vicki Lewis Thompson

P.S. A preview of what's in store appeared in July with a Blaze anthology entitled *Midnight Fantasies*. In that collection, my novella "Mystery Lover" is a lead-in to *Notorious,* so you'll want to find a copy if you haven't already discovered it. Enjoy!

1

GIRLS! GIRLS! GIRLS!

The electronic message on the billboard over the Pussycat Lounge expanded against a background of cascading fireworks, then disintegrated as a new message took shape.

ON STAGE NOW!

Noah Garfield walked past the entrance to the bar, located two streets over from the Las Vegas Strip. Although he had no intention of entering the place, he wouldn't be a normal guy if he didn't spend a moment picturing topless women dancing inside the darkened interior. Sexual adventure seemed more wicked when it was offered at two in the afternoon.

And sexual adventure still made him think of Keely, even after ten years. He could hardly believe so much time had gone by since she'd shocked the good folks of Saguaro Junction, Arizona, by posing for the centerfold of *Macho* magazine. With no trouble at all he could still see her stretched out in all her nineteen-year-old glory, smiling at him and about half a million other guys. Born to be wild, that was Keely Branscom.

He'd love to know where she was now. Maybe married with three kids, although he had a hard time picturing that. More likely she was performing in a club exactly like the one he'd just passed. That wasn't so hard to imagine.

The bachelor party tonight would be at a similar kind of place, and Noah wasn't really looking forward to it. He didn't have a steady relationship with a woman like the other guys in the wedding party, which meant he was sexually on edge. It wasn't a good idea to watch a lot of semi-naked women bobbing around when you were in that state.

The heels of his boots tapped out a steady rhythm as he continued on his way. The last time he was in this town for a pro rodeo about five years ago, he distinctly remembered a little neighborhood-type bar in this area. No dancers, no loud music, just cold beer and a couple of outdated slot machines.

Now he couldn't find it.

He'd counted on that little bar to be his hidey-hole over the weekend, whenever the festivities for his good buddy Brandon threatened to overwhelm him. He was glad, honored even, to be a groomsman—he really was. But Brandon and Jenny's engagement last fall had meant that Noah was the only one of his rodeo buddies who hadn't found himself a wife.

To top it off, his little brother, Jonas, had become engaged, and of all people, he'd picked Keely's sister, B.J. Noah wouldn't mind getting married. In fact, he would *love* getting married. But he'd been kept busy with the ranch, and Saguaro Junction wasn't exactly overrun with eligible females. Until recently, any that happened along had been instantly appropriated by Jonas.

Well, maybe now that Jonas was settling down, Noah would have the time and opportunity to find a wife of his own. But, in the meantime, here he was, smack-dab in the middle of Sin City at a time when he was feeling especially vulnerable to suggestions.

You could do just about anything you wanted to in this town, and that was way too much freedom for his taste. After only a few hours here he could already feel the sexual pull of the city, the urge to do things you'd never think of doing in your own hometown. It made him nervous.

Keely had affected him that way, all those years ago, and he'd wisely decided to steer clear of her. If he could just get that centerfold picture out of his mind, he'd be all set.

But this was the sort of place to freshen that memory, not erase it.

At the next intersection he paused and glanced around at a passel of gift shops, liquor stores and pawnshops. No neighborhood bar. It had probably gone out of business. With a sigh he turned around to retrace his path to the hotel.

The hotel had several bars, but they were all too trendy, too noisy. He hungered for worn vinyl stools and a little country music. Someplace like the Roundup Saloon in Saguaro Junction.

It was a pitiful thing for a man of thirty-two to be homesick, but that's what he was. He wouldn't even mind mucking out stalls right now if he could be back on the ranch looking forward to a barbecue this evening and a sunset that would make your eyes water with its beauty. He loved that ranch the same way his daddy had, and his daddy before him. It was Garfield land, and Noah always felt better when his feet were planted on it.

He was so caught up in his daydreaming that he wasn't paying any attention to the other people on the sidewalk. It took him a while to realize that the redhead walking toward him looked a lot like Keely. But his mind was probably playing tricks on him, considering he'd just been thinking of her.

With his hat pulled low to shade his eyes, he could study her more closely without being caught at it. Yep, sure reminded him of Keely. The blue flowers decorating her dress looked sweet and innocent, but the dress itself, filmy and cut to midthigh, was anything but. The skirt flounced around her smooth legs with every step she took.

It was a mouthwatering dress, clingy enough to allow every curve to make itself known when she moved. It laced up over her breasts, and although the neckline didn't show much cleavage, the dress revealed a hell of a lot of leg. Bare, brightly painted toes peeked out of a pair of high-heeled sandals. Keely could wear high-heeled sandals like nobody else.

Of course, this *wasn't* Keely. But this woman could be her twin. Same full, pouty mouth; same determined chin; same "I Gotta Be Me" stride.

She wore sunglasses, so he couldn't see her eyes. The eyes would be the clincher. No other woman in the world had Keely's eyes. Some people said green was a soothing, cool color. Not on Keely. She could scorch a man's heart with one glance. A few thought the devil himself stoked that blaze, and it could well be. Looking into her eyes, a man might consider selling his soul.

The Keely look-alike paused outside the dance club and Noah paused, too. Of course she wasn't Keely, but now he had to be absolutely positive before he could walk on past.

She dug in her shoulder purse for something and came out with a small leather notebook. Flipping it open, she shoved her sunglasses to the top of her head while she studied whatever was written there. Snapping the notebook shut, she thrust it back into her purse and stepped toward the entrance.

"Excuse me." He moved toward her and came up with the first line he could think of. "Could you tell me what time it is?" Damn, she even *smelled* like Keely. She'd been partial to raspberry-scented body lotion.

Without looking at him, she glanced at her watch. Then she raised her head and gazed in his direction. "It's two-fif—" She stopped abruptly and stared at him.

He gasped and his heart began to hammer the way it always did in reaction to her. Those eyes. God, they were more potent than ever.

"Noah?" Her mouth gaped open. "Noah Garfield, is that you?"

"It's me." The shock of seeing her made his head buzz.

"Wow." She let out a breathless little laugh. "I can't believe this."

"*You* can't believe it? *I* can't believe it. I was just thinking about you and then bam, you showed up." Whoops. He shouldn't have said that.

"Really?" Her kiss-me-now mouth curved in a smile. Her lipstick was the color of a ripe peach, and she must have recently put it on, because it still had a gloss that made her mouth look wet. "After all these years? How flattering."

"Well, I—uh…" Damn it all, now he was blushing.

Her smile widened. "Couldn't be the sign flashing over our heads that reminded you of me, now, could it?"

As usual, she knew right where to press to make him squirm. "Now, Keely, that's the sort of thing best forgotten, don't you think?"

"It's obvious *you* haven't forgotten it." She reached out and patted his arm. "That's okay. It's not every day that the girl you used to chase around the stock tank decides to bare her all in a centerfold. Folks in Saguaro Junction aren't used to that kind of thing. I guess it would tend to stick in your mind."

"I think most people have forgotten about it." Not true. Mention Keely Branscom anywhere in town and eyebrows still rose. He struggled to get some purchase on the conversation. "So how've you been?" Now *there* was an original question.

"Fine."

"That's good." Another brilliant comment. He had to admit she looked fine. Saucy as all get-out, the way she'd always been. Judging from the way the dress fit, she hadn't put on an extra ounce in ten years.

"How about you?" she asked.

"I'm good." He wondered how she made her lipstick look like that, as if she'd just licked her lips. He shouldn't be looking at her mouth, but her eyes weren't any safer a place to rest his glance. Well, he could look lower, at her breasts rising and falling under the thin, flowery material. That wasn't such a good idea. Better concentrate on her mouth, even if it did remind him of the one time she'd kissed him.

"What brings you to Vegas?" she asked.

He had to stop and think. Oh, yeah, Brandon. "A friend of mine's getting married."

"Really? Anybody I know?"

"I don't think so. He's from Wyoming. We met up on the rodeo circuit a few years back. I don't think he ever made it to the ranch, but we've kept in touch."

"That's nice." For a split second she sounded a little wistful. Then that cocky tone of hers took over again. "So what's up with you, Noah? Found yourself a salt-of-the-earth ranching woman yet?"

"Nope." Once again she'd managed to hit a subject he was touchy about. "Been a little busy." He hesitated, not sure how much he wanted to reveal. After all, she'd been the one who'd decided to break off contact with everyone in Saguaro Junction, including her father and sister. But finally he decided to tell her some of the news. Couldn't hurt. "My dad died a couple of years ago."

"Oh. Oh, I'm sorry." She gazed up at him, her green eyes filled with sadness. "He was a nice man."

"Thanks. He was." He couldn't ever remember seeing sympathy in her eyes before. Defiance plenty of times, devilment nearly as often and, once, on a very memorable night, desire. Never this soft, endearing sympathy.

He'd always thought of her as being so tough, but maybe she wasn't. Ten years ago he hadn't allowed himself to see past her cheeky bravado. Life had been safer that way. But he was older now, and he wondered if he'd missed a few things about Keely. He should have tracked her down, just to make sure she was okay.

"So you and Jonas are running things?" she asked.

"Yeah." He could say that now. Six months ago he couldn't have, back when Jonas spent more time chasing women than chasing cows. But B.J. had settled Jonas down considerably. "That's another thing that's happened," he said. "Jonas will be getting married soon."

"Get outta here!" She grinned. "Shotgun?"

"Nope. He's marrying your sister."

Disbelief flashed in her eyes, but it was quickly replaced with a touching vulnerability. She glanced away. "Well." Her throat moved in a hard swallow before she looked up, her gaze guarded. "She always was sweet on him, but she's making a huge mistake."

"A few months ago I would have agreed with you, but you'd be surprised at how Jonas has changed. He's getting more responsible by the day."

"What a shame."

The old irritation that had always been a part of his conversations with Keely pricked him now. If everybody had Keely's carefree attitude toward life, the work would never get done. "*I* happen to be glad for him."

She gave him that saucy smile, the one that always warned him that a smart-ass remark was coming. "You would be," she said. "You were born old."

His jaw clenched. Keely had a real talent for getting under his skin. She always had—in every department. "Everybody has to grow up sometime. Even you."

"Not if I can help it. And as for B.J. and Jonas, they should have years ahead of them before they have to settle into some boring routine. But no, they're shackling themselves to each other and that blessed ranch. I hate to see it."

"Nobody asked you to." Now, that was a low blow and he hadn't meant to deliver it. But he couldn't take it back, and he didn't know how to smooth over what he'd just said.

Her eyes registered the hurt. "No, I guess nobody did." She slid her sunglasses back on, and when she spoke again her voice sounded more brittle than bright. "And I suppose my father's as crotchety as ever?"

He was touched that she was brave enough to ask about Arch. She and her father had fought bitterly all through her teenage years, and he'd practically thrown her out after the centerfold incident. He hadn't been serious about sending her away, but with her nineteen-year-old view of the world, she'd taken it seriously. Neither of them had been able to swallow their pride long enough to make the connection again.

"Arch is fine," he said gently, wanting to reassure her of that much, at least. "In perfect health."

"I'm not surprised," she said with a grimace, although she sounded relieved. "He wouldn't tolerate the presence of an infirmity." She straightened her shoulders. "Well, now that we're all caught up, I'd better be going. I have an appointment."

He'd nearly forgotten where they were standing. Before he'd stopped her she'd been about to go inside this dance club. He had a sinking sensation that he knew why. "An appointment?" he asked, trying to keep the question casual.

"Yes. An interview."

"Oh." His gut churned. A job interview. The centerfold picture flashed through his mind again and he knew without a shadow of a doubt that she was trying to get a job dancing on the stage in there. She planned to take off most of her clothes and twirl those little tassel gizmos for the men who patronized this club.

He eyed the entrance once more and noticed chipped paint around the door frame. The rock music coming from inside sounded more sinister than it had a moment ago, and he heard loud male laughter. He hoped this place was a step down from what she'd been doing before and not a step up. But whichever direction she was headed, it looked like the wrong road to him.

"Listen, I'm already late, but it's been fun seeing you," she said. "What a coincidence, huh? Take care of yourself, Noah." She turned toward the shadowy entrance.

Without taking time to think about it, he grabbed her arm. "Don't go in there."

She glanced up at him in surprise. "Why not?"

"There have to be better ways to make a living." His breath hitched. Her bare arm felt warm and smooth beneath his fingers. She had wonderful skin, he remembered now.

And she was planning to show way too much of it to strangers.

With her free hand she pushed her sunglasses to the top of her head. Then she gazed at him as if fascinated by this turn of events. "What do you think I do for a living?"

"I'm...I'm not sure, and to tell the truth I'd rather not know. I'm just asking you not to go for that interview. I've been in places like this. I know how they expect the women to—"

"Do you, now?"

He released her arm as if her skin might burn him. "Damn it, Keely. You know what I'm talking about."

"I'm not sure I do. I'm still getting used to the concept of Noah Garfield in a topless bar. Did someone trick you into going in?"

"No!" The woman sure had a way of getting his goat. "I went in under my own steam. I'm not a saint."

A slow smile spread over those peach-colored lips. "Couldn't prove it by me."

"Look, Keely, I know we haven't always seen eye to eye on things. Years ago you seemed determined to head in a certain direction, and you wouldn't listen to anybody who tried to talk you out of it. But I'm asking you right here, right now, to reconsider. Maybe you met me on this street for a reason. Maybe it's time to think about alternatives."

She folded her arms and looked at him. Mischief lurked in her eyes. "Let's make sure I understand. Instead of going inside and getting a job wiggling my ta-tas for the customers, you want me to reform and go into a more respectable line of work. Is that the gist of it?"

"You're making fun of me, but yes, that's the gist of it."

The gleam of devilment grew brighter. "You want to save me from myself."

"Aw, hell, Keely." He figured she was going to roast him for this attempt to do the right thing. "It's not that topless dancing is so terrible. I know you think I'm some sort of prude, but I'm not. And I understand that you've always wanted to kick the status quo in the butt. But isn't this getting a little old? I should think you'd have moved on to something else by now.''

"I'm not even thirty!"

"Damn close."

"Ten whole months away, buster."

"See, it's the perfect time to make a change." He was thinking she looked years younger than thirty. Because they'd grown up together he knew exactly how old she was, but a stranger would think she was in her early twenties. No doubt her body would look good on stage for a long time to come, but he didn't intend to say that. He didn't even want to think that.

"And what sort of job should I do?" she asked, tapping the toe of her sandal against the pavement.

"I'm not sure." He rubbed the back of his neck. Now that he'd jumped into this white-knight routine, he didn't know how to proceed. "Maybe we could kick around some ideas."

"And when could we do that? You have a wedding to attend, as I recall, and I need to make a living."

And there was the heart of the matter. If she was looking for a job, she was probably short on cash. He couldn't very well tell a woman like Keely to forget about the money she'd make dancing topless and take a job flipping burgers instead. She'd laugh in his face. He wasn't going to convert her to a different lifestyle during one conversation on the street corner.

He stalled, trying to think what to do. "How long have you been in Vegas?"

"Just got here yesterday."

"Okay." He thought quickly. One step at a time. "I understand the economic realities. You just came to town and you need a job, but could you hold off for the weekend so we could talk about it? I could cover your expenses for the next few days."

"You mean, pay for my room and board? I don't think so."

"Then how about this? Cancel your room reservation and move in with me for the weekend. Would that save you enough so you wouldn't have to work right away?"

"You want me to share your hotel room?" She eyed him with interest.

That look triggered a vivid memory. She'd kissed him with the passion of a woman that night in the barn, even at the tender age of sixteen. "Strictly as friends," he said quickly. "It's a minisuite. I'll take the couch and you can have the bed. This isn't a proposition, Keely."

"Are you sure?" The mischief had returned to her green eyes. "I realize you're not in the habit of kicking over the traces, but we're not in Saguaro Junction anymore. No one from back home has to hear about this. And we all know what a naughty girl I am."

Warmth flooded through him. She really had a knack for saying exactly what would bring a reaction. "That's the kind of thinking you need to get away from," he said. "Life is about more than sex." At the moment he couldn't think what else it was about, but he'd get his bearings again soon.

"Let me make sure I understand. You're inviting me to stay in your room for the weekend, but you have no intention of us fooling around. Instead, you're going to do some career counseling for me."

"That's right." Not that fooling around with Keely didn't hold some appeal. But she apparently thought that's all she was good for, and he didn't want to reinforce that notion.

She frowned in confusion. "I asked you if you had a wife back home and you said no. But is there a serious girlfriend? Because I can imagine you would be totally loyal once you committed yourself to somebody."

"No serious girlfriend." Come to think of it, he hadn't even had a date in months.

"Noah, are you gay?"

He nearly choked to death. As he was coughing and sputtering, he shook his head and gasped out his denial.

She ticked off her conclusions on the tips of her fingers. "You're not committed to anyone, you're not gay, and you don't want to have sex with me, even if no one back home would ever find out."

"That's right." He did want to have sex with her, always had, but that was a white lie he could live with.

"Then you surely must be a saint who has dropped down out of the sky to save me from my wicked ways. Okay, I accept."

He cleared his throat and tried to look more confident than he felt. "That's great." Now that she'd pointed out to him that only a saint could be expected to resist her, he'd begun to think this whole idea was doomed. But if he could somehow find the strength to keep his hands off her, then maybe she'd develop a new image of herself. And that was worth doing. After all, his brother was marrying her sister. She would be family soon.

"We should probably go pick up your stuff," he said. "Is your hotel far from here?"

She looked suddenly worried. "Uh, the thing is, they, um…lost my luggage. You know how that happens. I don't have any stuff."

"Oh." So it was worse than he thought. Obviously she was making up the story about lost luggage, so that must mean she was staying in some fleabag motel and didn't want him to know it. Worse yet, her belongings were pitiful enough to be embarrassing to her. As together as she looked now, the outfit she wore was probably the only decent thing she owned.

Knowing that fact renewed his resolve to pull her out of this nosedive she was in. "Okay, then!" he said with more heartiness than the situation called for. He sounded like a damn used-car salesman. He cleared his throat and tried again. "Let's walk on back to my hotel. Then I can advance you a little money if you want to go shopping for a few clothes later.''

''We'll see about that. But before we leave here I want to duck inside and let them know I won't be keeping the appointment. I don't want a black mark beside my name, in case I need to come back someday.''

''I'll go with you.''

She smiled at him. ''I'd rather you didn't.''

''Why not?''

''In this neighborhood, if some guy is tagging around after a woman, looking like he's keeping track of her, people might think he's her pimp.''

As he wondered how she'd become so knowledgeable about such things, ice water shot through his veins. ''Keely, please tell me that you've never—''

''No. I've never. I may be a naughty girl, but I've never been that naughty.''

He sighed with relief.

''Yet.''

His muscles tensed all over again and he opened his mouth to deliver another warning.

Keely's musical laugh cut him off. ''Relax. I'm kidding. You were around for the first nineteen years of my life. You should know by now how much I love to tease people. Especially people like you.'' She fluttered a hand at him. ''Hold down the sidewalk. I'll be back before you know it.''

He watched her walk through the entrance into the cave-like interior of the club. That Keely. She always could get him going.

Then he blinked as if coming out of a trance. *He had just arranged to spend the weekend sleeping in a hotel suite with Keely Branscom.*

What the hell had he been thinking? He'd arrived in this place feeling on edge and sexually deprived. Now he'd invited the sexiest woman he'd ever known to stay with him in extremely close quarters. Less than four hours into his Vegas stay, and the city had him right where it wanted him.

2

KEELY HAD MADE a career of acting on impulse. This particular impulse—to play along with Noah's outrageous plan to save her—could be lots of fun, especially if she turned the tables and took him for a walk on the wild side, instead. So why this sudden attack of nerves?

Maybe she was still dealing with the news that her sister and Jonas were getting married. That situation would definitely take some getting used to. Yeah, it was the sudden word of their wedding that had her spooked.

Surely she wasn't still into Noah the way she had been at sixteen. And seducing him here in Vegas would be an awesome way to get revenge for the way he'd brusquely pushed her away at that tender age. But in order for that revenge to be sweet, she had to be certain she was completely over him. Well, she was. Of course she was.

Shaking off her uneasiness, she walked into the sparsely populated bar and glanced at the blond woman gyrating on the small stage. No, that wasn't the one. Her interview subject was a brunette.

"Would you like a table?" A thin man dressed in a white shirt and tight black pants appeared at her elbow.

"No, thanks. I'm Keely Branscom and I'm here to talk with Suzanne."

"Oh!" The man grew more animated. "You're the reporter from *Attitude!* She's in the back. Please sit down. I'll go get her."

Keely pulled out a chair at the nearest round cocktail table and sat. This might take longer than she figured. No doubt

Noah would be outside having a conniption, thinking she was secretly filling out a job application. But she couldn't be rude and leave without speaking to Suzanne.

The sound system in the bar wasn't very good, but the blonde on the stage was an excellent dancer. Keely counted five men in the place, all of them with their attention glued to the stage. She'd love to believe they were admiring the skill of the performance, but after years of reporting on the guy/gal scene for *Attitude!,* she could reasonably conclude they were fixated on the dancer's chest instead of her footwork.

In general, a man's motivation was pretty simple, which was one reason she was so intrigued by Noah's offer to reform her. His motivation was more complex. She really believed he didn't intend for them to have sex. Well, he just might have to reevaluate that decision.

"Ms. Branscom?"

Keely glanced away from the stage and saw that a curvy brunette in purple spandex exercise gear stood next to the table. Keely pushed back her chair. "Suzanne?"

"That's me." Suzanne held out her hand.

Keely stood and shook her hand. She had to practically shout to be heard over the pounding music. "Please call me Keely. Listen, it turns out now isn't a very good time for me to do the interview, after all. I wonder if we could reschedule."

"I guess so." Suzanne raised her voice and leaned closer to Keely. "The only thing is, I have, like, this horrific exam coming up in my psych class, so I need to spend most of my free time, like, inhaling the textbook. And tonight I'm dancing."

"Right." Keely was glad they weren't conducting the interview like this. It would give her a headache in no time. She wasn't sure when she'd stopped loving loud music.

She quickly considered how to work around Suzanne's schedule and her own interesting situation with Noah. He'd probably have some wedding-related thing going on tonight, so she might be able to slip over here.

"Do you get a break tonight?" she asked.

"Sure." Suzanne raised her voice as the music's volume increased. "About ten-thirty!"

Keely had to shout, too. "Are you planning to study during your break?"

"Nah! I'll probably kick back! I only get about fifteen minutes!"

Blissfully, the music changed tempo and became softer. "If you're willing, I could do the interview then." Keely couldn't get over how young Suzanne looked. Yet she was twenty-two, three years older than Keely had been when she'd posed for the centerfold.

"Tonight would be cool, but are you sure that's enough time?"

"Maybe not, but we'll get a start, anyway."

Suzanne glanced over at the stage. "Joy, she'd like to be interviewed, too. She's not going to college, like me, but she's going to beauty school. Does that count?"

"Sure does. Anybody who's dancing to earn tuition fits into the article."

"Cool. That's her on stage now." Suzanne watched for a moment and unconsciously began to wiggle in time with the music. "She has some dynamite moves."

"Yes, she does."

"That guy over there in the black T-shirt is her boyfriend. I am, like, so jealous. He is totally hot."

"He is?" Keely could only locate one person in a black T-shirt, and he didn't look like anything special. For one thing, she was getting sick of shaved heads and multiple piercings. And baggy pants did nothing for her these days, either. Plus, he looked more like a kid than a man.

"Yeah, he's awesome." Suzanne gazed at him in rapture. "Totally."

Keely glanced from Suzanne to the kid and reminded herself that this was her magazine's target audience. She needed to do a better job of relating. "He is pretty cute," she said. Cute was as far as she would go. And cute didn't do it for her anymore, unfortunately.

But someone who did do it for her stood right outside, waiting. "Well, Suzanne, I'll see you tonight, then," she said.

"Maybe Joy can come by so you can talk to her, too."

"That would be great. Thanks." Keely shook hands with Suzanne and hurried outside.

Noah was lounging against the side of the building, but he looked wary, not relaxed. He straightened and walked toward her. "I was beginning to wonder if something happened."

"Sorry. It took a while to find the person I needed." She gazed at him with new appreciation. Now here was an example of hot. His clothes might not be trendy, but they were classic turn-ons, at least for her. She'd grown up admiring the way a pearl-buttoned western shirt defined a man's broad shoulders and how smooth-fitting jeans defined even more interesting parts of his anatomy.

Noah looked mighty fine in that department. For years she'd dreamed of exploring the wonders so lovingly cradled by his Wranglers. From all indications he had a body built for serious sinning. Consequently he'd been a worthy challenge ever since she'd hit puberty.

But as luck would have it, when she'd gone for the gold that night in the barn, he'd turned her down. He hadn't been particularly gentle about it, either. For three years she'd tried to get even with him for that rejection, taking every opportunity to taunt him with what he'd missed. He hadn't cracked.

But she'd learned a few things since then, and they'd be sharing a hotel suite. It just might be Samson and Delilah time.

"You know, I've been thinking..." he said, his voice sounding tight.

Uh-oh. She lifted her gaze to his face and tried to look

innocent. "About what?" He must have caught her ogling. She'd have to be more careful not to overplay her hand. Some men loved being checked out. Apparently it made this particular man nervous. She slipped on her sunglasses to give herself more leeway.

"Why don't I see if I can get you a room on the same floor?" he said. "You'd probably be more comfortable with that."

Oh, he'd definitely caught her ogling. She had to take quick action. "No way, baby doll! I feel like enough of a charity case as it is! Tell you what, let's forget the whole thing."

"No, no. We're not going to forget the whole thing." He sighed. "Come on. The hotel's this way."

So he had a place on the Strip. She would have liked that, too, but the magazine had booked her at one of the less expensive places downtown. Maybe when he was otherwise occupied, she'd head over there and pick up a few things.

She fell into step beside him. "You know what your problem is? You think too much."

"Could be. But that's better than not thinking enough."

"Ah. That would be me you're referring to, wouldn't it?"

His mouth twitched with amusement. "I didn't mean just you."

"Oh, you probably did, but that's okay. I won't take offense. It you're talking levels of caution, on a scale of one to ten I'd be a minus fifteen."

He laughed.

"You, on the other hand, would be a plus thirty."

"You're exaggerating."

"No, I'm not!" She felt great walking down the street with Noah. Because she stood five-eight in her bare feet and had generous breasts, not many men could make her feel small and delicate. Noah had the height and breadth of shoulder to carry it off. Maybe it wasn't politically correct to enjoy that, but she did. She always had. *Always. Uh-oh. What if she wasn't over him?*

"If I'm so damn cautious," he said, "then why did I take up bull riding?"

"I thought about that. And it does indicate a streak of daring hiding in there somewhere." She had to be over him, she decided. After all, it had been years.

"See?" He looked pleased with himself. "I can be daring if I want."

"Yes, but you only have to maintain that daring for eight seconds or less. That's not a long time." She kept up the banter, but inside she was scanning for evidence, trying to decide if she was still hooked on Noah.

"Oh, yes, it is a long time. When you're in the heat of the action, eight seconds is an eternity. A lifetime."

"Really?"

"Really."

"Well, I sure hope that's not your attitude when you make love. If so, your lady friends must be *very* frustrated." There. If she could poke fun at him, then she was over him. Definitely.

He blushed. "We weren't talking about that."

"I was." That blush of his was so cute. The people she hung out with in L.A. were all pretty jaded when it came to sexual innuendos. Finding a man who could blush when he talked about sex was refreshing. And arousing.

He tugged his hat down lower over his eyes. "Well, I wasn't thinking about that particular subject, and you know it."

But he was now, and that was her goal. If only she knew for certain she could pull off this caper without getting hurt herself. "The fact is, I have no idea what kind of lover you are, Noah. You're a conservative guy, so when you talk about eight seconds being an eternity, I can't help wondering if you think that's plenty of time for—"

"Of course it's not!" He was really red now.

She'd forgotten how adorable he could be when he was flustered. "Well, good. Glad to hear it. Because most women need a whole lot more than eight seconds to become thoroughly—''

"I'm aware of that! Now, could we please change the subject?''

"Sure. Be glad to.'' She used to love teasing him like this. She loved it still. Probably too much, and she'd be wise to walk away from this whole setup. But then she'd never know if she could succeed in breaching his defenses. She had to know, no matter what it might cost her. And she was tough. She'd picked up the pieces before and could do it again. Damn the torpedoes. Full speed ahead.

"Thanks.'' He sighed in apparent relief.

Little did he know there was no relief in sight. "Oh, there's a drugstore,'' she said. "Would you mind if we stopped in there before we get to the hotel? I need a few things, and I'm sure they're more expensive in the hotel shops.''

"That's fine.'' He sounded grateful to be doing something as harmless as shopping. "I guess you would need a toothbrush and…other stuff.''

"A big bottle of lotion, for one thing. I'd forgotten how desert heat affects my skin. Back on the ranch I had to practically take a bath in lotion, remember?''

"Can't say as I do.''

Liar. "Oh, sure you do. You even commented about it one evening when I was on the front porch of Dad's house, slathering it all over my legs and arms. You said if I kept that up I'd slide right out of bed in the middle of the night.''

"Mmm.''

"My favorite is raspberry-scented, but they might not have that.'' She peeked at him as they walked through the door into the air-conditioned store to see if any of what she'd said was registering. He looked more than a little agitated.

Two years ago she'd done an article on scent as an arousal factor. All the guys she'd interviewed rated scent very high, and most of them fondly remembered how former lovers had smelled like cinnamon, or lily of the valley, or in one instance, chocolate. She was counting on Noah having the same response, and she'd used raspberry-scented lotion ever since she'd turned fifteen. If she couldn't find any in the drugstore, she'd smuggle over the bottle she had in her hotel room.

But raspberry lotion wasn't her primary target in the drugstore. She could hardly wait for the moment when Noah discovered what she planned to stock up on.

NOAH HAD BEEN in tight spots in his life and he'd always managed to come out okay. He clung to that hope as he followed Keely around the store and tried not to think of the scent of raspberries.

That scent had drawn him to her dad's porch on the night she'd mentioned. Dressed in cutoffs and a halter top, she'd stationed herself on the creaky old porch swing with a bottle of that damn lotion. To get near her, he'd made up some excuse about checking the area for snakes.

Keely wasn't the type to run off screaming at the mention of a snake, so while he'd swung a flashlight beam around and pretended to scout for rattlers, she'd nearly driven him crazy smoothing that creamy, fragrant stuff over her bare legs. They hadn't talked much, but he remembered crickets chirping and the rhythmic squeak of that swing, which could have passed for the sound of bedsprings. To this day he couldn't smell or taste raspberries without hearing that steady creak and seeing her hand slowly massaging the tender skin of her inner thigh.

That might have been the first time she'd discovered the stuff, but after that she'd used it constantly, trailing the scent of raspberries wherever she went. He'd come to dread that aroma, because it never failed to give him an erection, no matter how inappropriate the moment. More than once she'd glanced at his crotch and smiled, as if thrilled with her new power.

Then, a few weeks after she'd turned sixteen, she'd waylaid him in the barn. And she'd smelled exactly like a bowl of fresh raspberries. She'd tasted like that, too—juicy and moist, bursting with ripe sweetness.

He often wondered if she'd been a virgin then. If so, he'd bet she hadn't stayed one long after he'd turned her down. He'd probably given up the chance to be her first lover that night. Saying no hadn't been easy, considering she didn't look or act like any sixteen-year-old he'd known before or since.

But somehow in the midst of that hot, wet kiss, he'd remembered she *was* sixteen, and all the lust in the world wouldn't change that. He'd left the barn in a hurry, followed by the angry insults she'd hurled after him. At the time he'd thought she was furious. Now he wondered if she'd been more hurt than angry. He hadn't been particularly sensitive about ending the embrace.

Sensitivity hadn't been on his mind. Self-preservation had been all he could think about. God, how he'd wanted her. But giving in would have meant angering and disappointing two men he cared about—his father and hers.

Shortly after that he'd gone out on the rodeo circuit, figuring escape was the only answer. During his brief trips home over the next three years he'd noticed that Keely had gone overboard to become the sex symbol of Saguaro Junction. But innocent or wild, she turned him on like no one else. How ironic that he hadn't wanted to be her first lover, but later on he hadn't wanted to be the next one in line, either. With great difficulty he'd kept himself in check.

He was much older now and should have better control. But as he watched her scan the shelves looking for her raspberry lotion, he wondered if he'd changed at all where Keely was concerned.

All of a sudden she pounced on a bottle. "Look! Here it is!"

"Looks like it." He groaned to himself. *Wouldn't you know.*

"Okay, now a toothbrush." She moved quickly to that

aisle and grabbed a red one. "What kind of toothpaste do you use?"

He told her.

"That'll be fine. We can share, if that's all right with you."

"Uh, sure." He was aware of another customer, a matronly woman, giving them both the once-over.

"Great. The hotel shampoo will do for a couple of days, but I'll have to buy deodorant. I don't want some bracing, manly smell on my body."

His mind spun wildly as he followed her to the antiperspirants. What in God's name had he been thinking, proposing this scheme? How was he supposed to keep a level head while they shared the same shower, the same sink, and squeezed from the same toothpaste tube?

Dark red hair bouncing around her shoulders, she stalked through the rest of the store as if looking for something.

And like an idiot, he had to ask. "Is there something else you need?"

"Condoms."

He choked. "Why?"

"I'm surprised you would say that. Really, Noah, I'm beginning to wonder what kind of sex life you have. Ah, there they are, the little devils. Here, hold my stuff for a minute so I can look these puppies over." She shoved her lotion, deodorant and toothbrush into his hands.

Panic swelled within him. "Look, you don't need those things. I'm telling you, we are not—"

"Oh, these aren't for *you*."

"They're *not*?" The conversation had gone from bad to worse.

She studied the packages hanging on the display rack. "Not unless you change your mind."

"I won't, so let's just go, okay?" He glared at a teenage kid who was lingering nearby, obviously enjoying the show. The kid grinned and left. Noah lowered his voice. "Come on, Keely. Forget this stuff."

She ignored him. "These prices are really reasonable. Maybe I should stock up. You'd think men would look for inexpensive stores like this, but no. They like to be spontaneous, which usually means paying top dollar because they're in a rush. Or worse yet, suggesting we skip this step. Ha. As if."

He tried again. "All things considered, I don't think you really need to worry about—"

"I make it a habit to have some on hand in a couple of sizes, for emergencies. And we're here, after all. I really can't imagine a better bargain coming along anytime soon." She took a package from its hook and began reading. "'Ultra-comfort. Unique shape for more freedom.' I wonder what that means?"

"Keely."

"Noah," she mimicked. "Hmm. Maybe these are better." She unhooked another package. "It's so hard to know which ones are the best, with all these great descriptions— 'shared sensation, enhanced pleasure, ultimate feeling.' Oh, look. Here's one with a larger tip, and then there's the ribbed kind. Which do you think is the best?" She turned to look at him, a package of condoms in each hand, and devilment shining from those green eyes.

He ground some more enamel off his back molars. "Keely Branscom, you are doing this on purpose."

"Of course I am! I always budget money for a package of condoms."

"You're trying to get me going, is what you're doing."

"From the way you're breathing, I'd say I've succeeded." She grinned. "I really am buying the condoms, Noah. At least two packages of extra-large. And I'm giving you a chance to tell me which kind you like."

His jaw was clenched so tight his teeth seemed welded together. *"We are not going to need them."*

"Maybe not. But that's the thing about condoms. The packages are small and they store well. And there could be a time when you will thank me for planning ahead. Now give me my stuff. It's time to check out.'' She took her items from him and sashayed down the aisle with her lotion, her deodorant, her toothbrush and two kinds of extra-large condoms.

She obviously expected him to be wearing them before the weekend was over. It was a classic case of damned if he did and damned if he didn't.

3

KEELY HAD JUST LAID her purchases on the checkout counter when her cell phone rang from deep inside her shoulder purse. *Damn.* She'd forgotten about it.

She wheeled away from the counter, startling the young male clerk. "Forgot something!" she called over her shoulder to Noah, who, fortunately, was trailing her by a few paces. She figured he was embarrassed for the clerk to notice that she was buying condoms so he'd hung back from approaching the counter. Good thing. Maybe he hadn't heard her cell phone.

It rang again as she made a mad dash for the aisle labeled Feminine Products. If Noah had been schizy about the condom display, he surely wouldn't follow her there. Once she was safely surrounded by rows of tampon and sanitary-napkin boxes, she dug in her purse and took out the phone.

When she put it to her ear she heard the familiar voice of her editor. "Keely, sweetheart. Good news."

"Hi, Carolyn," she murmured softly. Trust her editor to call at the exact wrong moment.

"Why are you whispering? Are you in a movie theater or something?"

"No, but I can't talk loud. Or long."

"That's okay. This will be quick. Remember you mentioned expanding this article by interviewing some dancers in Reno, but I wasn't sure we should bother?"

"I remember, but can I call you back on this?" She glanced nervously behind her to make sure Noah wasn't there. "I—"

"I'll only be a sec. The publisher loves the Reno angle. I've lined up a couple of interview subjects for you there. You have a seven-forty flight out of Vegas on Monday morning. Got a pen? I'll give you the confirmation number."

"Carolyn, I—"

"Ready? Here it is." Carolyn rattled off the number.

Keely grabbed her notebook out of her purse and wrote down the number, but all the while she was thinking that this cell phone could blow her cover in no time this weekend. Carolyn expected her to keep the phone turned on while she was on assignment.

"Got it?" Carolyn asked.

"Got it, but Carolyn, you're fading out." Keely pressed the disconnect button a couple of times. "Carolyn? I think the phone's going on the blink. It's—" She broke off and ran the phone up and down the edge of a box several times, hoping the noise sounded like static. Then she put it back to her ear to gauge Carolyn's reaction.

"Keely? What's going on? Keely, can you hear me?"

"Barely," Keely whispered. *"I think it's—"* She dragged the phone around on the boxes some more before turning it off. Maybe she'd convinced Carolyn that the phone was dead. Keely buried it in the bottom of her purse again before heading back toward the checkout counter.

Looking extremely uneasy, Noah stood by the counter next to her items, which had been set aside while the clerk rang up another customer's purchases.

Keely smiled sweetly as she walked up to Noah. "Those prices weren't as reasonable, so I decided not to bother."

His eyes narrowed with suspicion. "What was that funny sawing noise?"

During her wild teen years, fast thinking had saved her more times than she could count. "I had an itch in the middle of my back. I used the corner of a box to scratch it." She gave a little wriggle. "All better."

He gulped. "Oh." His voice was strained as he attempted to sound casual. "That explains it."

Somehow she kept from laughing. One wriggle and he was gulping for air. She didn't remember him being so suggestible years ago. Apparently she had the advantage this time…so long as she kept her heart out of the equation.

"I can ring you up now, miss." The clerk, who couldn't have been more than eighteen, regarded her with adoration.

"Fabulous." She winked and sent him a high-wattage grin. "You have a very nice store here…" She paused to glance at his red plastic name tag. "Chad."

Chad grew as red as his name tag. "Thank you very much," he mumbled, and then he concentrated on punching the right numbers into the register. He had to clear his throat before he could tell her the amount. His gaze kept drifting to her chest and then he'd pull his eyes back with an obvious effort.

She opened her wallet and removed the money as quickly as she could. Her press pass was in there along with a gold card, but Noah would have had to be paying close attention to see either of them.

Chad took the money and handed over her change. "Do you, uh, live near here?" he asked eagerly. "I mean, would you like to be on our mailing list for…um…future sales?"

"Thanks, but I'm currently between addresses."

"Oh." Chad glanced over at Noah, then back at her, as if trying to decide if they were a couple. "Well, uh, feel free to stop in anytime. We always have specials."

"Thanks. I'll remember that." Picking up the plastic bag containing her purchases, she looked at Noah. "Ready?"

He gave a curt nod.

"Bye!" Chad called. "Come back anytime!"

She turned and smiled at him. "Bye."

Noah held the door for her as they left the store. Judging from the set of his jaw, she didn't think he was very happy. From all signs, he was a wee bit jealous—of a boy barely old enough to shave. Amazing.

Once upon a time she'd turned herself inside out trying to arouse Noah's jealousy, to no avail. Now it seemed that she'd done it with one hand tied behind her back. She decided to test the waters. "He was a nice kid," she said as they walked along the street.

"The way he was drooling I thought he might flood the store." Noah sounded quite irritated. "I think with a little more encouragement he would have asked you out, even though you're old enough to be his—"

"Big sister? He wasn't *that* much younger."

"Hell, he probably got his driver's license yesterday."

"He looked more like eighteen or nineteen to me. And by the way, men date women who are ten years younger than they are and nobody says boo."

He stared at her. "Don't tell me you're interested in him?"

She wasn't, not even slightly, but a jealous Noah was something she'd waited years to experience. She wanted to savor the feeling a little longer. "Well, he was very sweet, and he had the cutest dimple in his chin."

"You're putting me on."

"Okay, maybe I am. But, for the record, I don't think it would be the end of civilization if I happened to be interested in him. Some of my friends have deliberately taken younger lovers."

"Probably so they can lead them around by the nose."

Oh, this man had some things to learn, and she was just the gal to educate him. "I don't think that's the part of their anatomy they care about. A younger guy is usually so eager to please, and he generally has more…staying power."

Noah snorted. "Yeah, if you're into quantity instead of quality."

She pitched her voice lower, so it came out a sultry purr. "Quality can be taught. And young men are *so* coachable."

The sound that came from Noah bordered on a growl.

"What was that? I didn't quite understand you."

"Nothing."

She didn't think it was nothing. She thought it was the sound of a male animal whose masculinity had been challenged. From her experience, a man so challenged would be looking for opportunities to prove his prowess. Even if he hotly insisted otherwise.

Before long, Noah would beg to make love to her, and that would go a long way toward healing the hurt he'd inflicted, knowingly or not, when he'd rejected her sixteen-year-old advances. Maybe a few words of desperate need from him were all she needed to finally get him out of her system.

IT WAS ALL coming back to him now. Not only had he been tortured with feelings of lust where Keely was concerned, he'd also been ready to kill every guy who so much as looked at her. Leaving Saguaro Junction to follow the rodeo circuit had kept him away from Keely, but it had also saved a lot of cowboys from having their jaws busted.

Apparently he hadn't changed in that regard, either. The drugstore clerk was a mere baby, but when his hormone-driven attention had settled on Keely's breasts, Noah had been ready to take the kid apart. He'd have to work on that reaction, because men weren't going to stop looking at Keely during the next three days. Men were *always* looking at Keely.

The worst part was that he couldn't understand where his protective instincts were coming from. Maybe because he'd grown up with Keely, he had some big-brother feelings going on, but she'd never acted like a shrinking violet in need of male protection. The males probably needed protection from Keely, when it came right down to it.

That might be the heart of the matter, he realized with sudden insight. He hadn't been willing to face that his childhood friend had become an extremely sexy woman. Every drooling guy who hung around emphasized the very thing he didn't want to admit, so the answer was to keep them away from her. Knowing that she'd never tolerate that kind of protectiveness had been one of his major frustrations in life. The safest course had been to stay away himself, which had the added benefit of protecting him from his own sexual feelings for her.

He should have continued on that course today. But he couldn't have left her at the topless bar, knowing she'd have a job in no time and be dancing there by tonight, probably. The way things were going, the bachelor party really would end up at that exact bar and he'd have to watch his buddies and a host of strangers ogling Keely. The centerfold spread had been torture enough, but at least it hadn't been firsthand torture.

"Where are you staying?" she asked as they arrived at the Strip and turned left.

"The Tahitian." He'd been floored by the prices, but he had to admit the rooms were nice.

"That new place? Cool! I've been meaning to check it out. The cliff-diver show is supposed to be awesome at night. And don't they have an actual beach with surf in the courtyard?"

"I guess. I haven't seen it yet."

"You haven't? Everybody talks about it—white sand, saltwater waves lapping at the shore, palm trees swaying— the whole nine yards. I guess your room must not look out on that, or you'd have noticed."

"Nope. Mine overlooks the parking lot." He had a vivid mental picture of Keely lying at the edge of that lapping surf, the foam curling over her naked breasts and licking at her smooth thighs. Oh, boy. He was in trouble. He'd been denying her sexuality for years, but denial wasn't working anymore.

"In fact, considering you're staying at such a premier resort," she said, "I'm surprised you didn't want to hang out right there and soak up the atmosphere instead of wandering around in the heat on a basically boring side street."

"Well, the thing is, I—"

"Noah Garfield, were you planning to actually go into

that bar? Don't tell me that you're secretly a voyeur who pays to look at naked women?''

He winced as several people on the crowded sidewalk turned to stare at him. Taking Keely by the arm, he leaned down. ''No, I am not a secret voyeur, but now several people in this city think I am.'' He released his grip on her arm before the soft warmth under his fingers gave him even more ideas.

''Sorry about that,'' she said. ''You know I always tend to speak my mind.''

''I do remember that. Obviously you haven't changed.''

''Obviously you haven't, either. Still worried about what the neighbors think.''

She was baiting him. He knew that, but still she got his dander up. He wondered if he had any chance at all of changing her attitude this weekend. Probably not, but he had to try. He'd keep reminding her of her roots and see if that helped the cause. ''Where you and I come from, you'd better stay chummy with your neighbors if you expect to make it in the ranching business.''

''Well, I have no interest in making it in the ranching business.''

She scored another hit with that one. He loved his life as a rancher and took negative comments about it personally. ''I think you made that perfectly clear when you took the deal with *Macho*.''

''You noticed that.''

''Everybody noticed that.'' And that was the other big reason he'd better get his mind off the lovely body of Keely Branscom. He'd never been the kind of guy who could have sex for the hell of it. With him, a physical relationship with a woman needed to be going somewhere. With Keely, it could go nowhere. She didn't want what he could offer.

''Noah…about that centerfold…'' She sounded hesitant, which was unusual for her.

Surprised at the sudden shift in her manner, he glanced over at her.

She cleared her throat. "It was my ticket out." Her gaze slipped up to his face, but her expression was disguised by her dark glasses. "Can you understand that?"

"Sort of." Frustrated by not being able to see her eyes, he faced forward again. "I mean, if you wanted to get out of Saguaro Junction, posing for that magazine sure worked like a charm. And I can see why the town might seem too conservative for you. But to cut yourself off completely..."

"It was easier that way."

"Maybe, but growing up there wasn't all bad, was it?"

"No, of course not."

"Don't you ever miss the place?" He decided not to talk about missing the people for now.

She didn't answer for a long while. "Sometimes," she murmured at last. "Yeah, sometimes I do."

She was full of surprises. He didn't think she'd admit to that so soon. Maybe he had a chance, after all. "Then why not come back and mend some fences?"

"I don't fit in there, Noah. I'm too much like my mother."

He barely remembered Keely's mother, who'd died from complications surrounding B.J.'s birth. But Arch had said his wife had loved the excitement of the city and had been bored by country living. "I didn't mean you had to move back. But would it kill you to visit?"

"Maybe." She smiled wistfully. "Although I have to say, this business of my little sister getting married has me thinking. You never did mention when the wedding was."

"Let's see. It's...two weeks from Saturday," he said with some shock. "I didn't realize it was getting so close, myself. And I still don't have a gift bought, either."

"That soon? Are you *sure* this isn't a shotgun affair?"

"Absolutely sure. Jonas is the one who is pushing to tie the knot."

"I'm amazed." Keely shook her head. "B.J. must have really changed."

"Not a whole lot. She's still a better ranch hand than most men. Better at some things than Jonas, to be honest."

"Then I don't get it. She's so not his type. He likes girlie girls, and B.J. is about as far from that as you can get."

"Maybe your sister has hidden depths."

"Maybe she does."

"One thing's for sure—Jonas thinks she's fascinating. And B.J.'s still the same riding, roping gal as always, but there is something sort of different about her. It's like she's in full bloom or something."

"See? She's pregnant!"

"No, she's not, but I can see you aren't going to take my word for it." He paused. "Guess you'll have to ask her yourself."

After a long moment, Keely sighed. "I understand what you're trying to do, Noah, and it's very sweet, but...too much water's gone over the dam, or under the bridge. At any rate, there's been a heck of a lot of water running. I don't think I'd be a welcome guest at the wedding."

"I wouldn't be so sure." Noah was taking a chance saying that. But he had a hunch Arch and B.J. would love it if Keely showed up. Besides, he didn't see how the gap in the family could get any wider, so he thought it was worth the risk to suggest she go.

KEELY WALKED along silently beside Noah as they covered the last block before reaching the towering hotel that would magically transport them to the South Pacific. She was afraid to say too much more on the subject of her sister's wedding for fear Noah would figure out how much she longed to go back and see her father and sister. Maybe now her sister was old enough and experienced enough to understand what had happened all those years ago. Maybe they could be friends again.

Only two years apart, they had been friends once. Then Keely had launched into puberty like a rocket, leaving B.J. behind. Living on a ranch where the only other females were her boyish younger sister and the Garfields' housekeeper, Keely had found no one to help her through the confusing process of growing into a sexual person. She'd only had the dim memory of her mother to guide her, a mother who had apparently looked and acted just like her. Or so her father said.

Keely had developed early, B.J. late. And it had seemed to Keely that B.J. had tried to keep her tomboy image just to set her apart from her wild sister. Or maybe they'd split the parental influences between them, with B.J. becoming like Arch and Keely growing more and more like her mother. At any rate, B.J. had become the good daughter in their father's eyes, while Keely had continued to blaze a path toward bad-girl land.

But Jonas wouldn't be attracted to a woman who didn't have a touch of naughtiness, so maybe B.J. wasn't Little Miss Innocent anymore. Maybe she wouldn't be as mystified by Keely now. Then again, maybe she would turn her back on her rebel sister, and that would be painful. Keely had a real aversion to pain.

In fact, she gravitated almost exclusively to pleasure and living in the present moment. The past couldn't be changed and the future was a guess, but for the moment she had Noah Garfield right where she wanted him at last. As they approached the Tahitian, a ripple of anticipation made her shiver with delight. He had found her hard to resist in a drugstore. Once she got him inside this tropical paradise, he'd be a goner.

Set a distance back from the street, the hotel beckoned visitors to approach by leading them through a man-made jungle misted with thousands of tiny jets and cooled with countless tumbling waterfalls. The air reverberated with exotic birdsong and the steady beat of native drums.

"What fun," Keely said as they joined the throng headed toward the entrance.

"I'd hate to get their water bill," Noah said.

"Oh, for heaven's sake. Can you do me a favor for the

next three days and try not to think of practical things like that? You're going to ruin my fantasy if you insist on worrying about utility bills.''

To her surprise, Noah laughed. "You're right," he said. "Vegas is over the top, and you might as well accept that from the git-go."

"Very *good.*" She took off her sunglasses and slipped them into her purse as they approached a large clearing. "There's hope for you, cowboy. Maybe before the weekend is over, you—"

She forgot what she'd intended to say as the foliage gave way to a view of a granite cliff rising ten stories above them. "My God. They dive off this thing." She stood and gazed at the deep pool at the base of the cliff while she tried to imagine having the courage to hurl yourself into it from that height. "I definitely want to see this show tonight."

Noah glanced over at her. "I hope you don't mind watching it by yourself. I have a bachelor party I'm supposed to go to and it might run late."

That fit perfectly into her plans. She could squeeze in some interview time. "No problem," she said. "I'm good at amusing myself. But could we stop by the desk and get me a key to the room?"

"Oh. Sure." He sounded anything but sure.

"Would that make you uncomfortable?"

"No, no, of course not."

"You're worried that the people at the desk will think you picked up a call girl, aren't you? Just like Richard Gere picked up Julia Roberts in *Pretty Woman.*" She thought that was a good image to plant in his mind.

He looked uneasy. "But I'm not—I mean, we're not—"

"Tell you what. I'm going to help you out, here. In that movie, he told everybody the girl was his niece. So let's say I'm your cousin."

"Nobody will believe that."

"Of course they won't, but they'll pretend to believe it, and that's good enough, right?"

"I think if we say that you're my cousin they'll know we're lying and be even more sure you're a call girl."

Keely smiled at him. "Okay, then what do you want to say? That I'm a wayward woman and you're trying to reform me? They'll believe that even less. I'd better be your cousin."

He gazed at the cliff before looking back at her. "Maybe we could share a key."

"I don't see how that would work, unless you want me to hang around outside the room waiting for you to come back tonight. I don't think that would be too good for your image, either."

"I guess not."

"Noah, we're in Vegas, Sin City. So what if you have your cousin staying in your room? That's probably one of the tamest situations they've seen around here in ages. I'll bet an hour ago they gave a guy *two* extra keys because he ran into his *twin* cousins. And remember that not a single person behind that desk is your neighbor. So you don't have to give a care what they think."

He gave her a wry grin. "Point made. Let's go get the key." But as he started toward the large entrance doors decorated in brass bamboo, he suddenly turned back and grabbed her arm. "Come this way," he said.

"Why?"

"Just go with it. Head back the way we came." He hustled her down the walk past the crowd of pedestrians.

"Noah, I don't understand what we're doing."

"I'll tell you in a minute. Come over here." He stepped into the landscaping and pulled her in with him.

Instantly she was spritzed from head to toe. "I don't think we're supposed to be walking on the—"

"Down behind this rock." He pulled her to a crouch behind a large lava rock.

"Noah, I'm getting soaked from all those misters spraying down. What on earth is the matter?"

"The groom." He took off his Stetson and peered up over the rock. "Brandon."

"Ah." She gazed at Noah's tense profile. Despite her complaining, the mist felt kind of good after the warmth of their walk. "So you're planning on keeping me a secret from the bridal party?"

"I hadn't thought about it until you started talking about the extra key, but then I began thinking that it could be kind of awkward, trying to explain everything."

"Maybe you're right." Far from being insulted, she was delighted. One of her most popular magazine articles had dealt with secrecy in a relationship and how tantalizing the forbidden could become. She would love to be Noah's forbidden secret for the weekend. It would make her that much harder to resist.

"Here comes Brandon. Can you get down lower?"

"Sure." She got to her knees on the mossy ground and hunched down even more. The plants gave off a loamy, fertile scent that was quite exciting. And fortunately this wasn't *really* the tropics, so she didn't have to worry about putting her hand on an icky bug by accident.

Noah went down on his knees, too. Wrapping his arm around her, he pulled her in close.

Secrecy had all sorts of benefits, she decided as she snuggled against him. She'd only felt the hard press of his body once before and that had been wildly exciting. Yet he'd been a kid then, not much older than the drugstore clerk. She preferred this version. Maturity sat well on him—he had the solid strength and intriguing scent of a man in his prime. Their damp clothes seemed to melt against their bodies, giving the illusion of skin against skin. She could almost feel steam rising from where they were pressed together.

"I'm sorry you're getting all wet," he said softly.

"There are worse things." Like wanting to be kissed so bad she could hardly stand it. She studied his lower lip and longed to run her tongue along its length. She wondered if he'd moan the way he had the first time she'd kissed him years ago. And she wondered if he tasted more like a man than a boy. In order to find out, she needed him to tilt his face down toward hers, so she spoke his name. "Noah?"

Sure enough, he looked down at her. His eyes grew darker. "What?" he murmured.

"Lean closer," she whispered. "I need to tell you something."

His eyes grew darker still, and his lips parted as he drew near. "What?"

She slipped her hand behind his neck. "Jungle drums get me hot." Then she kissed him.

4

NOAH'S PROGRAM to reform Keely was seriously off track. Not an hour into it and he was making out with her in the bushes. For the second time in his life he'd succumbed to the temptation of her mouth, but he'd had some idea he could deal with it this time. For some unknown reason, he'd expected a repeat of the kiss she'd given him as a sixteen-year-old. He'd sadly miscalculated.

Oh, she'd had plenty of passion back then, too, but she hadn't been quite sure what to do with it. Now, she'd learned. Good God, how she'd learned. The pressure of her mouth was light at first. Warm. Soft. Taunting him.

His first reaction was to move in and take control. He fought not to do that, because if he took control, he'd never know Keely's plans for this kiss. He had a strong feeling she had plans...and he grew dizzy with anticipation.

Gradually she increased the pressure, coaxing his lips apart. The gentle flick of her tongue was slow and lazy, seducing him by degrees. His head spun as the kiss grew deeper...and deeper yet.

He cupped the curve of her hip and reaction surged through him. Her thin dress was so damp from the mist that she might as well not have been wearing it. He flexed his fingers, tightening his hold a fraction, and heard the change in her breathing.

They should stop this. They really should. But she smelled like raspberries and tasted wicked and delicious, like the candy he'd swiped from the corner store when he was six. He'd eventually had to pay for that candy. He had a hunch he'd have to pay for this moment, too. Something so good always came with a price tag.

Her mouth was moist and hot against his, and the spot where his hand rested began to grow warm. He stroked her in a gentle, circular motion and felt her tremble beneath his palm.

The steady drumbeats coming from the sound system vibrated the steamy air around them, and his blood seemed to pump in the same rhythm as it gathered in a very predictable area. But no matter how hard he became or how much he ached, he felt safe from temptation—safe to explore her hot mouth and dream of her hot body without worrying they'd get totally carried away.

After all, they were in a public place. They were hidden from view, but not even Keely would dare go further when they were a dozen feet from a sidewalk full of people. Not even Keely would make love in broad daylight in the middle of the hotel's landscaping.

Then she guided his hand from her hip to her breast, and he wasn't so sure.

Time out! his mind warned. Too late. Natural reflexes took over as he touched one of Keely's perfect breasts for the first time. Although he'd tried to ignore her breasts ever since she'd turned twelve and they'd begun to show, he'd dreamed about them anyway, long before they'd been displayed in full color for the world to admire.

The magazine picture had only confirmed what he'd suspected—Keely's breasts were a national treasure, a living work of art. Only a dead man wouldn't squeeze that handful of heaven when it was offered. He groaned with the tactile pleasure of closing his hand around so much ripeness.

With a low, throaty chuckle she arched toward him. Maybe there was a note of victory in that chuckle, but he was too lost in the bliss of fondling her to care. Then the front of the dress loosened, and he vaguely realized she must have pulled at the laces, untying them. While his racing pulse was still reacting to that development, a soft pop filtered through his dazed state, and he felt the taut material of her bra go slack.

Framing his face in her smooth hands, she leaned away from his kiss. "Be my guest," she murmured.

This was a mistake. A definite mistake. But he couldn't not look. Slowly he let his gaze travel downward. Her breasts, kissed golden by the sun, lightly freckled as if dusted with nutmeg, spilled out of her dress. Of course this woman wouldn't wear anything when she decided to sunbathe. He imagined her lying on her back, warm and relaxed by the heat, her body glistening with oil, the scent of raspberries heavy in the air.

Moisture gathered in his mouth. He was so hungry for her. As he continued to look, heart pounding, the mist gathered in tiny droplets on her skin and her nipples tightened and darkened to a deep rose. His breath caught. This was a mistake. And he was going to make it.

Slipping a quivering hand under the velvet weight of one smooth breast, he leaned down to taste paradise.

Snip, snip, snip. Noah froze. The sound of hedge shears was unmistakable. And it was coming closer. *Snip, snip, SNIP.*

He released Keely instantly. "Cover up!" he whispered urgently, getting his feet back under him and clamping his hat back on his head.

With a lazy smile, she casually pulled the cups of her pale blue bra over her breasts and snapped the front fastener. She seemed in no hurry whatsoever as she adjusted the straps.

The sounds of the gardener came even closer, yet Noah couldn't stop admiring her cleavage and wishing he had a little longer to enjoy it. But the guy would be upon them any minute. "Faster!" he urged.

"What's the matter?" Her eyes gleamed with mischief as she slowly pulled the laces of her dress closed. "Afraid of getting caught?"

He stared at her and realized that discovery didn't seem

to bother her at all. Maybe once she'd taken off all her clothes for the camera, she'd discarded the concept of shame right along with her clothes. She possessed a freedom that he could only imagine. To his amazement he envied her. He was also incredibly turned on.

Here was a woman who wouldn't balk at *anything*.

Keely tied the laces of her dress at the same moment an olive-skinned man in khaki work clothes came around the boulder pushing a small wheelbarrow mounded with clippings, a pair of hedge sheers resting on top of the cut greenery.

"Madre de Dios!" the man exclaimed. He nearly tripped over a giant fern as he backed up a step.

"We were just leaving," Noah said. He held out a hand to help Keely up and wished he looked as composed as she did. But he could feel the heat climbing up from his collar and he couldn't meet the gardener's shocked gaze.

Instead, he glanced at Keely, who was nonchalantly swishing bits of dirt from her shapely knees. She had never seemed more beautiful to him. The flush in her cheeks obviously came from pleasure, not shame. When she finished brushing herself off and peeked up at him, her eyes sparkled with remnants of desire.

He'd kissed off all that satiny peach lipstick, and her dress was rumpled, giving testimony to exactly what they'd been doing. Yes, he was embarrassed that they'd been discovered here, but in a way he was proud that he was the guy this gorgeous woman had been making out with.

While the gardener stared, Keely picked up her purse and the bag containing her drugstore purchases as calmly as if she were leaving a restaurant after a meal and the gardener was the busboy waiting to clear the table.

Noah thought of the boxes of condoms inside that bag and wondered what would have happened if the gardener hadn't come along. Noah suspected that if he'd been willing to make love to Keely's breasts, chances were he might have been coaxed to make love to the rest of her. The thought of the gardener coming upon them later and catching something even more involved made him break out in a cold sweat.

Swinging her purse strap over her shoulder, Keely flashed a winning smile at the gardener. *"Qué pasa, Jose?"*

For one startled moment Noah thought she might know the gardener, but then he glanced at the man's breast pocket and noticed the name embroidered on it.

Jose's shock and disapproval seemed to melt in the glow of Keely's smile. Slowly he grinned back and gave a little shrug. *"Nada, señorita."*

She winked at him. *"Bien. Adiós."* Then she picked her way carefully around the edge of the rock and headed for the sidewalk.

As Noah followed, he heard the gardener sigh with longing. Keely had made another conquest.

She was waiting for him at the edge of the sidewalk, and naturally she'd attracted a number of glances, both of the curious and of the lecherous kind. The way the damp dress clung to her was close to indecent and the moisture had turned her wavy hair into a mass of ringlets. She looked delicious.

When he stepped out from behind the foliage, several people stared openly. He tried to act as if prowling around in the hotel landscaping was a perfectly normal thing to do.

"Dr. Livingston, I presume?" she said with a grin.

He figured he had to get things straightened out right away. "Keely, don't get the wrong idea. What happened back there was—"

"All my fault," she said. "I know. I was a bad girl." She didn't look particularly sorry about that.

Bad girl. Damn, but that phrase made his blood race. But he had to control those impulses from now on, or he might as well forget about his plan to rehabilitate her. "No, it wasn't all your fault. After all, I'm the one who dragged you back there in the first place. From now on, I don't intend on anything like that happening again. I just want you to know that.'' He looked into her eyes so he wouldn't be tempted to notice how the dress molded to her figure. Fortunately, sunlight filtered down to the sidewalk and the material was beginning to dry already.

''All right.'' She looked far from convinced.

''I mean it, Keely. No fooling around. We're going to get your résumé in shape.''

''And I really appreciate that.'' She gave him a saucy look. ''I'm just worried that my résumé's not very well suited to what you have in mind. But if you're willing to massage it a little, maybe there's hope. I'm looking forward to your input.''

Heat flooded through him. ''Stop that.''

''Stop what?'' She widened her eyes in innocence.

''You know perfectly well. Your choice of words. Like *massage* and *input*. You're trying to make me think about—'' He realized the more he talked, the more aroused he was getting. ''Never mind. Let's go in.''

''Yes. Let's.''

Noah clenched his jaw and started toward the entrance. He would do this. The object was to set Keely on the right path, while being careful not to amble down the wrong one himself. They were only talking about three days. Surely he could manage to keep his pants zipped for three days.

THREE DAYS IN A PLACE like this would give her plenty of time and opportunity to corrupt Noah, Keely thought as they walked through the glittering lobby toward the reservation desk. She didn't need to win the war in the first two hours. She should probably cool it.

All things considered, she shouldn't have allowed matters to proceed so quickly in the underbrush. A kiss would have been plenty for this stage of the game. A kiss would have been quite enough of a sampling, thank you very much. But no, she'd gone completely out of her mind.

Apparently all those years of wanting Noah had created a powerful backlog of needs. If dear Jose hadn't shown up

she would have given away the farm right on the spot, behind a boulder in the front landscaping of the Tahitian. And
despite what Noah thought of her shady past, that sort of
stunt would be a first for her.

She wouldn't call it a bad idea, though. In fact, it was a
pretty good idea. Extremely creative. But the timing was all
wrong. Moving that fast, that soon, would have scared Noah
to death, once he'd done the deed and come to his senses.
She'd nearly blown her opportunity by overreacting. If she
wasn't more careful, he might reconsider his weekend plan
to save her.

And she so didn't want him to reconsider. After that kiss,
if she were a pinball machine she'd be on tilt. The heavenly
way his mouth had felt on hers had naturally made her think
of how perfect his mouth would feel on her breasts. And
she'd charged straight for that goal without thinking of the
consequences, forgetting that she might be sacrificing a
long-term gain for a short-term thrill.

Yet he was walking toward the reservation desk as if he
still had every intention of asking for another key. Maybe
after that last demonstration he was even more convinced
that he had to save her. Maybe letting her impulses get the
best of her hadn't been such a mistake, after all. Now he
really believed she was bad, through and through. Eventually, he wouldn't be able to resist being bad with her.

Feeling better about the future of the weekend, she decided to cut him some slack. "Why don't I wait over by
the potted palm?" she said. "That way you don't have to
feel so uncomfortable about asking for the extra key because
I won't be standing right beside you looking like your babe-
for-the-night."

He glanced at her, a gleam in his eyes. Then he looked
away, and when his gaze found hers again, the gleam was
gone. "That's okay. After the incident with Jose, this will
be a piece of cake."

"Really?" Now, this was an interesting development.
She had the urge to dampen her finger and chalk up a point

on an invisible scoreboard. In a very short time, she'd raised Noah's sexual daring a sizable notch. That was something to be proud of. At this rate, no telling what sort of adventures he might be willing to undertake by Sunday night. And though he'd tried to disguise it, she'd seen that gleam of desire when she'd mentioned being his babe-for-the-night.

Noah walked up to the desk, gave his name and asked for an extra key "for the lady."

Keely was majorly impressed. He hadn't even tried to pretend she was a relative.

"Certainly, sir." The desk clerk, a wholesome type of guy, didn't even blink as he called up Noah's account on the computer. But whatever he saw on the screen made his eyes widen. "Oh, boy. Good thing you stopped by the desk, Mr. Garfield. There's been a small problem with your room."

"What sort of problem?"

The clerk frowned at the screen. "I need to get the manager out here to talk with you. Excuse me a moment." He picked up a phone and punched in a number. "Mr. Garfield's at the desk. No, I don't think he's been up there yet. Right." He hung up the phone and turned to Noah. "Sorry for the inconvenience, sir. The manager will be right out."

Keely wondered if the delay, whatever was causing it, would make Noah more self-conscious about his request for a spare key. Apparently not, because he turned to her and shrugged.

"Mr. Garfield." A guy only slightly older than the desk clerk arrived and held out his hand over the counter. "I'm Martin Ames. Could we step down to the end of the counter for a moment? I need to inform you of our problem."

"Okay." Noah looked at Keely. "Let's go see what this is all about."

She hesitated. "Are you sure you want me to—"

"Yeah." He smiled and angled his head toward the end of the counter. "Come on."

"All right." *Congratulations, Noah,* she thought as she

followed him. From all appearances he was bringing a call girl up to his room, but he didn't seem to care whether the staff assumed that or not. His friends were a different story, of course, but his reluctance there was understandable.

Ames came out from behind the counter and glanced pointedly at Keely before returning his gaze to Noah.

To Noah's credit, he made no effort to explain Keely's presence. "What seems to be the problem?" he asked.

The manager looked uncomfortable. "We're a new hotel, as I'm sure you know, and in the rush to get it open on time, apparently the hiring process wasn't…what I mean to say is, the screening of applicants might not have been quite thorough enough. At least in the housekeeping department."

"And you would be telling me all this because…?"

"One of the housekeepers vandalized your room."

Keely gasped.

"*What?*" Noah stared at the manager in obvious disbelief.

"It was a case of mistaken identity," Ames said quickly. "The woman's in custody, and we've learned from the police that she's mentally unbalanced. It seems she formed an imaginary attachment to one of our guests, and when her interest wasn't returned, she attempted revenge by damaging his room and its contents. That would be bad enough, but she became confused and hit your room by mistake."

"What about my stuff?" Noah asked.

"I'm afraid it's pretty well ruined. She took a knife to your clothes and suitcase and smashed your toiletries. The police took it for evidence, so I'm not sure how soon you can retrieve it. But from what I saw, there's not much point in getting your things back."

"My God." Noah shook his head.

"We take full responsibility, of course," Ames continued. "If you'll give us an estimate of what you lost we'll write you a check immediately. And of course we've moved you to a new room, and you won't be billed for your stay.

If you should choose to move to a different hotel, we'll pay for that.''

"No, I won't move. My friend is getting married here tomorrow night.''

"Ah." Ames nodded. He seemed to be avoiding looking at Keely. "Then let me take you back to the desk and issue you a new key.''

"Two keys,'' Noah said.

"Oh.'' The manager slid a glance over toward Keely. "Of course.''

Keely could see that the discussion was drawing to a close. She was outraged on Noah's behalf. Her L.A. apartment had been vandalized once, and she knew the sick, violated feeling he was probably dealing with right now. Given the mental anguish, she didn't think a different room and some money to replace his belongings, some of which might be irreplaceable, was enough.

She cleared her throat. "Excuse me, but are you moving Mr. Garfield to another room that's similar to what he had?''

"Exactly like what he had,'' Ames said with a satisfied smile. "And there will be no charge, of course.''

"I think he should be given a substantial upgrade,'' Keely said.

Ames blinked. "An upgrade?''

"Now, Keely,'' Noah said, "the same sort of room will be—''

"I don't think so,'' Keely cut in. "You've been traumatized, whether you're willing to admit that or not. And I'll bet your feelings about this hotel are very negative right now.''

Noah gazed at her. "I wouldn't say I'm overjoyed with the place.''

"See?'' Keely turned to Ames. "I would suggest that you give Mr. Garfield an outstanding experience to take away with him, something that will at least partially cancel out the horrible thing that happened. I'm sure you have some luxury suites in this hotel. I would imagine at least one of them is vacant.''

Ames straightened his tie and glanced toward Noah. ''How do you feel about that, Mr. Garfield?''

Noah met Keely's gaze.

She lifted her eyebrows in a silent challenge. There was no doubt in her mind that he deserved this perk, but the Noah she remembered probably wouldn't have taken it. He would have scoffed at the idea of ''luxury'' accommodations, as if a rough-tough cowboy didn't need that kind of pampering. She'd love the chance to show him how wrong he could be.

Gradually a smile touched his lips. ''I think the lady's absolutely right,'' he said. ''Give us the best you can manage, Mr. Ames.''

NOAH WOULD NEVER HAVE agreed to a fancy hotel room for himself. After all, he only planned to sleep in it, so extras would go to waste, as far as he was concerned. But he was glad to get the nicer room for Keely's sake. God only knew the type of place she'd been living in recently.

Besides, a bigger room meant they'd have more space to spread out. He imagined the suite might have two bathrooms and maybe extra sleeping arrangements. If he wasn't bumping into Keely every five seconds he might stand a better chance of keeping his vow not to make love to her.

Ames gave them a new key folder and directed them to a special elevator.

''I'm so glad you told him you wanted a better room,'' Keely said as they stepped into the mirrored elevator. Soft guitar music began to play as the brass doors slid shut.

Noah laughed. ''I'm sure he didn't want to give it to me. These are the rooms they reserve for the high rollers.''

''So what? If they're going to screw up and hire a psycho maid, then they can compensate the poor guy who gets his stuff trashed. I'm really sorry about that, Noah. Did you lose anything special?''

"I've been trying to remember exactly what I brought. I don't think any of it was that important." Noah was having a hard time concentrating on the vandalism incident when more potent subjects stood right in front of him. As he faced Keely in the elevator, the mirrored walls gave him many stimulating viewing options.

On the left and right walls he could admire her figure in profile—the impressive thrust of her breasts, the narrow waist, the long slender legs made even more sexy by the high-heeled sandals. The back wall of the elevator gave him a different perspective. When she shifted her weight, the blue flowered material of her dress quivered against her firm bottom and flounced against her thighs. There was something very enticing about the backs of her knees....

And without warning, he was imagining Keely naked in this elevator, surrounded by mirrors. He could see her lifting her arms over her head, stretching, turning this way and that, while the mirrors reflected every spectacular inch of her. His breathing grew shallow.

"...forget to give him that," Keely said.

"Hmm? What?" Noah felt his face heat as he realized he'd missed half of what she'd just said.

She smiled. "The list of what you had in the room. You need to make that up as soon as possible."

"Oh. Right."

Her green eyes began to sparkle. "Are you enjoying the mirrors?"

Everything he was thinking was apparently written on his face. "I was wondering how they keep them so clean," he fibbed. "You notice there are no smudge marks."

"Now that you mention it, they are very clean." Her eyes danced. "Mirrors can be a lot of fun. Ever made love in front of one?"

"No!" And suddenly that seemed like the only thing he wanted to do.

"Too bad," she said. "Well, there's still time."

Way too much time, he thought. *Especially this weekend.*

5

KEELY'S PULSE RACED with anticipation as she took the key card Noah handed her and slid it into the lock that opened the elevator doors to the hotel's exclusive top floor. Moments later she used the same key for the double doors leading into the suite.

Spending the weekend in a hotel room with Noah had seemed promising from the beginning. Now that they'd be surrounded by luxury, she was beyond excited. No doubt about it, she was her mother's daughter when it came to enjoying the finer things of life.

"I hear water running," Noah said. "I hope nobody left it on and overflowed the sink or something."

"Now that the psycho maid is in custody, I doubt it." She stepped inside the spacious entry and sighed in appreciation. A waterfall in the entry was a very good sign indeed. This one cascaded down a wall of lava rock into a shallow pool rimmed with lacy ferns. Colorful seashells lined the bottom of the pool. "There's your running water."

"I'll be damned."

"Or there's some of your water, at any rate. I think there's more." The gurgle of another water feature drifted through the arched doorway ahead. "Let's go see what else they've dreamed up."

Walking into the living area of the suite, she drew in a breath. Whoever had created this setting understood how fantasy worked. She would love describing this place to her girlfriends. They'd be green.

Automatically her journalistic training kicked in as she

recorded details to take home. First of all, the walls resembled a rocky cliff face. Three separate waterfalls spilled down the rocks to gather in an actual, honest-to-goodness indoor stream that circled the room and flowed through an opening out onto a terrace. There it sluiced into a hot tub surrounded by rattan lounges and cocktail tables. She was speechless.

Inside, the designers had abandoned the idea of traditional furniture. A network of vines and splashes of red and pink flowers gave the impression of a jungle clearing. But this was a clearing with amenities. Velvet cushions in several sizes and shades of green lay in profusion on the smooth rock floor. Sand-colored concrete ledges mounded with more pillows created a raised seating area overlooking the stream. Pieces of driftwood topped with slabs of stone embedded with seashells served as end tables.

In order to get to the bedroom, she'd have to cross the stream on a bamboo footbridge. The concept was so cool that she hugged herself with delight. The bedroom would probably be awesome, too.

She walked over the tiny bridge and through another arched doorway into a haven of sheer white fabrics and romance. A white urn held waxy red anthuriums, but otherwise the room was so virginal-looking it slipped over the line to decadence. The huge canopied bed was draped with gauzy fabric and deep in pillows. Two overstuffed lounges, both slipcovered in white, sat in front of the floor-to-ceiling windows that repeated the view from the living area.

The simple elegance of the setting was a perfect contrast to the lusty mating of bodies she had planned. Seduction was going to be so sweet in this room.

Through another arch she glimpsed a large bathroom that gleamed with white marble and gold fixtures. Oh, yes. Noah was so dead.

But where was he, anyway? Maybe he was standing transfixed in the middle of the living area, unable to believe his eyes. Crossing over the bridge again, she found the room empty. Apparently he'd bogged down in the hall for some reason.

"Noah?" she called. "What are you doing?"

"Trying to figure out how this wall-of-water thing works," he called back. "Do you think we have to turn it off at night? I've been looking for a switch, but I can't seem to find—"

"I don't think you have to worry about how to turn it off." She swallowed her laughter as she headed back toward the entry. He sounded so adorably earnest. Staying in a place like this with a man who'd never experienced luxuries would be a real kick. But she'd do well to remember how different their preferences were when it came to living arrangements.

Sure enough, he wore a frown of concentration as he surveyed the entryway walls, looking for the on/off switch. "All this water running with no way to control it makes me nervous," he said.

"That's because you live in the desert." She also thought anything unrestrained at the moment, water or lust, would get to him. "I'm sure they don't want us fiddling with their waterfall," she said. "And this is only the beginning, anyway. If running water makes you nervous, wait until you see the rest. Come on."

"Well, okay." He walked toward the arched doorway. "But I'd still feel better if I knew how to control the—" His eyes widened at his first glimpse of the suite's interior. "Oh…my…God."

She stood there with a silly grin as his startled gaze traveled from the waterfalls to the miniature creek to the glass wall looking out on the terrace with its exotic hot tub. Beyond the terrace lay the jeweled fantasy hotels along the Strip and the powerful thrust of the mountain range flanking the town. By day the view was impressive. By night it would beggar description.

And they were here because she'd spoken up. She was

quite proud of herself. "A wee bit better than looking at the parking lot, wouldn't you say?"

He was obviously dumbstruck as he surveyed the room again, his attention lingering on the array of pillows and the footbridge leading into the bedroom.

She loved looking at him standing there, an Arizona cowpoke so delightfully out of place in the lush tropical setting. But get him out of those clothes and he'd fit in much better, at least for the weekend. Under those worn jeans and that faded chambray shirt was a body to die for, and soon it would be all hers to command. This unbelievable hotel suite would clinch her victory. A cowboy in paradise. What more could a girl ask for?

"I take it the bedroom's in there," he said.

Oh, yes. "Yes. It's a different style from this room, but it's still wonderful. And there's also an incredible bathroom, from what I could see. I didn't go all the way into the bedroom."

"And is that…all?"

She laughed in disbelief. "That isn't enough?"

"Don't get me wrong. I've never seen a place like this. It blows me away. But somehow I thought there would be more…space."

"The rooms are huge."

"I mean, more rooms."

"Ah." Now she understood. The more rooms, the less temptation. Oh, gee, too bad. "Sorry, but we seem to have an entry, a living room, a bedroom and a bathroom. And closets. Oh, and a terrace."

He looked out to the terrace. She could imagine the wheels turning as he tried to decide if he could sleep there, which was as far from the bedroom as he could hope to get and still be in the suite. She hated to tell him, but it wouldn't be far enough.

Finally he looked at her. "Do you like it?"

"Are you kidding?" She held out her hands and spun around on the smooth stone floor. "I *love* it!"

He smiled, although he still seemed a little on the nervous side. "Well, good. That's good."

"Don't you?"

"I..." He took off his hat and tapped it against his thigh. Then he ran his hand through his hair, combing it back from his forehead. "I don't know. It's so different. No couch, no chairs, no coffee table, no lamps. And where's the TV?"

If she had anything to say about it they wouldn't be watching any television this weekend, but he looked so uneasy she decided to find a TV for him. If imagining he'd be catching a ball game on the tube would ease his anxiety, then she was all in favor of locating the television set.

"I'll bet there's a TV somewhere." She figured the set was hidden, but a remote of some sort had to exist. Strolling into the room, she glanced around and finally found a remote-control unit lying on a rock ledge. "Here we are. 'Entertainment Center,'" she read from the list on the cover of the remote. When she pushed a button, precision motors whirred as a portion of one wall opened to reveal a giant screen.

Noah shook his head. "Amazing."

"Want me to turn it on?" She found the power button.

"No, that's okay."

"Let's make sure it works." Punching the button, she brought up a menu screen. Aha. Adult videos on Channel 14. That might be worth checking out. She didn't want Noah to get *too* comfortable.

She pushed the numbers one and four on the numeric keypad. An incredible sound system filled the room with seductive music. *Naughty! Sassy! No Holds Barred!* flashed on the screen.

"Keely, don't—"

"I'm just testing the system."

"Come on, turn it off." He advanced toward her.

"In a second." As the preview began, she held the remote behind her back.

"Give it here." He reached around her.

"Not yet." She danced away from him.

"Now, you know we don't need to see this." He grabbed for the remote again.

She twirled out of reach. "Just the preview, okay?" She managed to sneak a peek at the screen. Wow. The people were so big. It seemed to make them more naked, somehow. She didn't think she'd ever seen a skin flick on a big-screen TV. And the music was awesome. Must be some primo speakers disguised in the rock walls.

He sounded a little desperate. "Look, I'm not going to wrestle you for it."

"Too bad. That could be fun." She noticed he kept looking at the screen, too, and his attempts to get the remote away from her had become halfhearted.

"Just turn off the video, okay?" he pleaded.

"Right after this part." When the woman dropped to her knees and unzipped the man's pants in obvious preparation for oral sex, the camera zoomed in. The man's penis nearly filled the screen. "Oh, now, see that? I'll bet you dollars-to-doughnuts a man directed this video. You can tell, because a male director always concentrates on fellatio, while a woman—"

"Keely, for God's sake!"

"It's true! If you've watched enough of these you'd have to pick up on it!"

"Well, I haven't, okay? Saguaro Junction doesn't exactly specialize in adult-video arcades!"

"Then you should be delighted to have this chance to see some," she said sweetly. "Whoops, is that a phone ringing somewhere?"

"It sure as hell is, and I'll bet it's Brandon. God, I was supposed to meet him at—" He checked his watch. "Ten minutes ago. A fitting for the tux." He scanned the area frantically. "Do you see anything in this jungle that resembles a phone, or should I go answer that trumpet-flower thing? That's where the ringing's coming from."

"I'm sure that's a flower." She moved the petals aside and saw nothing but lava rocks behind it.

"This is ridiculous. We can't even answer the—"

"Oh!" With sudden inspiration, she looked at the remote in her hand. "Here's a button marked Fax/phone. Let's see what happens if I push it."

His eyes widened in panic. "Don't! It might be a video phone or something."

"Okay, then take it." She thrust the remote at him. "You push those little buttons and I'll leave the room."

"And go where?" he asked, sounding even more agitated.

"To the bedroom." She winked at him. "Maybe I'll slip into something more comfortable."

"But you don't have any other clothes!" He sounded very worried.

She glanced over her shoulder. "I know." Then she crossed the footbridge with her best eye-catching walk. Poor Noah. When she decided to make her move, he wouldn't know what hit him.

WITH TREMBLING HANDS Noah turned off the power to the big-screen TV, finally erasing the erotic images that had nearly driven him to do something he'd regret. Glancing uneasily toward the bedroom, afraid of what Keely might be up to in there, he pushed the button for the phone. Once again motors whirred as the rock wall parted and a shelf slid out, presenting him with a fax machine and a cordless phone.

Setting the remote on the shelf, Noah picked up the cordless and turned it on. "Hello?"

"Noah!" Brandon sounded relieved.

"Listen, I'm sorry I'm not down there like I'm supposed to be. There's been—"

"I heard about that. I dialed your room and couldn't get you, so the guys and I decided to go up there, because it's not like you to be late. That's when we found yellow crime-scene tape everywhere. Man, we went on a rampage, finally got ahold of the manager, Ames, and he told us what happened. I rescheduled the fittings for thirty minutes from now. Can you make that okay?''

"Sure. I could come down now if you want.''

"They have another wedding party in the rental shop right now, but we can go have a beer if you want to. Or we could all come up there and see your new room. Is it pretty cool?''

"It's okay.'' Noah didn't want to describe it because his friends would be up in a heartbeat to check it out. "The usual.''

"It must at least have a hot tub or something, right?''

"Well, yeah, it does.'' Noah picked up the remote to find out what else it controlled besides the TV and the Fax/phone cabinet.

"Where? In the bedroom? Our honeymoon suite has a hot tub in the bedroom.''

"Uh, it's on the terrace.''

"The *terrace?* Damn it, son, we don't even *have* a terrace, let alone one big enough for a hot tub. What's your view like?''

"Um, you know—town, the mountains, stuff.''

"I gotta see this. What's your number?''

"Well, I don't know if you can just come up. There's a special elevator.'' In his agitation Noah's thumb clamped down on one of the buttons on the remote. Another rock panel slid back to reveal a completely stocked wet bar backed by mirrored glass.

"A special elevator?'' Brandon cried. "Shitfire, you're on the high-roller floor, aren't you? We are so coming up!''

Noah tried to close the panel over the wet bar and brushed against another button that activated the lighting system. "Listen, why don't I meet you in that bar that has all the tropical birds in it?'' he said quickly as the colors bathing the room changed from cool blues and greens to purples, and finally to a very sexy red.

"You don't like tropical birds in your bars," Brandon said. "You told me that already."

"I think we should do it anyway, for the experience." The lights pulsed and glowed as they continued through their cycle. Orgy lights was all Noah could think as he watched them. "We'll get an umbrella drink," he said to Brandon. "I've been hankering for an umbrella drink."

"You have not." Brandon paused, letting the silence stretch between them. "Why don't you want us to see the room, bro?"

"You're right, you should see it," Noah said immediately. He couldn't risk hurting his friends' feelings. "You need to come up and see this room. Matter of fact, maybe we should switch rooms, you and me. After all, you're the bridegroom."

"You were afraid I'd be jealous because your room's cooler than mine, weren't you?"

"Well…" It was as good an excuse as any.

"Don't worry about it. And I appreciate the offer to switch, but I don't want to do that. Jenny told me she loves the idea of a hot tub in the bedroom, so we can go in it naked and fool around. I already have that picture in my mind and I'm really looking forward to it."

"I'll bet." And thanks to Brandon, Noah had a picture in his mind of fooling around with Keely in the hot tub.

"The thing is, I don't think she'd feel the same way about a hot tub on a terrace. She's kinda timid about things like that, getting naked outside and all."

Keely wasn't the least bit timid, Noah thought. She'd be willing to make love on that balcony. Now, if only he could forget that for the next three days, he'd be all set. But he didn't suppose he would, short of getting amnesia.

"Besides," Brandon said, "you earned this room, with all you went through. Are you gonna buy new clothes here, or do you want to borrow some things from us? I'm close to your size, and so's Clint."

"I hate shopping for clothes."

"Then just take the money and wait until you get home. We'll bring some things up when we come. Now, how do we get there?"

"I'm not sure. You can ride the elevator, but then you need a room key to get the door to open. I—oh, wait a minute. Maybe I do know how to do this." He glanced down at the remote and found a button marked Elevator. "Take the executive elevator. When you get to the top, I can open the doors from here. Go on into the hall, and it's the first set of double doors to your left."

"This is unbelievable. You're probably in the same damn room Garth Brooks stayed in when he played the Tahitian last month."

"I don't know about that." But Noah had no trouble imagining celebrities in this room. No trouble at all. And he wondered where a celebrity would stash his secret sweetie, if he had one.

"Okay, we'll be up there in a few minutes, after we grab some clothes for you."

"Great. Bye." Noah hung up the phone and headed quickly toward the bedroom. "Keely? Keely, the guys are coming up here. We need to figure out what to do."

She wasn't in the bedroom, but her dress and underwear were. She'd tossed them across the end of the white bed like pale blue warning flags.

He screeched to a stop. "Keely?"

"In here. I felt like taking a bath."

"Oh." He looked warily toward the bathroom. A heavenly scent drifted toward him, and he heard the sound of soft splashing, although he couldn't see what was going on, thank goodness. But he could imagine her lolling around in a bubble bath, with foam only partially concealing her golden skin, and her breasts bobbing on the surface of the water. Maybe imagination was more seductive than actually seeing her in the tub, but he wasn't going to take the chance on looking at the real thing.

"So your friends are coming up to the suite?"

"Yeah." He tried not to sound as panicked as he felt. "In just a few minutes."

"No problem." She splashed around some more and water gurgled, as if going down the drain. "I'll hide in the closet."

"Naked?" He didn't know why it mattered, but the thought of her hiding naked in the closet was ten times more anxiety-producing than if she put on clothes first.

She laughed and appeared in the doorway wearing a large white towel, her hair caught up in a loose topknot. "Naked in the closet. Now, that creates a real mental picture, doesn't it?"

He gulped. She'd wrapped the towel around her and tucked the end between her breasts. One flick of a wrist, either his or hers, and it would fall at her feet.

"There are two robes in that closet," she said. "I checked."

"I'll get one for you!" He nearly tripped in his eagerness to get to the closet. Of course the sliding door was mirrored, and the bed was perfectly reflected in it. Of course.

He pulled the terry-cloth robe from its hanger, rattling all the hangers on the rod in his haste to get her covered up. Then he turned.

"Thank you," she said, and let the towel drop.

Sweet Lord in heaven. He clutched the bathrobe and tried to remember how to breathe. No wonder people had been willing to pay for a glimpse of such beauty. Women with a body like hers had toppled empires, so maybe he'd be forgiven if he couldn't stop looking at her.

The fantasy atmosphere in the room must be getting to him. As he gazed at her, he started zoning out on weird thoughts of Keely making love to the sun, allowing it to kiss her skin until her body was golden and dusted with freckles. He thought of her lying under the sun being licked by tongues of flame until she was wet and eager.

She would be easy to arouse. He knew that from her response earlier this afternoon, and from the rapid, shallow way she was breathing now. Her nipples darkened and puckered, inviting him to linger in appreciation of her full breasts. Not long ago he'd touched, but he hadn't tasted.

Now he could. Now he could kneel before her and kiss the soft skin of her belly. He could explore lower, parting her auburn curls with his tongue until he reached…heaven. And then he could hear her cry of release, a sound he'd only imagined in his dreams. Then he would seek his own release from the hard, grinding pressure building relentlessly within him.

"The robe?" she asked softly.

He glanced at the robe, then back at her. If he didn't activate the elevator doors, his friends wouldn't be able to get onto this floor. He and Keely could be totally, completely alone for as long as they wanted to be, for as long as it took for him to satisfy this unbearable craving. His mouth grew moist as the possibilities beckoned to him.

"Now's not the time," Keely said, her voice gentle.

His voice rasped in his throat. "Why not?"

"You need to get fitted for your tux in a few minutes. I was only giving you a sneak preview." She reached over and took the robe from him. "We have all weekend, Noah."

While he watched, his body trembling with the urge to have her, she slid her arms into the sleeves of the bathrobe. The motion jiggled her breasts and he groaned. The robe gaped open a moment as she adjusted the collar, and her hour-glass figure was perfectly framed by the white terry lapels. That view was even more erotic than when she'd worn nothing at all.

Then she overlapped the lapels and tied the belt, eliminating his view. But like a bolt of lightning, the image of her perfect body was burned into his retina.

6

AFTER NOAH LEFT the room looking shell-shocked, Keely gathered up her clothes, purse and the drugstore bag before stepping into the closet. Sitting on the floor, she slid the door shut, leaned against the wall and closed her eyes. A smile tugged at her mouth. What a great moment that had been.

She hadn't planned to drop the towel, but it had started to slip as he'd turned to grab a robe from the closet. Rather than fumbling with her towel like a self-conscious virgin, she'd let it go.

Impulse had turned out to be more effective than inspiration. Although she wasn't about to let him ignore his wedding duties, she wouldn't mind having him think about her in the process. He would certainly think about her now.

Taking a bath had also been an impulse, but once she'd seen that huge tub, she'd looked at her somewhat grimy knees and decided to indulge in a quick soak while Noah dealt with his phone call. Yes, all in all her impulses were leading her in the right direction.

Rummaging through the drugstore bag, she took out her raspberry lotion, released the plunger and filled her palm with some creamy lotion. No reason to waste the time she was trapped in here.

Excited male voices filtered into her little hideaway. Noah's friends had arrived and were obviously impressed with the setup. She listened to them rave while she smoothed lotion over her legs. God, she loved this scent, and it seemed to be amplified by her confined quarters.

"We should have the bachelor party here, guys!" one of Noah's friends said. "I feel an orgy coming on."

"You always feel an orgy coming on," said another. "But it won't work, Clint, old buddy."

"Why not? It's perfect. It's decadent. It's—"

"And what about the entertainment, Einstein?"

Keely figured their idea of "entertainment" involved women wearing next to nothing and dancing around wildly for their benefit. She pumped another helping of lotion into her cupped hand.

"We could import the entertainment, couldn't we?" said the guy who was apparently named Clint. "This is Vegas! Girls, girls, girls!"

Then the conversation became a jumble of suggestions and countersuggestions. Keely pulled a foot into her lap and rubbed lotion into her sole and between her toes. She loved wearing sandals in the summer, but she had to keep massaging lotion into her feet every day to keep them smooth, plus she indulged in regular pedicures. She could just imagine what her ranch-foreman father would think of that extravagance.

While she applied lotion, she tried to guess how many men were out there besides Noah. She finally identified three. One was Brandon, the groom. Then there was Clint, who seemed to be the idea man, and a third person named Greg, who sounded like the joker of the group.

"I don't care if you want to use the place," Noah said at last, "but personally, I think it'll be a lot of extra trouble to bring in the entertainment."

Keely wondered what he'd do if she popped out of the closet and offered to take care of that for the boys. Have a heart attack, most likely. It was a fun concept, though. Noah was such a sitting duck for stunts like that. She'd have to be careful not to overdo it just because it was so easy to shock the pants off of him—literally. She rubbed lotion on her other foot.

"Noah's right," said Brandon from the living room. He

seemed to be the organizer. "Maybe we can just come back here to hang out afterward and drink ourselves silly."

Now, that could put a real crimp in her plans. She wondered if Noah would come up with something to kill that idea. After all, she had just given him a dramatic glimpse of what he could look forward to once they were alone tonight.

"That would be okay, I guess," Noah said.

Keely grimaced. He must be having another attack of conscience and wanted some built-in safeguards to keep him from acting on his urges. Corrupting Noah wasn't going to be quite as easy as she'd first thought.

She untied the robe and slipped her arms out of the sleeves so she could put lotion on her upper body. As she smoothed it over her breasts she thought of Noah's calloused hands caressing her. She was looking forward to a repeat of that experience.

"Then let's plan on coming back here," Brandon said. "We'll start the evening at that topless bar we picked out and then head back to the hotel. Oh, and these are the clothes Clint and I came up with for you, Noah. Two pairs of jeans and three shirts."

"You're sure you guys don't need them?" Noah asked.

Keely cupped her breasts and closed her eyes. She wanted to hear that voice of his murmuring in her ear. Soon. She'd figure out how to get rid of his friends tonight.

"I always pack too many clothes," Clint said. "Besides, Sharon and me are gonna be enjoying that saltwater beach. I bought some bathing trunks, and—"

"Trunks, my ass!" Greg chortled. "You bought yourself a Speedo, boy. You are into the Vegas lifestyle, big time!"

Clint laughed. "Why not? Hell, I can wear those cowboy duds anytime. This weekend I'm gonna be a beach bum."

Keely wouldn't mind seeing Noah in a bathing suit, come to think of it. She might have to include a shopping trip in her evening plans.

"And you make a great beach bum, old buddy," Brandon said. "Listen, we need to get down to the tux-rental place."

"I have to hand it to you, Brandon, for staging this shin-dig in a Vegas hotel," Clint said. "Tux rental, bridal shop, florist, chapel and reception hall, everything together in one building. When Sharon and I got married we ran all over the damn place."

"I remember," Brandon said. "I ran all over the damn place with you, and Greg and Tina's wedding was no better."

"Tell me about it," Greg said.

"Okay, guys. We gotta boogie," Brandon said again, sounding a little more impatient.

"Can't we see the bedroom and bathroom first?" Greg asked.

"If we make it quick," Brandon said. Footsteps sounded over the bamboo footbridge. "I'd love to know what this room goes for per night."

The closet was getting a little warm, Keely thought. Or maybe she was heating up the space with her lusty thoughts about Noah in a bathing suit.

"They don't charge for these kinds of rooms," Greg said, the sound of his voice coming closer. "The guys who stay here are the ones who fly in by private jet and drop thousands at the tables. Something you clowns can only dream about."

"Excuse me?" Clint said. "I did pretty good in the casino last night."

"Oh, you were awesome," Greg said. "That bucket of nickels sure impressed Tina and me. Any minute now they'll roll out the red carpet for a big spender like you."

"At least I had a bucket of nickels, while a certain cowboy I could mention had a whole lot of nothing in his bucket," Clint said.

Keely decided against putting the robe back on for fear she'd start sweating. She leaned her bare back against the wall, which was smooth and cool. Ah, that was better.

"Wow, will you look at this bedroom?" Brandon said. "It even smells good in here. Like raspberries."

She smothered a giggle.

"And the crime of it all is that Noah is staying solo in this layout," Greg said. "Hey, Noah, maybe you should look around tonight and see if there's anybody worth bringing back for the weekend."

Sitting up straighter, she listened for his response.

"I don't think so," Noah said.

She relaxed back against the wall.

"What do you mean, *you don't think so?*" Clint said. "This is Vegas, cowboy. Vegas girls. You're the only one of us who's free to sample. We were counting on you to perform for the group so we can get some secondhand thrills."

"I guess you'll have to get your thrills someplace else," Noah said. "I'm not in the mood."

Liar, liar, pants on fire, Keely chanted softly to herself.

"How can you not be in the mood?" Greg said. "This place cries out for a hot interlude with a temporary babe."

"Yeah," Clint added, "and you didn't exactly avoid that kind of experience when you were on the rodeo circuit."

Keely blinked. Noah had hot interludes on the rodeo circuit? That didn't fit her picture of him at all. Although the idea of him getting it on with another woman made her pea green with jealousy, she was dying to know the details.

"Yeah, I remember a certain lady in Cheyenne," Brandon said. "You two were holed up in that motel room for forty-eight hours at least. And there was that little gal in San Antone, the barrel racer. And then at the Pendleton Roundup, you—"

"Never mind," Noah said, sounding very tense. "No point in dredging up ancient history."

"Well, damn." Greg sighed. "Obviously our buddy Noah is over the hill."

"I am not! I just—"

"The facts speak for themselves," Greg continued. "We

need a moment of silence, boys, for the late, great Noah Garfield. The guy's in Vegas and he can't get it up.''

''Maybe he's not dead yet,'' Brandon said. ''Maybe staying in this passion pit will inspire him to regain his former glory.''

''God, you would think so, wouldn't you?'' Greg agreed. ''Look at that bed. It's criminal to sleep alone in that bed. And right across from that great bed, you've got mirrors on the closet doors.'' He sighed again. ''I had mirror sex once. It was great.''

''You had sex with a mirror? Are we talking self-gratification for the Gregster?'' Clint asked, laughing.

''*No,* I had sex with a woman in front of a mirror, lame-brain. And no, it wasn't with Tina, so I'd appreciate keeping this discussion between us.''

''Always is,'' Brandon said. ''Listen, y'all take your bathroom tour and then we're outta here. Time's getting short.''

''Wow.'' Clint's voice echoed slightly in the tiled bathroom. ''That tub's big enough for six *Playboy* bunnies. And look at this! Suds in the tub! Noah, did you just take a bubble bath?''

Keely clapped a hand over her mouth. She'd forgotten that somebody might notice that.

''*A bubble bath?*'' Greg said. ''Noah Garfield? This I gotta see. Oh my God. Looks like somebody took a bubble bath. Come to think of it, there was a towel on the bedroom floor. So the evidence mounts that a bubble bath was indeed taken. And the occupants of this suite are Noah Garfield, and...well, *nobody,* so the incriminating finger points to you, old buddy.''

''Gotta be Noah,'' Brandon said, laughing. ''No wonder you didn't want us up here, bro. Did you hide your rubber ducky? I don't see it anywhere.''

The laughter grew louder and the comments more crude. Finally Noah's voice rose above the hubbub. ''You morons should try a good soak in the tub once in a while,'' he said. ''Clears the mind.''

''It wrinkles your privates, is what it does!'' Greg said. ''Maybe that's your problem, son. Too many bubble baths. Only good time to take a bath is when you have somebody in there with you. I can't see the advantage in sitting there by yourself. Well, unless you're into that.'' More laughter followed.

''This has been most edifying,'' Brandon said, ''but we really have to leave. Want me to put these clothes in your closet, bro?''

Keely froze. Then she fumbled around frantically as she tried to put her arms in the sleeves of her robe without making any noise. She couldn't seem to find the armholes.

''You can just leave them on the bed,'' Noah said quickly.

Keely tried harder, but the robe was hopelessly twisted.

''The shirts are on hangers,'' Brandon said. ''I might as well—''

''Okay, then I'll do it,'' Noah said.

Keely sagged against the closet wall with relief.

''Sheesh. You always were a bossy son of a gun,'' Brandon said. ''Here.''

''Thanks. I appreciate the loan of the clothes.''

Keely held herself very still as the closet door slid partly open. She found herself staring up at Noah's crotch as he blocked the opening with his body. She had the biggest urge to whisper *peek a boo* and give him a little tickle on the zipper of his fly, but she controlled herself.

His gaze flicked down to where she sat, and she waggled her fingers at him. His quick gasp told her he'd noticed that she'd slipped out of the robe. No doubt he thought she'd done it on purpose to torment him, but this time she was innocent. Well, sort of innocent.

Abruptly he hooked the hangers over the rod and shoved the door closed so hard she was afraid he'd crack the mirror.

''Boy, that raspberry smell sure is strong,'' Clint said.

"They must have hung one of those sachet doo-dads in the closet."

"Must have," Noah said. "Come on, let's go."

She waited until there was nothing but silence outside the closet door before she shoved it open and crawled out, leaving the bathrobe in a heap on the closet floor. Grinning, she stood and stretched, all the while wondering what Noah was thinking about right now. Naked women in closets, most likely. The cool air felt great on her skin, and she decided that this suite was made for walking around naked. She crossed the footbridge into the living room.

So Noah had been a wild man out on the rodeo circuit. That made her mission to corrupt him even more important. He'd moved home to the ranch, shouldered all those responsibilities and lost his spark. It was encouraging to know that he used to have a spark. And she was just the girl to rekindle it.

This hotel suite was the very place to light such a fire, she thought as she surveyed the cushions spread everywhere. But she needed some more ammunition. Originally she'd planned a quick trip to her hotel to get the rest of her clothes, but they weren't naughty enough for what she had in mind. This hotel would undoubtedly have a couple of shops that would be perfect for the occasion, and she could pick up Noah's bathing suit at the same time. But first she had to find out if Noah had thought to leave her a key.

They hadn't had time to discuss where he'd put the extra one. Considering his condition after she'd dropped her towel, he wouldn't have been able to focus on such matters, anyway. But she hoped he'd thought of it before he left.

Ten minutes later, she stood gazing out the sliding doors to the terrace and fanning herself absently with the empty key folder. The key wasn't anywhere. He'd probably taken both keys without thinking about it. Or maybe he had thought about it and didn't want her venturing out yet. Either way, she didn't intend to let the lack of a key stop her. She'd simply have to go find him.

Until she went shopping she'd have to make do with the dress she had, but she longed for fresh underwear after that nice bath. Finally she decided to rinse out her panties and dry them with the hair dryer. She could skip the bra. After all, she was in Vegas, as Noah's friends had pointed out more than once.

She touched up her makeup with supplies she kept in her purse, put on her slightly damp panties and pulled her dress over her head. Then she released her hair from its topknot and finger-combed it into place. Time to go find the Romeo of the Rodeo Circuit.

SHE'D ENDED UP naked in the closet, after all, Noah thought as he stood in the tux-rental shop and buttoned the vest he'd be wearing as a groomsman. Now all he could think about was how she'd looked. He should have guessed she'd be in there putting on her raspberry lotion.

When he'd opened the closet door he'd been hit with a double whammy, a naked Keely and the overwhelming scent of raspberries. How he'd managed to close the door and walk out of the bedroom as if he were a sane person, he'd never know. He could still see her there in the dusky interior of that closet, smiling at him and wiggling her fingers in greeting.

She was a devil woman. And she wanted to tempt him the way she'd tempted others before him, but it wasn't going to work, damn it. Somewhere he'd find the strength to resist and demonstrate to her that at least one man valued her for something besides sex. He would show her there was another path she could take and that her spectacular body didn't have to dictate her future.

But he'd have to be careful. He'd nearly cracked when she'd dropped that towel. If he were completely honest with himself, she'd been the one to call a halt, not him. If she'd given him even the slightest encouragement, he would have aborted his plan and been all over her. He knew it and he suspected she knew it, too.

That damn raspberry lotion wasn't helping, either. He couldn't very well tell her not to use it if that's what she liked. And he wouldn't want to be responsible for the dry air damaging that soft skin. That satiny, golden, sweetly freckled...

"Yo, Garfield!" Brandon clapped him on the back. "Just two more buttons and you'll have that vest together. Work with me, man. Button, buttonhole. That's it. I think you've got it now."

Noah's neck grew warm with embarrassment. No telling how long he'd been standing there staring off into space. "Can't a guy take a moment?" he said. "These weddings are big medicine. I've got some deep thinking to do."

Brandon laughed. "That sounds like my line. Anyway, you'll have plenty of thinking time later, when we all have a beer in our hands. Right now we have to find out if your monkey suit fits. Here's the coat."

Noah stuck his arms in the coat Brandon held for him. "Why does everybody always get rigged up like this for weddings?" he asked.

"Because it gets the women hot," Greg said as he adjusted the lapels of his coat. "Right, Brandon?"

"So I've heard."

"It's true." Clint checked out his reflection in the three-way mirror. "Chicks can't resist a guy in tie and tails."

"If you say so. You all could pass for city slickers, if that's what you're after." Noah grinned as he watched his three friends walk around in their rented finery. Looking at them now, nobody would guess that Clint and Brandon were two of the finest bareback riders in the country and that Greg could rope and tie a steer faster than almost anyone on the circuit.

Clint and Brandon were as close as brothers, but they'd never pass for biological brothers. Clint was tall and blond and Brandon was short and dark-haired. Greg, a freckle-faced redhead, had developed a slight beer belly now that he'd reached his thirties, but he was strong as an ox.

"I think I look like a high roller," Greg said, sucking in his stomach. "Maybe this getup will convince somebody to give me a suite on your floor, Noah."

"This from a guy who bombed out on nickel slots," Clint said.

Immediately Greg wanted to debate the possibility of a system for playing slots. Noah tried to concentrate on the conversation, but Greg's mention of the suite had derailed him. Once again all he could think about was Keely.

He could even smell raspberries. Amazing how a scent could stay with you like that, even when the source was... Wait a minute. He turned toward the door of the tux shop and, sure enough, Keely had just walked inside.

She didn't look at him. His heart raced as he wondered what she was up to. If she'd meant to blow his cover, she would have come right over and greeted him. Instead, she wandered around the shop gazing at the displays, while his three friends stared openmouthed at her.

He couldn't blame them. With her tousled hair and short, flirty dress, she was a traffic stopper, all right.

The clerk hurried up to her. "May I help you with something?"

She turned her high-wattage smile on him. "I'm getting ideas."

Noah would bet the ranch on that one.

The clerk nodded happily. "When is the happy occasion?"

Keely's glance flicked ever-so-slightly in Noah's direction. "Soon." Then her attention swung back to Noah with more purpose. "And, you know, that's quite a bit like what I had in mind, right there."

Noah forced himself to breathe normally as she came toward him. He didn't have to look to know that his buddies were watching intently.

Her green eyes held that sparkle of devilment that was pure Keely. "*Very* nice," she said, giving him the once-over. "Would you turn around, please, so I can see how it looks in back?"

He really didn't have a choice. He turned.

"Yes," she murmured. "Exactly what I'm looking for."

He faced her again and hoped the red in his face didn't clash too much with the dove-gray coat. "I need to get changed." He winced at the obvious catch in his voice.

"Thank you for letting me look." The corners of her mouth tilted up. "The *key* is in the fit of the trousers, don't you think?"

She was torturing him and she knew it. He heard muffled laughter coming from the back of the shop where his friends had gathered to observe the action. No doubt they thought he was being picked up, assuming he was willing to be picked up.

"We think of ourselves as the premier tux shop in town," the clerk said, puffing out his chest with pride.

"And accessibility certainly is a *key* factor in that," Keely said. "Accessibility and availability are the *keys* to success in any venture, in my opinion."

"Absolutely," agreed the clerk.

Noah was afraid he'd sweat through this outfit if he stood there much longer listening to her sexy comments. "If you'll excuse me, I'll go take this off," he said.

"Now, there's something else I need to know," Keely said. "Do your dressing rooms have *keys?*"

Noah nearly came unglued. He couldn't look at the clerk. "I'll be in the back," he said. And if Keely followed him into the dressing room and tried anything, he'd…well, he'd do something. He wasn't sure what. At the moment the idea of Keely in the dressing room with him was causing a problem with the fit of his trousers, and he had to get away from her.

"I'll bet that man is a *key* player in whatever he does," she commented as he hurried toward the short hallway leading to the dressing rooms.

"I couldn't tell you," the clerk said. "Now, how many tuxedos will you be requiring for your event?"

Noah didn't pause to hear her answer.

"Told you the monkey suit works," Greg said in an undertone as Noah barreled past his friends without looking at them. Then all the guys just about killed themselves laughing.

Noah went into the dressing room where he'd left his clothes and closed the door firmly. Sure enough, there was a lock and he twisted it shut. She was not going to seduce him in the tux-shop dressing room, damn it, not even if it would be about the most risky, exciting thing he'd ever experienced in his life. His fingers trembled as he started taking off the rental clothes.

A soft knock sounded at the door.

"Busy!" Noah called out.

Loud male laughter greeted his statement, along with various comments about his lack of sex drive.

He walked over and opened the door to find his friends grinning at him. "What you think was happening was not happening," he said.

More laughter.

"We know that," Greg said with a chuckle. "The lady was trying to score, but nothing was happening. Garfield, have you lost your mind?"

"Or some other significant body part?" Clint added. "That woman was *hot,* and she was coming on to you, and you acted like some damn virgin!"

Brandon shook his head sadly. "This is not the Noah Garfield we've come to admire."

"She's nuts, is what she is," Noah said. "Did you hear her? She wanted to know if the dressing rooms had *keys,* for crying out loud."

"Yeah, she sure did." Greg sighed and looked longingly into the distance. "A woman with imagination is a beautiful thing. In one of these dressing rooms you could have three-way-mirror sex, not to mention sex in a forbidden place."

"These monkey suits are dynamite." Clint said. "She was pulled right in, and what a catch! I'll bet she's a dancer." He waggled his eyebrows. "You know, a *dancer?*"

"And she picked you right out, bro," Brandon said. "Did you hear her say she thinks you're a *key* player?"

And finally Noah got it. Keely wasn't here to sneak into a dressing room with him and have three-way-mirror sex. He felt almost sad that her motivation hadn't been naughty, after all. She'd been trying to tell him she needed the extra key. Apparently, in his agitation, he'd left the suite with both of them.

She probably needed some money, too, if she planned to do a little shopping this afternoon. He'd left her pretty much high and dry up there. Well, high, anyway. Nothing was dry about that suite.

Greg peered around the corner into the shop. "She's still out there. You might be able to salvage this situation if you go talk to her."

"Okay, I'll get dressed and go talk to her," Noah said. "But I'm not having sex in one of these dressing rooms, and that's final."

7

KEELY WASN'T SURE whether or not all her signals about keys would get through Noah's sexual fog. No matter how many times she vowed not to tease him, she continued to do it. He was such a delicious target, and each time she scored a hit, the painful memory of his rejection all those years ago faded a little more. She'd give anything for a snapshot of his face when she'd asked if the dressing rooms had keys.

Another of her features for *Attitude!* had dealt with unusual places to have sex, and dressing rooms had been one of them. She'd never personally tried it, though. In fact, she hadn't personally tried many of the adventures she wrote about in the magazine. This weekend seemed tailor-made for those kinds of adventures.

Getting a glimpse of Noah in a tux had doubled her determination. What a babe magnet. With those baby browns of his and that killer physique, he could well have left a trail of broken hearts on the rodeo circuit. But now he was stuck in Saguaro Junction, and she knew from experience that the action was skimpy around those parts. She'd give him a vacation from the deadly-dull social life of a small town.

But she really needed the extra suite key in order to keep this operation smooth. If Noah took off with his buddies before slipping her the key, she might have to try something more blatant. She didn't want him leaving for the evening while she was locked out. Yes, she could always go back to her own hotel if necessary, but it wasn't exactly next door.

As she continued to talk to the clerk about her imaginary "big event," she heard laughter from the dressing-room area and figured Noah's buddies were giving him a hard time. Those guys were a kick, a goofy bunch she'd like to make friends with if the situation were different. She'd matched up the voices with the bodies, so she'd pretty much tagged each one of them.

Greg was the redhead with the cute little belly. The tall blonde with the all-American good looks had to be Clint, and then there was Brandon the bridegroom—short, dark and adorable. Too bad his life would be over in a couple of days, once he'd tied the knot.

Both Clint and Greg already wore wedding rings. Poor guys. This bachelor party might be their only chance to break away from the tedium of their constricted lives. No wonder they wanted dancing girls tonight and hoped Noah would act out their fantasies this weekend.

And speaking of the fantasy man, he was strolling out of the dressing room, his arms full of rental clothes. He handed the stuff to the clerk who took it toward the counter, then headed in her direction. Thank goodness. He'd figured out her code.

"Nice to see you again, cowboy," she said.

"Sorry to be so dense." He held out his hand. "Here," he said, keeping his hand closed over the key. "The guys think you're propositioning me, by the way."

"I am." She took what was in his hand and realized money had been folded around the key. "You don't have to give me this." She slipped the key into her purse and tried to give him back the money.

"You need some clothes, right? For God's sake, put that away. And don't move to the right or left. If you stay right where you are, I'm blocking their view of you, so they won't see what we're doing."

"Really?" She lifted both eyebrows and ran her tongue over her lips. "So what do you wanna do?"

His mouth twitched, as if he might be holding back a laugh. "Nothing, okay?" he said in a low voice. "Now get rid of that money."

"All right." She tucked the money down the front of her dress. Fortunately, the lace-up bodice gave her some cleavage, even without wearing a bra. The gesture would have lost impact if the bills had fallen through her dress to the floor.

"*Keely.*"

"Noah, you're so funny. From what I heard, your rep could use some polishing. This little conversation we're having could do your image a world of good if you put the right spin on it. In fact, I don't know why we're keeping secrets from these guys. They seem like an open-minded bunch to me."

"I can tell you where their minds are. Listen, they want to come up to the suite after the bachelor party tonight. I didn't know how to tell them they couldn't, but I'll have to figure out some way to keep them from doing that. You can't very well spend the night in the closet."

"Oh, I don't know." She winked at him. "I had a good time in there."

His face reddened.

"But I have to admit that after a while it did get pretty hot."

"Keely, is it possible for you to talk about something besides sex?"

"Sure, but what fun is that?" She chuckled at his pained expression. "Look, why don't we just tell your friends that you're being a good Samaritan and helping me find a new and less interesting career?"

"Because they wouldn't believe it. If they knew you were staying with me, they'd leap to one conclusion and one conclusion only. We'd never be able to convince them otherwise."

"Would that be so terrible? Apparently you're no stranger to the wild-weekend concept."

He frowned. "So you heard all that."

"Clear as a bell."

"I want you to know I cared about those women. It wasn't the way they made it sound."

She would rather have heard that the women meant nothing to him. "Noah, I'm the last person in the world who would judge you for enjoying a little healthy sex. And your friends won't, either."

His frown deepened. "I don't want them thinking that about you."

"Why not?"

"Because...because we grew up together, damn it, and I don't like it when guys think those things about you."

"Noah, what they're thinking, that I'd be fun in bed, has some basis in fact. I'm not that kid you grew up with. Not anymore."

He flushed an even darker color of red. "I don't care," he said, sounding a bit like a kid himself. "Nothing's going to happen between us."

She chose to let her smile answer that one.

"It's not! I forgot myself a couple of times, but I won't forget myself again."

"If you say so." She continued to smile at him.

"I do, and that's that." He crossed his arms over his chest. "I'm going to find some way to keep the guys from coming up to the suite tonight. I don't know how, but I'll think of something. Now, please go buy some clothes. And work on your résumé. Tonight we'll go over it and come up with some ideas."

"Sounds promising."

He blew out a breath in obvious exasperation. "You don't think I can pull this off, do you?"

She managed to control a burst of laughter. "What an interesting, and very Freudian, choice of words." She drew a slow circle on his arm with one finger and watched the material of his shirt quiver as the muscles in his forearm bunched. "Forgive me for not understanding why you can't give me job counseling *and* a really good time in that suite. I'm not your sister, Noah. I never was." She looked up at him, enjoying the darkening storm in his eyes. "So why does it have to be black and white, either-or?"

He opened his mouth as if to answer her, then hesitated, apparently reconsidering what he'd been about to say. "Because we need to focus on your job situation," he finally muttered.

She didn't think that was all of it. "You've never heard of multitasking?"

"I—"

"Or could it be that you're a coward?" she murmured.

"What do I have to be afraid of?"

"Letting go. Letting go of your old image of me, letting go of your old image of yourself."

"That's ridiculous."

"You're right," she said. "Absolutely ridiculous. Well, I must be off. I really do need to buy clothes, especially underwear. I realized when I started to dress to come down here that I didn't have anything clean, and I really hate to put on previously worn underwear after a bath."

His attention drifted to her breasts and he swallowed. "So what did you do?"

"I'll bet you can tell if you look closely. It's cool in this shop, which is making my nipples—"

"I can see that." He sounded hoarse. Slowly his gaze lifted to her face. "Are you—" He cleared his throat. "Are you telling me you don't have anything on under that dress?"

"I'll let you figure that out. See you around, cowboy." She turned and sashayed out of the shop, giving her hips an extra twitch because she knew he was watching the movement of her skirt and picturing her naked under it. And if she knew men at all, he was drooling.

She thought he might as well give in now, because the

outcome of this weekend was a foregone conclusion. But he was a stubborn sort and it looked as if he had quite a bit more fight left in him. Come to think of it, she was enjoying the challenge. His resistance would make his final surrender that much sweeter.

In the meantime, she'd look for a few outfits that would guarantee success. Before she left for Reno Monday morning she'd return Noah's money, but in the meantime she'd pretend to use it to buy new clothes.

Spying a racy-lingerie shop, she headed for it. Between shopping for clothes and interviewing Suzanne and Joy over at the topless bar tonight, she'd be a busy lady. And then there was the cliff-diving show. She didn't want to leave the Tahitian without seeing that at least once. Considering that the weekend could get a tad complicated, she should probably try to see the cliff divers tonight before Noah returned.

MANY HOURS LATER Noah headed back to the hotel on foot with his three friends and several of the male wedding guests. They were a happy, slightly drunk bunch of guys, with the exception of Noah. He'd gone easy on the beer, knowing he had some tricky maneuvers ahead of him.

First of all he had to convince his buddies not to turn his suite into party central without offending them. Assuming he accomplished that, he had to spend the night with Keely without making love to her. That feat alone required him to stay stone-cold sober.

For about the millionth time, their last conversation played in his head. When she'd asked him why sex couldn't be a part of this weekend, he'd come close to giving his white-knight speech, the one in which he promised to show her that at least one man on the planet wasn't after her body. Maybe that would boost her self-esteem enough that she'd have the courage to try a career that didn't depend on sex appeal.

But he wasn't sure how she'd take that kind of statement.

After all, he was implying that she was too insecure to consider any job that didn't trade on her physical attributes. He hadn't wanted to take a chance on insulting her when they'd have no chance to talk it out. Besides, she'd probably laugh at him. So far he'd done a damn poor job of ignoring her body.

He planned to improve for her sake. Of course it was for her sake. Her suggestion that he was a coward, that he was afraid of letting go, of admitting that she was a desirable woman, was pure hogwash. He was perfectly capable of letting go with her or any woman and then getting control of himself again. On the rodeo circuit he'd proved that more than once.

But he'd never really tested himself with Keely. A part of him didn't want to know that she was a spectacular lover. Childhood friends weren't supposed to turn into spectacular lovers, especially when they were as far out of reach as Keely.

As the men navigated the busy sidewalk along the Strip, most everyone in the group was singing, or trying to sing "Let Me Entertain You" from *Gypsy*. Apparently the topless dancers had inspired them. They could afford to be inspired, Noah thought. Not a one of them had the sexual challenge that waited for him once he was alone again with Keely.

He'd never been so sexually frustrated in his life, or so unlikely to have that frustration eased soon, unless he wanted to abandon his principles. None of the strippers at the bar had been half as beautiful as Keely, but they'd kept his mind firmly on the subject of sex with every bump and grind.

Brandon slung a friendly arm around Noah's neck. "Hey, you bull-riding son of a gun. I'm glad you could tear yourself away from that ranch long enough to see me get hitched. I know how much that place means to you and how you hate to leave it."

Noah grinned at him. "Anything for you." Brandon was

about as plowed as a bridegroom should be on the night before his wedding, Noah decided. He was plenty loose, but not falling-down drunk.

"Y'know that plan we had, all of us goin' up to your place for the rest of the evening?"

"Yeah," Noah said. "And the thing is—"

"I know what the thing is," Brandon said with a chuckle. "We all do. We were gonna pretend we were goin' up there so we could watch you squirm, but back at the bar we had a confab and decided not to torture you. So relax. We'll close out the night in the bird bar so you can have a little R and R upstairs."

Noah stared at him. "I don't have the foggiest idea what you're talking about."

Brandon smiled. "The woman in the tux shop, buddy. That's what I'm talkin' about."

"I told her I wasn't interested." Which, in a manner of speaking, was true.

"Uh-huh. And that's why you gave her a key? And money?"

"What makes you think I did that?" He was sure he'd blocked their view of the transaction with his body.

"There's this cute little security camera in the shop. We watched the action on the monitor."

Noah groaned.

"And we're happy for you, buddy. You're carrying on the tradition for those of us who are no longer able. Way to go, bro." He gave Noah's neck a squeeze and released him.

"Brandon, listen, I—"

"Enjoy the bachelor life while you can, Noah, old pal." With a wink, Brandon turned away and made a megaphone of his hands. "Hey, you guys!" he shouted. "If we get a move on, we can make it for the last cliff-diving show of the night!"

Noah sighed. He hadn't a clue how to respond. Nobody who saw him give a key and money to a woman who looked like Keely would believe that was an innocent arrangement. But it would be, damn it. And somehow he'd find a way to explain that to the guys. But he might as well forget trying until tomorrow.

"Yeah, come on." Greg flicked an imaginary rope over the group. "Get along, little doggies. Let's go see the diving."

"Aw, what's the big deal?" Clint said. "It's just some guy showing off."

"No, it's a guy and a gal," Brandon said. "They're supposed to be star-crossed lovers or something. There's a whole story that goes along with it. It's a pretty cool show. Jenny and I watched it last night."

"So is the gal topless?" Clint asked. "I'm not interested unless I can see her ti—"

"They're diving, you sex maniac." Greg whacked him on the shoulder. "The dive takes about one second. You wouldn't see anything, anyway." He chuckled as he glanced over at Noah. "You're under no obligation to stay for the show, lover boy."

"But I want to see the show," Noah insisted.

"Sure you do," Greg said with a smirk. "And then you want to go play bingo, and after that you'll be ready to get steak and eggs at the coffee shop. No chance. Don't try to kid a kidder, buddy."

"I do want to see the show."

"Then you're drunker than I thought," Greg said. "Come on, then."

Noah followed his friends as they mingled with the crowd heading for the cliff and diving pool. On the way he walked past the large rock where he'd kissed Keely that afternoon. The misty jungle atmosphere and the wildly beating drums rekindled a vivid memory and created all kinds of dangerous sensations in his body. The longer he put off going up to the suite, the better. "In fact, I'm going to the bird bar with you guys," he said over the sound of the drums.

Clint snorted. "The hell you are! You get your fanny up

to that room and do your duty. You owe it to us, now that we're out of the game.''

Noah decided it was pointless to argue. Tomorrow he'd straighten everything out. Somehow.

"Look!" Greg said. "There they are, ready to dive!"

Glancing up, Noah saw an olive-skinned couple in scanty swimsuits standing at the edge of the cliff. Each wore a lei and a crown of flowers. Torchlight glinted off their burnished bodies as they held hands and gazed into each other's eyes. Then they embraced, bodies writhing in passion.

Great, Noah thought. More suggestive behavior to stoke him up.

Then two warrior types came from either side of the cliff and pulled the couple apart. As the drumbeats softened, a gentle woman's voice described a Polynesian version of Romeo and Juliet—lovers from warring families who were forbidden to marry.

As the narration continued, the couple pantomimed begging for permission. Finally, according to the narrator, the father of each family agreed to a test of the couple's devotion. If the lovers could survive a leap from the great cliff called Nooki-Nooki, they would be allowed to wed.

"And I thought Jenny's dad was a hard sell," Brandon murmured.

Clint elbowed Noah in the ribs. "A cliff called Nooki-Nooki. That's where you're gonna hang out tonight, cowboy."

"Oh, ease up on him," Greg said. "From the way he's acting, you can tell he's out of practice. If you keep after him he's liable to develop a case of performance anxiety."

Clint hooked an arm around Noah's shoulder. "It's like riding a bicycle, buddy. Once you hop on, I promise you'll remember what to do."

"I appreciate the advice," Noah said. The conversation was not helping his state of mind. "Now, are you two going to watch this dive or stand around flapping your gums and miss the whole thing?"

"Guess we might as well watch it," Greg said, turning toward the cliff. "But God knows what you're doing here, Garfield, when you could be upstairs doing the horizontal hokeypokey with a woman who could be Julia Roberts's twin sister."

Personally Noah thought Keely was better-looking than Julia Roberts. As the drumbeats swelled to a crescendo, he scanned the crowd. She'd said she wanted to watch this show. His pulse rate quickened at the idea that she could be here in the crowd, maybe only a few feet away.

And then he saw her.

She stood about fifty feet from them, her face lifted as she watched the couple at the top of the cliff. And she'd been clothes shopping. But if Noah had hoped for outfits that wouldn't stir him to new heights of lust, he was out of luck.

Her new dress was pale green and strapless. He couldn't for the life of him figure out how it stayed up. From the appreciative glances Keely was collecting, several men in the crowd were hoping it *wouldn't* stay up. The slinky material hugged her hips and ended at the middle of her golden thighs.

With Keely standing there looking as delicious as a frozen daiquiri, Noah couldn't imagine how any male in the area could concentrate on the divers. He certainly couldn't. When the splash came he didn't even glance over at the pool.

"That was amazing," Clint said. "And now our friend Noah can—oh, will you look at that?"

"What?" Noah quickly swung his gaze to meet Clint's, but he knew he was dead. Clint had caught him gawking at Keely.

Clint grinned at Noah. "Spotted her, did you? Hey, guys, Noah's sweetheart, ten o'clock. And raise your heat shields, boys. This gal's hotter than the space shuttle on reentry."

Greg whistled low through his teeth. "Wouldn't you love to find that prize at the bottom of your Crackerjack box?"

Brandon chuckled. "And if you two are real good to me, I promise not to tell Sharon and Tina what you just said."

Noah definitely didn't appreciate his friends ogling Keely. In fact, he hated it. It might be hopeless, but he had to take a stab at setting the record straight. "Look, I know what you guys all think about her, but here's the truth. She's between jobs and short on money. I offered her a place to crash for the weekend while she decides what to do. We're not going to have sex."

His friends nearly split a gut laughing.

"Yeah, right," Clint said as he wiped tears from his eyes. "I'll tell you what, old buddy. If you spend the weekend with that woman and don't have sex, I'll give you all my leather-bound issues of *Hustler* and see if I can locate a hotline for Dr. Ruth, because you obviously need serious therapy."

"It's true," Noah insisted. "She's…well, I knew her a few years ago. She's like a sister to me." That lie didn't come easily.

"A sister," Brandon said, his tone skeptical.

"Yeah, a sister," Noah repeated. Maybe if he said it often enough even he'd believe it. "We grew up together."

"No kidding?" Greg seemed impressed. "Then you picked the right place to grow up. Nobody I grew up with turned out like her."

"So she's really a friend?" Brandon asked. "Then you should bring her to the wedding, man."

"Uh, I don't think that's a good idea." He'd begun to look at this weekend as sort of a surgical strike—do a good deed and then get the hell out of the area. The only way he could deal with the temptation Keely provided was to keep her isolated from the rest of his life.

"I think that's a *great* idea," Clint said. "Let's go ask her right now before she leaves. What's her name?"

"Keely," Noah said. "But don't ask her. I don't think she'd feel comfortable about coming."

"That's not the impression I get from the lady," Greg

said. "She looks like the kind of person who'd be comfortable *anywhere*." He waggled his eyebrows.

"See, that's why I don't want her to come to the wedding," Noah said. "You guys would be tripping over your tongues, and your wives would get mad, and it would ruin the whole event."

"You let us worry about that," Clint said. "Come on. Let's go see Keely and invite her to the wedding."

"Back off, Clint." Noah hated when situations got out of control, and that seemed to be happening a lot lately. "If anybody's going to ask her, I will."

Brandon grinned. "A little territorial, are we?"

"No, I'm not." A guy who became territorial about Keely had nothing but heartache ahead. But the feelings churning through him were too damn familiar. That protective streak that had caused him so much trouble many years ago hadn't died the way he'd hoped it had.

"So you'll ask her," Brandon prompted.

Noah felt trapped. If he didn't agree to ask Keely they wouldn't believe that she was an old friend. "Okay, I'll ask her, but don't expect to see her there. She's not a fan of weddings."

"Then she's gorgeous *and* unusual," Greg said. "Noah, you've picked a winner this time around. Lots of great sex with no commitment required is a helluva combo, my friend."

"We're not having sex, damn it."

"Hey, buddy," Clint said. "I think the woman you're not having sex with might be heading back up to that lust chamber you call a hotel room."

Noah glanced over toward the place where Keely had been standing. Sure enough, she was walking away, and nobody made an exit like Keely. She'd perfected that walk by the time she'd turned sixteen, and it caused grown men to whimper like babies.

"*Ay, chihuahua,*" Clint moaned, right on cue.

"I can't look," Brandon said. "I have to keep my thoughts pure for Jenny."

"Well, I'm looking," Greg said. "That's what I call poetry in motion. In fact, I feel a poem coming on. I'll call it 'Ode to Keely's A—'"

"Never mind the odes, Shakespeare," Noah said.

"So," Brandon said, a knowing smile on his face. "Are you gonna go up to your suite or hang out with us?"

"The thing is, I have to go over Keely's résumé tonight."

"Her résumé?" Greg chortled. "I can't believe you said that with a straight face."

"I can't believe you're still standing here," Clint said. "Go handle that résumé, buddy."

"I really am helping her figure out a game plan for her career." Noah edged away from his friends. "I know you don't believe me, but that's exactly what we'll be doing."

His friends all nodded as if they were convinced he was a nutcase they needed to humor. They probably didn't believe that Keely was a childhood friend, either.

"Really," he said.

Clint gave him a thumbs-up. "See you in the morning, stud."

8

KEELY WAS in a funky mood as she rode to the top floor of the hotel in the brass and glass mirrored elevator. She'd seen Noah and his buddies at the cliff-diving show and she knew they'd seen her. No doubt they were still trying to talk Noah into hooking up with her for the night.

But they weren't encouraging him because they thought she was a nice girl. Quite the opposite. Normally she'd take satisfaction in their view of her. She'd been thumbing her nose at stuffy convention for so many years that it was second nature to her now. Her strapless dress was designed to raise eyebrows and she'd bought it for the purpose of making Noah's eyes bug out. She was reasonably sure it had.

But lately the thrill of shocking and titillating people was wearing thin. Difficult as it was to admit, she was growing tired of always being the bad girl, the rebel, the outsider. Interviewing Suzanne and Joy had been like taking a trip back in time to attitudes she'd held dear when she'd posed for the centerfold.

In those days she'd dared anybody to stop her from doing what she wanted, when she wanted. If baring her body could get her where she wanted to go, then she'd take her clothes off with pride, and to hell with anyone who disapproved. Suzanne and Joy felt the same way about dancing topless to earn college tuition.

Keely applauded their gutsy decision and wasn't sorry she'd made a similar one so many years ago. The money had helped her get a journalism degree and the moxie she'd shown in posing had influenced Carolyn to hire her at *At-*

titude! Because of that centerfold, she'd left Saguaro Junction far behind, which had been her goal.

She'd snagged the trendy apartment in L.A., mingled with the cool people, had all the sexual freedom she could want. She wouldn't trade her life for anything, and yet at the moment she felt restless and out of sorts, wishing for something she couldn't identify.

Using her key, she activated the elevator doors and stepped onto the lush, jewel-toned carpeting of the hallway. She needed to shake off this mood if she expected to seduce Noah tonight. But as she walked to the suite and went inside, the falling water in the entry reminded her of the cliff divers. Maybe the show was to blame for her weird thoughts.

For all its sappiness, the narration had touched something in her. It was only an imaginary story, but still she wondered what it would be like to love somebody so much that you'd risk your life to be with them. She'd never taken a relationship with a man that seriously.

Maybe she wasn't capable of such deep passion. Maybe she didn't want to be capable of it. Passion that intense had tremendous power to wound. Or to trap. Like her mother had been trapped in Saguaro Junction. Her father had admitted that his wife had been unhappy on the ranch, and more than once he'd said that Keely was just like her. Keely had no intention of making her mother's mistake and letting love coax her into a life she wasn't suited for.

But while she'd watched Noah and his friends from the corner of her eye and thought of the occasion that had brought them all together, she'd felt a moment of…could it be envy? Surely not. She didn't want any part of that white-lace-and-promises routine. Let other women turn into Betty Crocker if they thought it would satisfy them. Her sister, B.J., was welcome to that role, but she had no intention of becoming an apron-wearing, muffin-baking, floor-scrubbing drudge.

Still, loving someone so much you'd jump off a ten-story

cliff for them—now, that would be something to experience.
Once upon a time, as they said in fairy tales, she'd imagined
herself that much in love with Noah. But at sixteen every
emotion had been hung with heavy drama, each moment
carried the weight of life and death. Noah had rejected her,
and guess what? She'd survived just fine. Okay, so she'd
leaped at the chance for revenge, but that didn't mean she
still had a thing for him.

And he wouldn't reject her this weekend. Not with what
she had planned.

Now that he'd viewed her slinky green dress, she could
move on to the next item in her shopping bag. Walking over
the footbridge into the bedroom, she nudged off her sandals
and shimmied out of the dress.

In moments she'd slipped on the black thong bikini she'd
bought. She'd considered greeting Noah naked, but there
was still the chance that his buddies would come back to
the suite with him. Besides, minimal coverage often played
with a man's mind more than complete nudity. She'd done
an article on the subject three years ago.

Come to think of it, over the years she'd gathered plenty
of ammunition on the most effective ways to seduce a man.
And that's why Noah was going down.

She'd explored all the options of the remote earlier in the
evening. Taking it from the ledge, she turned on the colored-
light show, the adult movie channel and the hot tub, which
was nicely positioned for viewing the giant screen. She
clicked through the movie options and chose one called
Playmates in Paradise. That should start his engines.

The well-stocked bar included some excellent champagne. She filled the ice bucket, opened the champagne and
settled it into the ice. Wrapping a bar towel around the
whole arrangement, she carried the bucket and two crystal
flutes out to the terrace. After retrieving the remote and plac-
ing it within reach of the tub, she poured herself a glass of
champagne and climbed into the bubbling water.

Easing down onto a molded seat, she glanced to her left

and there was the glittering Strip stretching toward the downtown area where her hotel was located. If she turned her head in the opposite direction, she could watch three busty women get naked with one well-endowed surfer.

Keely took a sip of champagne and watched the movie action for a while. Stimulated by bubbles and the erotic behavior on the screen, she began to really look forward to Noah's arrival. The movie was fairly classy, yet here was yet another film directed by a man. A woman would have reversed the equation. Keely had never made love with more than one partner at a time. In real life it might be very confusing and she wasn't sure she'd like it, but she didn't mind including that scenario in her fantasy life.

Then the man who'd played several roles in her fantasy life walked into the living room. He glanced out to the terrace and then looked at the screen.

Keely picked up the remote and muted the sound of the movie. "I'm relaxing," she said. "Unwinding from a long, busy day. How was your bachelor party?"

He cleared his throat. "Okay. Listen, Keely, it's…uh, perfectly obvious what you have in mind here, but I have no intention of—"

"Oh, I *know* that," she said. "You don't plan to have sex with me, right?"

"Right." He sounded hoarse.

"Well, don't worry about it. I can take care of myself." Her natural talent for improvising kicked in. "In fact, that's what I was doing just now, before you arrived. The movie got me in the mood, and then the jets in this terrific hot tub did the rest. Somebody knew exactly how to position the nozzles. It's the best design I've ever experienced." There. That should turn his crank.

He stared at her and swallowed hard. "Oh."

"It seemed a shame to let all this go to waste." She took another sip of champagne to keep from grinning in triumph. "I admire your principles and all, but the mood of this suite really gets me hot. I needed to blow off some steam. Now

I'm all mellow and ready to brainstorm my career options. Did you know that a good orgasm can make you think more clearly?''

"I...never heard that."

She'd never heard it either, but it made sense, considering how sex improved a person's circulation. Maybe that would be a good subject for a future magazine article. "Well, next time you have a particularly big problem to work through," she said, "you could try masturbating first and see if you don't come up with a solution afterward."

He coughed and gazed out at the city lights. "Right."

"So how about it? Shall we brainstorm in the hot tub?"

He glanced at the movie again. "With that going on? I don't think so."

"Sorry. I forgot it was still on." She clicked the remote and turned the movie off. She figured it had served its purpose of putting him in the right groove, but she didn't want him to be distracted from the real thing by a filmed version.

"Thanks." He seemed relieved that the film wasn't playing anymore.

"You should try this hot tub," she said. "I mean, think about it. How many chances will you have to sit in a hot tub on a terrace overlooking the Las Vegas Strip? Psycho maids who break into your room and destroy your stuff don't come along every day, you know."

He glanced around the terrace and back at the hot tub. "Okay, maybe I will try it."

"Good. I promise we'll talk about my career options." She tried not to look overconfident. Once he was in the bubbles with her he was so going to be seduced.

"I'll go put on my—" He paused in the act of starting toward the bedroom. "I don't have a suit."

"I thought of that."

He sent a piercing glance in her direction. "And before you suggest it, I'm not going in without one."

"I didn't think you would. When I was shopping for mine I realized you wouldn't have one, either. In fact, I realized you wouldn't have underwear. I took the liberty of picking up a few things for you. I estimated you have a thirty-four waist. Is that close enough?''

"I guess so, but you didn't have to go buying me underwear." His cheeks turned the color of brick.

"What were you planning to do about that?"

"I, uh, hadn't thought about it."

"Well, now you don't have to." She took another swallow of champagne. "You'll find everything lying on the bed."

"Okay." Looking very uneasy, he turned and walked into the living room, over the footbridge and into the bedroom.

She figured in about five seconds she'd get a reaction. It only took four.

"Keely, this underwear is way too small!" he bellowed. "And it's *colored*."

"It's not too small if you're a thirty-four waist," she called back. "It stretches. And don't you get tired of wearing white all the time?"

"No."

"Well, this is Vegas, Noah. It's tough to find boring underwear in a resort boutique. I did the best I could."

Silence. "I guess I can make do with these for the weekend," he said at last.

"Good."

"I mean, it's not like anybody will see them."

Except me. She smiled and finished off her champagne.

"Where's the bathing suit?"

"On your—uh, on the pillow." Earlier in the evening she'd turned down the bed and draped his skimpy suit over one of the pillows. The suit was black, to match hers, and she'd enjoyed the way it looked against the fine white linen pillowcase. But she'd known it would look even better cupping Noah's generous equipment.

Reaching for the ice bucket, she took out the champagne bottle, poured another glass for herself and filled Noah's flute. The party was about to begin.

She knew he'd found the suit when he began to laugh.

"I double dare you," she called out, surprising herself with the same phrase she'd used to taunt him when they were kids. And he'd risen to the bait every time except one, and they hadn't really been kids anymore by then. On that hot summer night when she'd double dared him to make love to her, he hadn't taken the dare.

For one panicky moment she wondered if that iron will would assert itself again. She couldn't let that happen. A flash of insight told her that success had become very important to her, maybe too important. But it was too late to worry about that now.

"It's that or come in naked," she said. "The underwear won't work. It becomes transparent when it's wet."

When he didn't reply, she tried to think of more inducements. "If you go back home and tell Jonas you stayed in a room with a hot tub on the terrace overlooking all of Las Vegas and you didn't sit in it even once, you'll never hear the end of it. You don't have to mention me at all. Just tell him you were sitting there sipping good champagne and enjoying the view. That will drive him nuts. He—" She stopped speaking. She nearly stopped breathing. Noah stood in the doorway wearing the suit.

Dear God, the boy she remembered had become a man. And what a man. The women in that skin flick could have their pretty-boy blond surfer with his carefully shaved chest. She'd take this broad-shouldered cowboy with chest hair the color of burnt sugar. No gym had shaped this body. He'd earned those muscles and scars during years of riding and roping.

As her gaze traveled over him, she was filled with gratitude that he'd agreed to wear the suit. She was virtually certain few women had seen him like this—all that masculine beauty punctuated by a coal-black exclamation point outlining the most intriguing aspect of his physique.

Thanks to his talkative friends, she knew that on the rodeo circuit he hadn't been shy about using his considerable endowments to give pleasure to the women he'd met. And now fate had given her a chance to discover his talents before he chose a proper ranch wife and settled down to a life of dull married sex.

She couldn't remember the last time the sight of a nearly naked man had left her speechless with yearning. Finally she forced herself to say something. "C-come in. The water's perfect." She couldn't help the stutter. He was so magnificent she couldn't think straight.

"And we're going to talk about your career."

"Of course." She'd agree to talk about Einstein's theory of relativity if he'd just get in the hot tub with her.

"I guess we have to talk somewhere. And you're right. If Jonas finds out I didn't take advantage of the stuff in this suite, he'll carry on something fierce." He walked over to the tub and climbed the steps. "But that's not why I'm doing this."

She gazed up at him and wondered if she'd died and gone to heaven. Talk about a great camera angle. She swallowed. "So why are you?"

"Because I figured out that I wanted to. It's been awhile since I did something just because I wanted to." He stepped down into the swirling water.

"Oh." It was the most she could manage as the bubbles inched up his body. When he finally sat across from her she had to work not to whimper because her view had been obliterated by the damn water.

"This feels good." He leaned back against the edge of the tub and closed his eyes. "Damn good."

She almost groaned out loud. She could imagine something else that would feel damn good, but she didn't want to scare him off right when he was beginning to relax and enjoy what came his way. "I guess the ranch is quite a responsibility," she said.

"Don't you know it." He opened his eyes and glanced over at the view of the Strip. "I truly love that place, and

I don't begrudge all that I put into running it, but I haven't had a vacation since I took over two years ago."

"Then it's about time." She handed him the champagne flute. "Here. This goes with the view."

He took the delicate crystal, his hand brushing hers, his gaze holding hers for a precious moment. "Thanks. I guess it does." Then he cleared his throat and took a drink of the champagne. "It tastes expensive."

"It is." She leaned over and lifted the bar towel to show him the bottle.

He shook his head. "I'll have to take your word for it. Looking at the brand won't tell me anything. I'm not into champagne." He took another swallow. "But this isn't bad for being a girlie drink."

"I'm glad you like it, because once you open a bottle this pricey, it's criminal not to finish it off." She didn't want him to get drunk, but she wouldn't mind having him loosen up a little more.

He rolled the stem of the flute between his fingers. "Why do I have the feeling that you want to sit here and drink champagne instead of talk about your career plans?"

"There you go again, setting us up for either-or. We can do both. I think talking about career plans while drinking expensive champagne is a great idea."

"Okay, then let's start by you telling me what jobs you've had since you left the ranch."

She'd thought about this and was ready for the question. "I've waited tables, taken on some light secretarial work. Then there was the telephone soliciting."

He nearly dropped his flute. "Telephone *what?*"

Excellent. His mind was firmly in the gutter. "I made cold calls for a carpet-cleaning company," she said.

"Oh. That kind of soliciting."

"What did you think I meant? Phone sex?"

"No! Of course not. I mean—" He paused to gulp some more champagne. "Hell, never mind. Carpet cleaning. Okay. What else?"

"Let me put a head on that for you." She lifted the bottle from the ice bucket and waited until he held out his glass.

He hesitated.

"You said it yourself. It's a girlie drink. Not much punch to it."

"Yeah, you're right." He extended his glass so she could fill it again. "So, what else have you done?"

"A little bartending."

He nodded. "What else?"

She adjusted the straps on her bathing-suit top for no reason other than to jiggle her breasts and make him notice. "You probably don't want to know *all* the jobs I've had," she murmured.

As she'd planned, his gaze drifted to the twin triangles of black material that barely covered her nipples. "Maybe not," he said, a thread of huskiness winding through his voice. "How did the…uh…carpet-cleaning job work out?" Bringing his attention back to her face appeared to take great effort.

"Not too bad. People seemed to respond to my voice on the telephone. Want to hear my sales pitch?"

"Sure." He took another big swallow of champagne.

"I think I can remember it. Let me concentrate for a second." Keely really had spent about a week calling for a carpet cleaner, and she'd had such bad luck in the first day that she'd modified the phone message they'd given her without telling them. Then her calls had been wildly successful as long as she'd talked to the man of the house. But when the president of the company had discovered what she'd been saying, he'd fired her. The man had completely lacked a sense of humor.

"Here goes," she said, holding his gaze across the foaming water and lowering her voice to a sultry purr. "'Hey, there, big guy. Can we talk dirty? Dirty carpets, that is. Your carpet needs your attention, it craves your attention. It deserves to be stroked firmly, massaged and caressed until it ripples beneath your hand, and then, my friend, it needs to be washed clean and...sucked...thoroughly and completely, until it springs up, aroused to its full...potential. How soon would you like this done...to your carpet?"'

During her recitation Noah's breathing had become labored and his gaze turbulent.

She wasn't completely calm, herself. If he didn't make a move soon, she was going to be in bad shape. "So," she said, smiling brightly, "what do you think? Do I have any talent for sales?"

"I think..." He paused and cleared the huskiness from his throat. "I think you need to go to bed."

Her pulse raced with anticipation. "And you will...?"

"Not."

Damn. "But you want to," she murmured, willing to bet a year's salary that beneath the foaming water he was completely erect.

The muscles in his jaw worked. "Yes. I want to."

And so did she. So very, very much. She was going crazy with the wanting. "Noah, what could it possibly hurt? We're two free, consenting adults. Both of us are dying to consent. I don't understand why we can't go into that bedroom and have a wonderful time. For that matter—" she slipped the straps of her bathing-suit top off her shoulders "—we could begin the fun right here."

"Keely, don't."

"Don't what? Enjoy the movement of the water against my skin?" Putting down her champagne flute, she unhooked her top and allowed it to float away. A girl could only hold herself back for so long before she cracked. She wiggled out of her bottoms and they floated to the surface, too.

"You know what I mean," he said in a tight voice.

"Yes, and you know what I need." Cupping her breasts, she rose to her knees on the bench seat so that the foaming surface tickled and played with her nipples until they were taut with desire. "This feels good, Noah. Do you think it's wrong for me to like it?"

Never taking his gaze from her breasts, he shook his head.

"And right above this bench there's a water jet. If I position myself just right, I can enjoy that, too." She found the pulsing stream and tilted her pelvis back. There. Mmm. It wasn't Noah's touch, but he still seemed to have scruples. "Is that wrong?"

His tortured gaze held hers. "No," he said, his voice rasping low in his throat.

"I want you, Noah." The pulsing water worked quickly on her already aroused body. Her breathing grew shallow and her heart pounded with excitement. She'd never dared so much in front of any man, but now that she'd begun this little exhibition she found that it packed its own kind of thrill.

She could tell he was going insane watching her. Good. He deserved to go insane.

"Yes, I really want you," she whispered. "But if I can't have what I want…" She closed her eyes and ran her tongue over her lips. "I'll take what I can…get." As the tremors of her orgasm overtook her, she squeezed her nipples hard and gasped with pleasure. Knowing he had watched every second intensified the sensation more than she would have believed. Breathing hard, she leaned back against the edge of the tub.

Slowly she opened her eyes and looked at him.

He was destroyed. She'd never seen anybody in such agony in her life.

Taking a long, shaky breath, she braced a hand on the side of the tub and coaxed her rubbery legs to support her as she stood. "Well, that sure was fun," she said. "You really should have come along." Retrieving the two pieces of her suit, she climbed out of the tub and walked dripping and naked into the living room and over the footbridge.

9
***

NOAH HAD NEVER EXPERIENCED anything like the rush of watching Keely making love to the hot-tub jets. And the fact that she'd deliberately done it while he was sitting there totally fried his circuits. If he'd come upon her when she hadn't known he was there—well, that would have been wild enough. But she'd *chosen* to have him see this, knowing full well how much he wanted her. She'd hoped he'd break.

He would not break. In this charged moment he couldn't remember the reason, exactly, but he knew control was very important.

Until Keely had snuggled up to that water nozzle, he'd thought he understood sexual frustration. He'd kidded himself that he was strong enough to deal with it, no matter what the temptation. But the frustrations he'd lived with in the past were small change compared to the gut-wrenching, groin-pounding urges that shook him now. Keely had pushed him into unknown territory.

The water churned around him, teasing him, taunting him with liquid fingers that had brought Keely relief while he remained in straining agony. A jet of water gurgled against his back, suggesting possibilities, beckoning him to follow Keely's lead. Beneath that scrap of material some idiot designer called a bathing suit he swelled until it seemed the tiny garment couldn't hold him any longer.

In a wild frenzy he reached beneath the water and ripped it away, tearing the seams in his eagerness to be rid of the restraint. His penis surged free. With a moan of surrender he stood and turned toward the rippling stream of water.

Hands braced against the edge of the hot tub, he eased his rigid flesh into the outer swirl of the pulsing jet. Oh, God. This wouldn't take long. The lights of the Strip blurred into a river of color as his climax crept ever nearer.

Finally, holding back a groan with clenched teeth, he gripped the edge of the tub and shuddered as the milky evidence of his passion rose and merged with the bubbling water. Struggling for each breath, he let his head sag between his still tense shoulders.

"Nice going," she said softly from the doorway behind him.

He refused to turn around. "Go away," he whispered hoarsely.

"I will. I only came back out to bring you a robe, so you wouldn't get chilled."

His laugh sounded like a rusty saw against a fence post. Chilled. Never in a million years.

"I'm leaving it here on a chair."

Still he didn't turn around. No telling what she was wearing, or not wearing. And if he looked at her, he would want her again as much as before. The picture of her making love to the jet of water was too fresh for him to even think of blotting it out of his mind.

"That little teaser of relief won't be enough, you know," she murmured. "At least, it wasn't for me. You're such an endearingly stubborn man, Noah. But if you decide to bend that iron will of yours, I'll be in the bedroom. We could have a very good time."

He wondered if she'd have a very good time without him. Once again he tried to remember why he shouldn't make love to her. He was positive he'd had a good reason, back when he could think. And because he knew that eventually he'd be able to think again, he was determined to wait out this period of insanity.

When he heard nothing more from the vicinity of the

doorway, he cautiously looked over his shoulder. She wasn't there. Climbing out of the tub he felt shaky as a new foal. Sure enough, a white terry robe lay across one of the rattan patio chairs.

He picked it up but couldn't seem to make himself put it on. All his nerve endings felt tender, as if the slightest contact would send shock waves through his system. On some level he realized that he was standing naked on a terrace within view of several high-rise hotels. Naked and still partially erect.

His nakedness didn't seem like the most critical issue. As long as he stayed out on the terrace and Keely stayed in the bedroom, he might be able to quiet the roaring in his ears long enough to reason this through. He spread the white terry robe open on the cushioned rattan chair and eased down on it. God, his skin felt sensitive, as if he could feel each individual loop of the plush terry caressing his butt and his balls.

Gingerly he leaned back in the chair and gazed out at the sparkling, churning kaleidoscope that was Las Vegas. The combination of this city and Keely Branscom would corrupt any guy with a pulse.

But he had to resist, anyway. He didn't like to think of himself as the kind of man who would meet a childhood friend and promptly jump into bed with her even if she invited him. His brother, Jonas, was a different story. But Noah had taken his older-brother role seriously. His mother had told him to set a good example for Jonas and he'd tried to do that. He'd tried especially hard after his mother died, for her sake.

But it hadn't worked that way in the motherless Branscom household. In that case, the younger one, B.J., had turned out to be the responsible kid and Keely, the oldest, had been hell-bent-for-leather from the beginning.

Maybe it had nothing to do with circumstances and everything to do with personality. Keely and Jonas were cut from the same cloth. Noah was extremely grateful that he was here instead of Jonas, because if she'd made Jonas the same offer she'd made him, Jonas would have grabbed it. Well, maybe not now that he seemed to be in love for the first time in his life.

And maybe not ever, come to think of it. Jonas hadn't talked about wanting to get Keely alone and have some fun. She was about the only woman he hadn't gone after, though. Noah and his father had lived in constant fear that Jonas would get all the county's eligible girls pregnant. It was a miracle that no one had come to the ranch insisting that she carried Jonas's baby.

The issue of birth control aside, Noah couldn't claim much success with Jonas's personal development. Maybe little brothers were programmed to be contrary. At any rate, B.J. seemed to be accomplishing what he'd failed to do— Jonas was finally becoming a grown-up.

Noah wondered if that had anything to do with his own restlessness lately. He wasn't required to model good behavior anymore. Or maybe it was simply Keely getting under his skin the way she'd always done and bringing out the devil in him. Maybe it was time to admit he'd always been a little afraid of her, because when she was around his control began to slip.

And maybe it was time for him to let go, at least for a weekend, but he had the wrong woman for that. Keely didn't need a man who was ready to let go, no matter what she said. She needed a man who would be steady and responsible, a man who would guide her to make some better decisions.

That was what he'd been trying to remember—keeping his hands off Keely was for her sake, not his.

A cool desert breeze drifted across the terrace. It blew gently over his body, drying the drops of water that still clung to the hairs of his chest and groin. He considered putting on the robe, but the night air felt too good. And there was a certain forbidden thrill sitting here under the stars without a stitch on.

There was nothing really wrong with it. He was on his own private terrace where he should have the right to do this if he wanted. Anyone who wanted to spy on him would need a pair of binoculars to see anything.

And yet a sense of freedom and sexual excitement washed over him as he sat there naked gazing out at the city bustling around him. He wondered if Keely had felt that excitement and freedom when she'd posed nude for *Macho* magazine. The more he thought about it, the more he believed that might have been the attraction, maybe even more than the money.

Today when she'd unfastened her clothes so that he could touch her breasts as they kissed behind the boulder, she'd seemed to relish taking that risk. He'd never met a woman more willing to celebrate the wonders of her body without shame than Keely. And encouraged by her, he longed to take a few sexual risks, himself.

But he liked to think he knew where to draw the line. From all indications, Keely didn't. If he hadn't come along, she'd be bumping and grinding in some bar like the one he'd visited tonight with his buddies.

He hated the thought of that. Keely had more to her than a gorgeous body and an uninhibited attitude. She was creative, funny, brave and endlessly optimistic. There had to be a career that would make the most of those qualities—a safe career that wouldn't put her in the path of drunken, sexually aroused men every night of her life.

He had approximately forty-eight hours to come up with suggestions for her. And part of that time he'd be tied up with the wedding, so he didn't have the entire forty-eight hours. He'd forgotten to ask her whether she wanted to go to the wedding. Oh, hell, she probably wouldn't be interested. So he'd take care of his wedding duties by himself, and use the remaining time to discuss job options with Keely.

Daylight would help him stay on the subject. Coming upon this scene tonight had nearly eliminated his defenses, but in the morning he'd be in better shape to handle her constantly seductive behavior.

Curving his spine, Noah scooted lower in the chair and laid his head against the back cushion. He needed to get some sleep. Tomorrow promised to be one very busy day.

As KEELY LAY against the soft cotton sheets and listened for Noah's approach, she finally decided he planned to spend the night on the terrace. If she were scoring this battle of wills, she'd say they were about even. Maybe she hadn't gotten him into a condom yet, but he'd worn the sexy bathing suit she'd picked out and he'd given in to the seduction of the water jets.

Oh, how he'd given in. She'd watched him lean toward that pleasure and a rush of moisture had dampened her silk bikini underwear. When he'd come, she'd nearly climaxed, herself. She'd never watched a man masturbate before, except in X-rated movies. For that matter, she'd never allowed a man to watch her do the same thing. Noah might think that tonight's demonstration was commonplace for her, but it was a real first.

Of course, she'd never met a man who could sit in a hot tub with her and keep his hands to himself. When she'd begun her game with the jets she'd assumed that eventually Noah would get into the act. His continued resistance had left her no choice except to follow through. It seemed the more Noah held back, the more she dared. She'd discovered she liked this dynamic.

But she wouldn't want it to go on for the entire weekend. No, at some point she wanted him to become the aggressor. And he would. He'd already made some strides in that direction.

Although still aroused, she was beginning to get sleepy, too. She'd had a long and fascinating day. Tomorrow promised to be even more fascinating. Cuddling into a premium goose-down pillow, she drifted to sleep.

A RINGING TELEPHONE woke her the next morning. Fuzzy from sleep and sexy dreams, she blinked and tried to find a phone. The room had nothing so ordinary as a bedside table with a phone on it. Finally she remembering seeing one hanging over the tub. It looked like a seashell, but she'd noticed that it was plastic, and a place like this wouldn't have a plastic seashell on the wall. She'd lifted it and discovered that, sure enough, it was a phone.

Heading for the bathroom, she took the pink shell from the wall and pulled out the retractable antenna before punching the connect button. She cleared the sleep from her throat and put the shell to her ear, half expecting to hear the sound of surf. "Hello?"

"Keely, this is Brandon! Listen, sorry to disturb you two, but Jenny needs to know for certain if you're coming to the wedding. She wants to make sure she has enough leis."

"The wedding?" She combed her hair back from her face and glanced in the mirror to find Noah standing in the bathroom doorway wearing the white robe and looking dangerously sexy and unshaven.

Turning, she faced him. "I didn't know I was invited," she told Brandon.

"Noah didn't ask you? Oh, well, he probably has a lot of things on his mind." There was a thread of laughter running through Brandon's voice. "You are definitely invited. Noah says you grew up together."

"We did." She noticed Noah's attention on the thrust of her breasts under the white silk of her tank top. Looking him straight in the eye, she slipped her hand under the top. "He's like a brother to me." Slowly she caressed herself.

Noah sucked in a breath.

"That's what he was trying to tell us. Anyway, can you make it tonight?"

"I'd love to." She watched the desire build in Noah's dark eyes as she continued to stroke her skin. She was getting pretty excited, herself. "What time?"

"Seven. Oh, and there's a short rehearsal at eleven and

a rehearsal lunch. You're welcome to come to that, too. We had to compress things because we're cramming it all into one weekend. I'm glad you'll be there!''

"So am I. Do you want to talk to Noah?"

"Is he available?"

"I'm not sure. I'll check." She took the phone from her ear. "Are you available?" she murmured.

He made a sound low in his throat.

"I'll take that as a yes." With a smile, she handed him the seashell phone. "Think I'll hit the shower." She peeled off her tank top as she walked toward the glass enclosure. When she glanced back to see if Noah was still there, he'd left the room.

He didn't reappear while she showered, washed and dried her hair, and put on her next killer outfit, stretch capris and a halter top that left her midriff bare.

When she was dressed she followed the scent of coffee to the living room and discovered him there with a cup in his hand and a room-service tray on one of the driftwood-and-stone end tables.

He glanced at her outfit and sighed. "Not gonna let up on me, are you?"

She laughed at the pitiful resignation in his voice. "Noah, I am going to have you before this weekend is over. You know it and I know it, so you might as well give in and get it over with."

He put down his cup and stood. "And I'm telling you that you're wrong. I intend to prove to you that there's at least one guy out there—namely me—who is interested in you without needing to have your body as part of the arrangement."

She had to admit the concept was touching. Doomed to fail, but touching, anyway. "And what will that accomplish?"

He took a deep breath. "Now, don't take this wrong, but I'm hoping it will convince you to do something with your life that doesn't involve sex or the suggestion of sex."

"I see." So he was determined to sacrifice himself so that she'd get her head screwed on straight. And touching or not, his attitude was also pretty damn superior. He thought he knew what was good for her. She simply had to foil his plan, if only to make him a little more humble. Noah had a lot of good points, but humility wasn't one of them.

"I ordered up a few things." He gestured toward the tray. "Help yourself while I shave and shower. We need to leave for the rehearsal in twenty minutes."

She gazed at him. Maybe tomorrow morning she'd find out what his beard felt like against her skin while he kissed her all over. No use trying to organize such a maneuver now and make him late for the rehearsal.

"How are you going to shave?" she asked, remembering that he hadn't replaced any of his toiletries.

He picked up a small zippered pouch from beside the breakfast tray and started toward the footbridge. "I asked them to send up the basics so I could shave and brush my teeth."

"You'd have been welcome to borrow my toothbrush." She held her ground and made him walk around her to get to the footbridge. "Once a guy's had his tongue in my mouth, sharing a toothbrush doesn't seem like a big deal."

"That won't be happening again," he muttered as he stomped over the bridge.

"Pity. You're very good with your tongue when it comes to kissing. I was hoping to find out if you're as talented when you use it elsewhere."

His groan as he went into the bedroom made her smile.

IF NOAH HAD EXPECTED any awkwardness between Keely and his friends, he'd been mistaken. During the rehearsal and the lunch that followed, Keely seemed to be getting along well with everyone. She made a special effort to charm both Brandon's and Jenny's parents and he remembered something he'd forgotten about Keely—she could talk to literally anyone.

The meal was served at a long table at the hotel's trendy Coral Reef restaurant, where the waitresses dressed in tight scuba gear and the menu included mostly fish. In the hubbub of getting seated, Noah was separated from Keely, who ended up at the opposite end of the table. His position allowed him to observe her technique for drawing people out. No question about it—she had quite a talent for that.

Once the food arrived, Clint's wife, Sharon, squeezed lemon juice on her tuna and accidentally shot some down Keely's front. Keely laughed and patted her chest, spreading the drops around. "Squirt some more over here. I've always wanted to smell like a freshly waxed table."

Sharon grinned. "You know, so have I," she said, and baptized herself, too.

Suddenly lemon wedges were at a premium as everybody started spraying juice around. Keely gave as good as she got, never for a minute seeming to consider that she barely knew these people she was tagging with streams of juice. It turned into a raucous lunch, and before it was over, Keely was as much a part of the group as if she'd been around for years.

And for all the seductive moves she'd made when they were alone, in public she acted like Noah's kid sister. In fact, she behaved as if sex was the farthest thing from her mind. A few suggestive jokes made their way around the long luncheon table, but none of them started with Keely. She laughed along with everyone else, but she didn't take the opportunity to send him one of those smoldering looks he'd been getting whenever they were alone.

In some ways he was a little disappointed about that. He had to admit that having Keely come on to him all the time had been damn good for his ego. He found himself becoming impatient for the lunch to end so he could have her to himself again. They'd discuss her job possibilities, of course. He'd realized that whatever she did should include interacting with people. Her small-town background and outgoing personality made her naturally good with people.

He was going through some options in his mind and anticipating a return to the suite with Keely when Jenny shot down his plans.

Standing, she turned to Keely. "Barb, Sharon, Tina and I have appointments for a manicure and pedicure at the hotel salon," Jenny said. "You have to come with us and tell us every embarrassing story you can remember about Noah. And if you want a manicure and pedicure, I'm sure the salon can squeeze in one more person. We've monopolized them for the afternoon, anyway."

"Sounds great," Keely said with a smile as she left the table and headed out with the women. Almost as an afterthought she turned and waggled her fingers at Noah. "See you later, big guy."

"What a terrific person she is," Brandon said after the women had left. "But I don't get this platonic thing you two have going."

"Yeah," Clint said. "You have to work yourself past that one, buddy. I realize you two grew up together, but the point is, you did grow up. And so did she."

Greg sighed wistfully. "Did she ever." Then he glanced down the table at the two dads sitting there. "I mean that in the most respectful way. I'm crazy about my wife."

Jenny's father chuckled. "We're all crazy about our wives. But when a woman like Keely comes along, you'd have to be dead not to notice her."

"Amen to that," Brandon's dad said. "I keep thinking she looks familiar, somehow. Has she been in commercials or something like that?"

"Not that I know of," Noah said. But that was another idea to add to his list of career choices. He wondered if Keely had ever tried to break into television.

"I know what you mean about her looking familiar," Clint chimed in. "I've had the feeling I've seen her before, too."

Noah didn't want any of the men to keep following that

line of thought. "Maybe it's because she looks like Julia Roberts," he said.

"Well, she does, but that's not why," Brandon's father said. "I could swear I've seen her before. Even the name sounds like one I've heard. Give me some time. Before the weekend is over I'll make the connection."

Noah sincerely hoped not. Now was not the time for anyone to remember seeing Keely with a staple in her navel.

"Hey, who's ready to hit the beach?" Brandon asked, and the party started to break up.

As the men all prepared to leave the restaurant, Clint nudged Noah in the ribs and spoke in an undertone. "I hope before the weekend is over you'll be able to make a connection, too, buddy. And I'm not talking about a mental connection, either."

10

KEELY COULDN'T REMEMBER the last time she'd hung out with married women, and apparently she'd been guilty of some stereotyping. Jenny, Barb, Sharon and Tina didn't remotely resemble Betty Crocker. Instead of trading recipes, these women wanted to trade sexual fantasies as they sat around taking turns having their toenails and fingernails buffed and polished.

"We spent the afternoon exchanging fantasies before Tina and Greg's wedding last year," Jenny explained to Keely. The bride sat with both feet in sudsy, whirling water in preparation for her pedicure. "And we all promised to do it again at my wedding. It's a lot more fun than having a surprise stripper, and we all get to play."

Keely nodded. "I like it."

"It's up to you if you want to tell us one of yours," Jenny added. "You can think about whether you want to or not while you're listening. Okay, here's mine."

Trying not to let her mouth drop open, Keely heard Jenny—a blonde with innocent-looking blue eyes—describe her fantasy of being carried off by a sheik and sold into sexual bondage. While Josette buffed and massaged Jenny's feet with some sort of tangy-scented herbal cream, Jenny provided details of what the bondage would involve. When she was finished, everyone, including Keely, applauded.

"Me, next!" Tina said, raising the hand that had recently been tipped with Mango Madness. "Ooh, I love this one I came up with. Here goes." An olive-skinned Italian beauty, Tina sketched a scene in which she commanded male slaves to do her bidding. And she had an impressive list of duties for them to perform.

Keely joined in the applause for this one too and wondered if she'd forever associate the bracing smell of nail polish with women's sexual daydreams. She wished she could take notes. An article on female fantasies might be an excellent project for *Attitude!* magazine.

Then Sharon, a well-rounded brunette, detailed a fantasy that involved making love to a handsome stranger in the back of a moving limousine. Sharon was followed in the rotation by Barb, a tall woman with black hair. Barb wanted to be rescued from a burning house while wearing a negligee and then afterward to have sex with each of the gorgeous firemen as an expression of her gratitude.

"Do you want to tell us one?" Jenny asked, turning to Keely after Barb had finished and collected her applause. "You don't have to, but it's fun."

"I can see that." Keely was rethinking her assumption that marriage dried up your sexual imagination. As the only single woman there, she felt obligated to hold up her end of the game. "How's this? I am a beautiful queen, and my page is in love with me but he dares not show it because of his lowly station. I figure out that he's in love with me, so I begin subtly coming on to him."

"Oh, that's good," Jenny said. "And slowly he begins to crack."

"Right," Keely said. "And, being a normal man, eventually he can't help himself and he has to have me, but he knows he could be killed for it. So he risks his life to make love to me. At night. In the throne room. And it's raining outside." She found herself getting into the fantasy.

"And of course you tolerate it," Sharon said, her dimples flashing.

"Well, yeah," Keely replied. "I mean, the guy is hung like a horse."

Jenny laughed. "Naturally. And you don't have him killed."

"No, I only threaten it if he doesn't do his level best to please me. Night after night after night."

"Excellent!" Tina said. "He either produces multiple orgasms, or off with his head!"

By this time both manicurists were begging to add their fantasies to the collection, and then everyone decided they needed a second round.

Keely managed to come up with a second fantasy, but she loved the first one far more. And it wouldn't take a degree in psychology to figure out why, either. Oh, yes. Noah's ultimate surrender to his desire would be sweet.

"So, Keely, what was it like growing up with Noah?" Jenny asked as the women sat in the salon letting their fingernails and toenails dry.

Keely thought about that as she admired her fingers and toes tipped with Lotus Blossom Pink. "Well, his younger brother, Jonas, and I were the ones who always got into trouble, and Noah had to bail us out so we wouldn't get busted. Like the time Jonas and I took the tractor for a joyride before either of us knew how to drive it. We ended up in a ditch, of course, and broke some part or other. Noah used his dad's truck to pull the tractor out and then told his dad that he'd put the tractor in the ditch, not me and Jonas."

"I can picture Noah doing that." Tina wiggled her toes. "He seems like the protective type. So were you two ever involved?"

"Uh, not really."

"She's blushing!" Jenny said. "Dish, girl!"

Keely couldn't believe that she'd given herself away like that. "It was only kid stuff. You know, down by the barn. Nothing ever came of it."

Tina glanced at Keely. "I think something could come of it now. If you're interested, that is. He looks at you like a chocoholic would look at a box of Godiva."

Jenny laughed. "I'll bet all the guys do when they think we don't notice. That's a killer bod you have there, chick."

Keely felt her blush deepen. "Oh, this old thing. I've had it for ages."

"You wear it well," Tina said with a nod. "And I still say Noah's interested. I mean, *really* interested."

"Yeah, but he doesn't want to be," Keely said before she could stop herself.

Sharon's brown eyes opened wide. "Why ever not?"

Keely sighed. She hadn't meant to say even that much, but these women had a way of making her forget to guard her words. "He might be sexually interested, but he doesn't want to act on that because nothing could ever come of it and he can't just walk away from me when it's over. My dad and sister still work for him, and his brother is marrying my sister. So it's complicated."

"Back up a minute," Jenny said. "Why couldn't anything ever come of it?"

"Because." She paused and glanced around at these funny, intelligent women, all of them probably living out in the sticks somewhere with their cowboy husbands. "Don't take this wrong. I think you guys are fantastic. But I'm not the type to be a ranch wife."

Jenny burst out laughing. "Oh, yeah. The ranch wife. That wholesome woman who never wears makeup and brings in fresh eggs from the chicken coop every morning."

Tina joined in the laughter. "Oh, yeah, her. The one who bakes all her own bread and whips up gingham curtains for every blessed window in the house. Oh, and she makes tablecloths and napkins, too, to match the curtains."

"Don't forget putting up the preserves and making the quilts," Sharon added with a grin. "And helping with the branding in the spring and the roundup in the fall."

"And in between times she drives all over the countryside doctoring the sick and cheering the infirm," Barb said.

Jenny glanced at Keely, her blue eyes twinkling. "That's the one you're thinking of, right? Martha Stewart in boots and spurs?"

"I guess. I mean, maybe your picture is a little extreme, but that's about the size of it."

"Well, the thing is, that ranch woman—" Jenny winked at her sister and two friends. "Hit it, girls."

"*She's so last century!*" the women shouted in unison.

"Long live the new ranch wife!" Jenny shouted, punching a fist in the air. "She gets pedicures!"

"She serves fast food!" Barb raised her own fist.

"She shops at Nordstrom's!" Tina waved a fist in the air.

"She hires a cleaning service!" Sharon put both fists in the air and leaped up to dance around the salon, Rocky style.

Keely laughed in delight. "Good for you. I'm impressed. Obviously you all have it together. But you've never lived in Saguaro Junction."

"I don't think the place matters," Jenny said. "Women everywhere are changing. It's the millennium, and drudges are out of fashion. Hey, if a woman *likes* doing some of that, great. But you can live on a ranch and still have lots of the goodies of life. I don't plan on going anywhere *near* a chicken coop. Times have changed."

Keely still had trouble picturing such liberation on the Twin Boulders Ranch. "Somebody ought to tell that to Noah Garfield."

"Yep," Jenny agreed. "And I think you're just the gal to do it."

The salon party broke up after that. Keely excused herself so that she could use the second half of the afternoon to finish up the interviews for her magazine article. Because she didn't have time to conduct them in person, she had to risk using her cell phone. To make sure she wouldn't be caught doing that, she walked to the hotel next door and found a relatively quiet nook in the coffee shop.

On the way out of the hotel she passed a boutique that displayed a stunning dress in the window. Realizing that she needed something a bit more dressy for the wedding, she went inside. While trying it on, she gazed at herself in the mirror. Was this the image of the new, liberated ranch wife? Could a ranch wife be someone who'd posed nude for a men's magazine?

Of course not. And she had no business thinking like that, anyway. No matter how the image had changed, it still involved the tedium of marriage, that boring institution that sucked the life right out of a sexual relationship, right? But the women she'd met today didn't seem to be sucked dry. They were juicy ladies. And getting into bed with Noah every night didn't sound like such a bad deal, either.

Yeah, like he'd ask her to consider that option. The man didn't want to let himself climb into bed with her tonight, let alone for the rest of his life.

But he *would* go to bed with her tonight. She turned in front of the mirror. Definitely.

NOAH BOUGHT HIMSELF a pair of shorts so he could spend the afternoon playing volleyball on the resort's sand court with the guys. Throwing himself into the physical activity felt great. Maybe if he played hard enough, maybe if he spent the whole afternoon getting hot, sweaty and tired, he'd be too exhausted to be tempted by Keely in the suite tonight after the wedding.

He didn't go back to the suite until he had to change into his tux. Bracing himself for Keely to be parading around in something sexy or in nothing at all, he discovered she wasn't even there.

While he was taking his shower and getting dressed, he expected her to show up at any moment. Eventually his curiosity turned to irritation. She'd been invited to this wedding, and she'd damn sure better not be late. Then his irritation changed to concern. What if she'd gone back to the topless bar and taken that job, after all?

When he'd seen her last she was headed off toward the hotel's salon, but maybe she'd ducked out of that. He almost called Greg and Tina's room to find out if Tina knew where Keely might be. But he didn't really want to do that.

Standing in front of the bathroom mirror, he struggled with his bow tie. In the few times he'd ever worn a tux, he'd never really learned how to tie the damn thing. With a growl of frustration, he pulled it loose and started over.

A second before Keely spoke, he smelled her raspberry lotion. Instantly his groin tightened.

"Need some help, cowboy?"

He looked in the mirror and she was reflected there, leaning casually in the wide arch separating the bedroom and the bathroom.

Her purse was slung over her shoulder and a shopping bag dangled from her hand. She looked as if she'd been outside—her hair was tousled and her cheeks were pink from the heat. She was also breathing fast, despite her relaxed pose against the doorway. The crocheted halter top she wore quivered with each breath she took, and he wondered if she'd hurried up here because she was running late or because she was eager to see him again.

"That bow tie seems to be getting the better of you," she said. "Don't you have to be down there in a few minutes?"

"Yep." He met her gaze in the mirror and weighed the risk of having her help him tie it. "Are you going to have time to get ready?"

"Sure. I have at least a half hour more than you do. I'll get dressed after you leave. But you can't go with your tie looking like that." She put down her purse and her shopping bag and came toward him. "Turn around and let me see what I can do."

He assumed she'd learned the skill from hanging out with guys who regularly wore these monkey suits. Knowing Keely, she might be planning to turn this into a very seductive operation. Filled with misgivings, he faced her. "How was the manicure session?"

"Lotus Blossom Pink." She held up both hands to show him her nails.

They were covered in a pearly color that reminded him of the inside of a seashell. Or the inside curve of her ear.

Or the inside of...places he'd do well not to think about. Damn, but she smelled good.

She stepped closer and took the ends of the bow tie in her pink-tipped fingers. "Now hold still," she murmured.

Oh, he'd hold still. He didn't dare move a muscle. He just hoped that involuntary reactions wouldn't take over. Some things he couldn't control.

Staring at a point over her head, he tried to block out all sensation, but he wasn't having much luck. He was very much aware of the light, whispery sound of her breathing, the brush of her fingers and the scent of raspberries. If she leaned forward a fraction, her breasts would touch the front of his white pleated shirt. He clenched his hands at his sides.

"Shoot," she muttered.

He glanced down and knew immediately that was a mistake. Keely could be the most provocative, tempting woman in the world when she tried. But right now, to his complete amazement, she wasn't trying. And he discovered she could be just as irresistible when she didn't try.

All her concentration was on his tie, and she'd tucked her tongue into the corner of her mouth while she worked. Apparently she didn't know much more about this process than he did, but she'd been willing to jump in and help. He found that endearing.

Frowning fiercely, she pulled the tie this way and that.

"Want me to try again?" he asked.

"No, I'm going to get it. I'm just out of practice."

That meant she hadn't been doing this favor for any man recently. Noah was glad to hear it.

"There!" She stepped back with a huge smile of triumph. "I did it!"

A lump of emotion stuck in his throat. He remembered seeing that expression on her face when she was nine years old. As a self-important twelve-year-old he'd been teaching her how to rope her horse as the gelding circled them in the corral. When she'd finally settled her loop over her horse's head, she'd given him that exact grin.

Her grin had turned to surprise when the rope had tightened and jerked her off her feet. He'd forgotten to tell her what to do after she'd roped the horse. Her skinned hands and knees were all his fault that day, and he'd blamed himself for weeks.

He'd been worried about resisting Keely when she turned on her sexual charm, but he might have an even tougher time resisting her when she reminded him of the eager, happy little kid she used to be.

"You look very nice, Noah," she said softly. There was no taunt in her green eyes this time. Her compliment was simply and sincerely given as if she had no ulterior motive.

He was lost. "Keely." He gripped her arms, his fingers registering the warmth and smoothness of her skin.

Awareness blazed in her eyes. "You have to go," she said, her voice husky.

"I have to kiss you first."

"Noah—"

"I have to." He settled his mouth over hers with a groan of relief. Yes. How he'd needed this kiss, ached for it. Yet it was a different kind of ache from the one he'd had the night before. There was a sexual edge to this longing, but it was more about cherishing her than making frenzied love to her. It was the kind of ache that scared the hell out of him.

Ah, the joys of Keely's mouth—lips plump against his, responding, moistening, parting to let him stroke his tongue inside. His grip on her arms tightened, his fingers massaged that silky skin. And before he knew it, he'd slid both hands to her neck and untied her halter top.

And then…then he went a little crazy, filling both hands with her magnificent breasts, kissing his way over her jaw and down her throat. Braced against the edge of the counter, he leaned down and claimed his prize.

He grew dizzy from the pure pleasure of her breast in his mouth.

And she tunneled her fingers through his hair and held

him close. "Noah..." she said, gasping out his name. "You have to...leave."

Oh, no. He couldn't leave now. Not when he'd found heaven.

"You...should go."

With a murmur of protest he lifted his mouth and caressed one wet, erect nipple with his thumb while he moved to dampen the other with his tongue. Men had died for less reward than this. He could barely believe he was really cupping the weight of her beautiful breasts. Squeezing them with trembling fingers, he gave thanks for his good fortune as he tasted and tasted again, his mind numbed by the wonder of what was happening. The sensations bombarding him made his head buzz and his ears ring.

And ring, and ring. Wow, that was some sensation, like a...telephone.

Keely backed away from his embrace. "Sorry," she mumbled.

Dazed, he stared at her as she went over to get her purse and then proceeded to dig through it. A man could go crazy watching uncovered breasts like hers quiver. Finally she pulled a cell phone from the bottom of her purse.

A cell phone?

She pushed a button and shoved the phone back in her purse. Then she glanced up at him. "You'd better go," she murmured.

"What—" He paused to clear his throat. "What was that?"

"Nothing."

"You have a cell phone?"

"Yes."

"Why?" He couldn't fit the cell phone in with her supposed rootless living style. Topless dancers moving from city to city didn't have cell phones. Or did they?

"It's for work," she said.

Everything clicked into place for him. "Keely, are you a call girl?"

"No, I'm not."

He should have guessed she'd deny it, both now and the first time he'd asked her. What had he expected her to do, confess such a thing? "You are, aren't you? And you were afraid to tell me."

"No, really. I—"

"It's okay." He couldn't blame her, not when every time he looked at her he wanted to take her to bed. After years of getting that reaction from men, she might have become convinced that was what she was born to do. "It's not your fault that men want you," he said. "Hell, look at me. I can't keep my hands off you, and I promised myself I would."

"Noah, I'm telling you I'm not a call girl."

"And I'm telling you that I understand. We'll work around it."

She threw up both hands. "Okay, believe what you want. But right now, you'd better get downstairs." She stood. Her halter top had fallen until it was draped around her waist, but she made no move to retie it around her neck.

"Yeah, I'd better get going." But he couldn't seem to stop looking at her. Light from the overhead fixture in the bathroom picked up the sheen of moisture on her breasts, moisture left there by his eager mouth. God help him, he wanted more.

A call girl. That made it even more important that he not make love to her. She needed a completely platonic relationship with him if she had a prayer of changing her life. And so far he'd completely bombed out on the platonic thing.

Gazing at him, she pulled the halter top off over her head and shook out her hair. "Unless you want a quickie before you go. On the house."

"No!" He backed toward the door, while his whole body screamed with frustration. "Listen, I should never have kissed you. I should never have gone beyond kissing you." But, oh, God, was it fantastic. He could still taste her on his tongue. "Tomorrow we'll map out a job strategy. I'm thinking something in sales."

She arched her eyebrows. "Because I already have sales experience, you mean? I guess that makes sense. If I can sell my body, I can sell widgets."

"That's not what I meant!"

"I must not be very good at selling my body, though." She kicked off her sandals and began to peel off her capris. "I've offered it to you several times now and you keep turning me down."

His heart thudded in his chest as he watched her take off the last of her clothes. A quiver of need passed through him. "It's very, very hard."

She laughed and glanced at his crotch. "I can see that."

"Hey! I didn't mean—"

"Men have told me all sorts of lies, Noah, but all I have to do is look at the fly of their pants and I know exactly what they're thinking. It's like those witching sticks some people use to find water. Men get around me and—boing!— that witching stick points right in my direction." The devilish gleam was back in her eyes when she met his gaze. "If you decide you want to drill for water, come and see me. I'll give you a special rate."

It took incredible willpower for him to turn away from a very naked, very tempting Keely and walk out of the suite. Somehow he did it.

11

NOAH WENT THROUGH the motions of seating people in the rows of white folding chairs on the grassy courtyard where the wedding would be held, but his thoughts were still back in the suite with Keely. He'd been stupid not to see the truth immediately. The interview she'd been going to in the topless bar might have been with some sort of Las Vegas madam. Or worse yet, a pimp. The thought made him shudder.

Well, he was going to save her from that kind of life, just the way Richard Gere had saved Julia Roberts in *Pretty Woman*. Except Richard Gere had hired Julia Roberts for sex in the first place, so that had been part of the deal from the beginning.

If you decide you want to drill for water, she'd said, her skin flushed with desire, her eyes issuing a definite invitation. Was he a total fool to be so chained to his principles? Probably. His friends would certainly say so. Keely would certainly say so.

Then something else occurred to him. In her chosen profession as a hired lover, she wouldn't go to bed with a man because she wanted him. Having sex because she wanted to might be a real treat for her, a vacation from the same-ol', same-ol'.

Now, there was a dangerous concept. If he truly believed that, he could start thinking that he'd be doing her a favor, giving her a chance for some mutual satisfaction for a change. That might be the only motivation he'd need to send him over the edge.

Then Keely appeared and he wondered if he hadn't toppled over the edge some time ago.

If he hadn't, this latest dress of hers would do the trick. A rush of possessiveness heated his skin as if he'd just opened an oven door, and he hurried over so that he'd be the one to escort her to her seat.

She smiled as he approached. The smile was sly and seductive, and it put the final touch on a picture designed to bring him to his knees. She'd tamed her wild curls, pinning them on top of her head for a regal, sophisticated look. But it wasn't any less sexy than the tousled style she usually wore. Maybe it was even more sexy, because he could imagine the fun of mussing her up.

Rhinestone earrings and a small rhinestone-trimmed shoulder purse sparkled in the light from the tiki torches surrounding the courtyard. But the fit of her dress was the real showstopper. It shimmered over her body like mercury, outlining her hourglass figure to perfection. Made of an iridescent material, it rippled and flashed like a hologram with her every movement.

Although the dress had a high-necked collar, a diamond-shaped cutout beneath the collar showed an impressive amount of cleavage. And the back of the dress was nonexistent except for that little band of a collar. Beneath it was a spectacular view of supple, golden skin sweeping down to her waist.

Her skirt was ankle length, but a slit up the side ran to midthigh. Another few inches and it would graze the edge of her panties. That was assuming she wore any tonight. She had a wicked gleam in her eyes, so absolutely anything was possible.

Pulse racing, he offered his arm. When she slipped her hand through and moved in close, he took a deep breath and nearly zoned out on raspberry lotion. "Where do you want to sit?" he asked.

"On your lap," she murmured.

"Keely." He thought his heart would pound right out of his chest.

"Is that a yes or a no?" She flashed him another of her I-dare-you smiles.

"You're outrageous."

"And you're turned on. I'll bet your witching stick is twitching. I'll bet you're picturing all the possibilities right now."

"Pretty sure of yourself, aren't you?" And she had a right to be. She was dead-on accurate about the state of his mind and his body.

"It's a safe bet that you'll be thinking about me straddling you instead of listening to the ceremony. And speaking of that, I'll sit on the groom's side of the aisle. He asked me to the wedding, after all."

Taking another deep breath, Noah escorted her to the seats on the right side of the aisle.

"And I can tell you're just dying to know, so I'll end the suspense. I'm not wearing panties. They ruined the line of the dress and it was too hot for panty hose. You can think about that while you're standing at the altar trying not to look my way."

Swallowing hard, he halted near a row of chairs with a vacant seat. He noticed that most of the men in the vicinity had their attention firmly fixed on Keely. He lowered his voice. "Are you planning to throw out lines like that all night?"

"I'm only trying to live up to your expectations, Noah. Do you like the dress?"

"It's…um…tight."

"Well, that's on purpose, because if it was too loose you'd be able to see right down the front." She drew closer and dropped her voice to a low purr. "I'm not wearing a bra, either."

He struggled for his next breath.

She ran her index finger along his sleeve. "Does looking at me in this dress make you hot?"

He cleared his throat.

"I'll take that as an affirmative. Besides, I know it does. I can tell by the way you're breathing, sort of rough, like a car that needs to be tuned. I'd be glad to give you a tune-up, Noah."

"You'd better take your seat."

"Guess so." She squeezed his arm briefly before turning toward the row of chairs. Then she glanced over her shoulder. "See you later, big guy," she murmured, puckering her lips in a phantom kiss.

Moments later he took his place at the altar with the other groomsmen. As the minister led Jenny and Brandon through their vows, he tried to pay attention to the ceremony. After all, that was the reason he was here—to witness his buddy getting married.

But instead, he spent the entire ceremony exactly as Keely had predicted he would. He tried not to look at her, but he couldn't help it. And every time his attention strayed in her direction, he thought about how little separated him from her naked body. Only one tight, silvery dress. A dress with no back and a slit up the side. Once the collar was unfastened, she'd be bare to the waist. And if they were alone, he could easily push aside that skirt....

KEELY BECAME more caught up in the ceremony than she'd expected to be. She'd meant to concentrate on Noah and complete the seduction she'd started with her entrance. Instead, she found herself listening to the words of the ceremony, and for some stupid reason they were making her cry.

She blinked back her tears. Maybe B.J.'s upcoming wedding was hitting her harder than she wanted to admit. When she thought of B.J. getting married without her being there, her stomach felt hollow. Years ago they'd talked about being maid of honor for each other. It had been a given. She wondered if B.J. had chosen her friend Sally for that job.

Discarding that depressing subject, Keely focused on

Brandon and Jenny. They seemed so damn happy, as if they didn't mind a bit that they were severely narrowing their options with this move. Keely had always believed in keeping her options open. Any man who had dared mention the ''M'' word had been dropped.

By keeping her options open, she'd remained free to fly to Paris if she wanted, free to party wherever the music was the hottest, free to sleep with a gorgeous hunk who suddenly appeared on her radar. Jenny was giving up those options. And yet the life that Jenny had chosen didn't seem so bad at this moment, and all of Keely's options seemed to have lost their luster.

It was Noah's fault. Seeing him again had stirred up those childish dreams of living with one man—Noah Garfield—for the rest of her life. No other guy had ever inspired those dreams, and when Noah had rejected her, she'd decided it was a stupid idea in the first place.

And it was still stupid. Jenny and her friends might think the world had changed enough to allow a woman like Keely to live happily ever after in Saguaro Junction, but Keely, who'd inherited her mother's craving for excitement, knew better. So did Noah, which was why he'd never consider her as his life companion.

Life companion. God, did Noah have that written all over him. Any woman fantasizing about a man who could see her through all the joys and sorrows fate could dish out would recognize Noah as the real deal. He made her mouth water as he stood up there in his tux. He made her yearn for things that were beyond her reach. But early on she'd taken a clear-eyed inventory of herself, and now she had to have the courage to accept who she was...and who she wasn't.

In the meantime, however, she could have one weekend of lovemaking. Another woman would be lucky enough to have him for a lifetime, but Keely had been allowed this weekend and she intended to make the most of it.

She was aware that the dynamics between them had

changed since she'd accidentally left her cell phone on and
he'd assumed that a cell phone meant she was a call girl.
She wasn't sure exactly what was going on in that fertile
brain of his, but she had the definite feeling that his resistance to her was weakening. It could be the effect of the
dress, of course, but she thought something else was happening.

Whatever it was, she wouldn't question it. If thinking she
was a call girl allowed him to let go and make love to her,
then she'd let him think she was a call girl. She didn't care
how he perceived her, so long as the end result was hours
and hours of wild sex. And then they would part. It was the
only way this could end.

She blinked back another rush of tears. Damn. Maybe one
of the reasons she hated weddings was that they always
made her cry.

"OH, MAN, will you look at that." Clint handed Noah one
of the two piña coladas he'd brought over from the bar
before turning to face the action—Keely doing the limbo in
her tight, silver dress. "Tell me you're not letting that go
to waste."

Noah took a cooling sip of his coconut-flavored drink,
hoping the icy concoction would quench the fire in his belly.
Or better yet, maybe the rum would short-circuit his brain.
But the drink seemed to have no effect whatsoever and he
was still in agony as he gazed at Keely sliding under the
pole, her body moving rhythmically to the beat of the music
and the clapping hands urging her on. "You have a one-
track mind, son," he told Clint, although the comment applied to him, too.

"Every other track gets shut down when a woman built
like Keely does the limbo," Clint said. "Any man with
breath left in his body would respond to a sight like that.
But you're the only guy here with a chance of acting on
that impulse. I just need to know you're up to the job, so
to speak."

"You might need to know, but you're not gonna know." Noah kept his tone casual, disguising the fierce emotions that had gripped him from the moment the luau reception had begun and Keely had made it clear that she planned to party.

When Keely partied, sexual sparks flew in all directions. She'd drawn the attention of every man in attendance, with the possible exception of Brandon, who was understandably preoccupied with his new bride. For a solid two hours Noah had fought his own sexual bonfire. At the same time he'd tried to stamp out the smaller blazes of jealousy whenever he caught a man looking at Keely the way Clint was doing right now.

"I guess you don't really have to tell me anything." Clint kept his gaze on Keely while he took another swallow of his piña colada. "It's a foregone conclusion that something's gonna happen between you two."

Noah had pretty much concluded the same thing, but he wasn't happy about it. He should be stronger, nobler, wiser. Then he'd be able to keep his hands off Keely and be in a better moral position to help her turn her life around.

But he'd been forced to admit his own weakness and her greater strength. Before much longer, she would get her way. He couldn't hold out anymore. He'd tried to justify it as a pleasure that Keely deserved, after all those times when she'd only been doing her job. As a justification it didn't work very well. In his heart he knew that this would be about his needs, not hers.

By the time he'd finished his piña colada Keely had won the limbo contest, adding her prize to the one she'd picked up for taking first place in the hula contest. She turned in Noah's direction and blew him a kiss.

Clint chuckled. "Like I said, a foregone conclusion. At lunch I wasn't sure about the chemistry, but tonight she's on your trail, buddy." He clapped Noah on the back. "How does it feel to be the envy of every guy here?"

"Just wonderful."

"Funny, but you don't look as happy as I would expect you to. Is there a problem?"

Noah looked at his friend. Clint had no idea how many problems were connected to this situation, but Noah wasn't going to enlighten him. Instead, he grinned. "Clint, Keely's a woman. Of course there will be problems."

Clint nodded. "Point taken." He glanced at Noah's empty glass. "I think we need a refill. Let's—"

"Ladies and gentleman," Greg crooned into a wireless microphone, "may I have your attention, please."

"Damn, but he loves that mike," Clint said. "I think he believes he's the next David Letterman."

"Don't complain," Noah said. "Better him as the emcee than either one of us."

"True."

Greg glanced around at the crowd. "It's now time to play a special version of that old favorite, musical chairs, better known in this case as musical laps!"

Noah remembered having fun playing the game at Greg's wedding. The guys sat in a circle and the women moved around the circle ready to grab a lap when the music ended. But Keely hadn't been a part of the game a year ago. He didn't want Keely sitting on any lap but his.

"Finally something I can do," Clint said. "Come on, Noah. Grab yourself a chair."

He was going to hate this. Really hate it. He picked up a chair and set it beside Clint's. Greg organized the women, making sure there was one less man in the circle than there were women walking around it. To the melody of "Ukelele Lady," the women started to move around the group of seated men.

Whenever Keely passed Noah, she slowed down and gave him a secret smile. Then he watched helplessly as she cruised by with that killer walk of hers. The music stopped.

Amid breathless squeals from the contestants, Keely settled quickly in another man's lap. Noah didn't know him, but that didn't matter. He hated his guts.

Sharon plopped down in Noah's lap. "Hi, cutie," she said, turning to smile at him. "Having a good time?"

"Sure." He unclenched his jaw and smiled back. "How about you?"

"I'm having a great time watching you watch Keely. I've never seen you with that look on your face."

"It's indigestion. I should never have eaten that poi junk."

"Uh-huh. Indigestion and lovesickness look about the same on a man. I can see where I could get confused."

"You're confused, all right." Lovesickness? He'd better not be coming down with that disease. Catching it from a woman like Keely could be fatal.

Greg commanded the microphone again. "Okay, ladies, that's enough lap dancing for this round. On your feet."

Sharon slid off Noah's lap. "We all like her, you know," she said.

He played dumb. "Who?"

She rolled her eyes and glanced at her husband sitting next to him. "Did you find out anything interesting?"

"He's not talking," Clint said. "I did my best, but—"

"We have to eliminate a lap," Greg said. "Clint, come on out of there."

"Aw, *man,*" Clint grumbled as his wife began to laugh. "I never get to have any fun." Muttering to himself he hauled his chair off to the side and Greg started the music again.

Once again Keely passed by Noah, her hips swaying in time to the music. He ground his teeth and suffered. The tune continued and she approached for the second time, still wearing that secret little smile. When the music abruptly ended, Noah reacted without thinking. Grabbing her around the waist, he pulled her down to his lap.

"Oof!" she gasped, startled.

Heat climbed up from Noah's starched tux collar. He really hadn't meant to do that. On the other hand, he was very glad to have that silky silver bottom planted firmly on his lap instead of another guy's. Maybe a little too glad. In fact, a certain part of him was getting way too glad.

"I want a ruling on that!" Jenny, the woman left with no lap, stomped over to Noah and Keely. She attempted to look disapproving, but a grin was trying to break through. "I think that was some kind of interference on Noah's part." She turned to Greg. "And possible collusion on Keely's part. How would you call it?"

Greg nodded soberly. "Definitely a lap violation, and possibly a moving violation, as well."

"I'm innocent, Mr. Judge, sir," Keely snuggled down a little deeper.

"It's all my fault," Noah said. And his automatic reaction had also been a mistake. Not only had he telegraphed his feelings to everyone in the immediate vicinity, he wasn't going to be able to hide his erection if Keely didn't stop shifting her weight around.

"I say they're both guilty as sin," Jenny said, her lips twitching with laughter. "Throw the book at 'em."

Greg's eyes twinkled as he stroked his chin. "The bride has spoken, and tonight she's the law around here. I'm afraid I have to eliminate both of you from the competition."

"Sounds fair, right, Keely?" Noah stood immediately, hauling Keely up with him.

"If you say so," she said cheerfully.

He released her and backed away, hoping to hell nobody would notice the bulge in his pants.

"No hard feelings?" Jenny asked, winking at him.

"Uh, no." He just knew she'd used the word *hard* on purpose, and no doubt his face was pink as a flamingo.

"Then I have a favor to ask," Jenny said. "Would you two please go find the caterer and ask her to bring out some more fresh pineapple for the buffet table? I noticed we're running low. Just go behind the waterfall and straight down the hallway to the end and you'll find her. Her name's Julie Osaka."

"Uh, okay," Noah said, not sure he should venture anywhere with Keely at the moment.

"Let me get my purse," Keely said.

"All right." He couldn't very well order her to stay at the reception, so he waited until she'd retrieved her purse before he headed toward the waterfall at a brisk pace.

"Are we going to jog all the way to the caterer's office?" she asked, hurrying after him.

"Can't have Jenny running out of fresh pineapple."

"Okay, but if the two of us arrive in her office panting like racehorses, no telling what the caterer will think we've been up to."

He realized he was overreacting, besides behaving like an uncivilized jerk. He slowed down. They were going in search of the caterer. Surely he could keep his act together for a simple errand like that. "Sorry." He held the glass door open for her.

"That's better." She linked her arm through his as they strolled down a carpeted hallway. Then she glanced up at him. "All that work to get your bow tie together, and you've spent the whole reception with it hanging loose and your collar unbuttoned."

"I was hot." He quickly backpedaled. "I mean, warm. The night's very warm."

She slipped in closer so that the side of her breast nudged his arm. "Actually, I think a guy looks sexy with his tie undone. It's a tease, like the first stage of undressing."

"Hmm." He didn't dare try to carry on a conversation. Even though they were strolling at a leisurely pace now, he had trouble breathing normally. The most outrageous ideas stampeded through his fevered brain. She was wearing nothing more than that dress. All he needed was a dark corner. Surely there was one of those nearby. He'd already noticed a couple of places where the hallway branched off. God, he was depraved. And she'd done that to him.

A trim woman with Asian features came out of a doorway and started toward them.

When she was close enough for Noah to read her name tag, he realized they'd been lucky enough to run into the caterer. "Excuse me," he said. "We're from the wedding party, and the bride asked if you could see about putting out more fresh pineapple."

The caterer smiled. "Of course. You can't have a decent luau without plenty of fresh pineapple. I was just heading down there to check on things. I'll stop by the kitchen and take care of that first. Anything else?"

"That should do it," Noah said.

"So the reception's going well?"

"It's lovely," Keely said. "Everyone's having a great time."

"Good. Then I'll let you get back to the party." The caterer headed down one of the side hallways.

Keely gazed up at him. "Mission accomplished."

"Right." He looked into her green eyes and found heat simmering there. The accessibility she'd built into that dress was driving him wild. "Now we can go back."

"Right." She ran her tongue over her lower lip. "Would you mind if I stopped by the powder room first?"

"I'm...not sure where it is." His heart pounded. He didn't think the powder room was what she had in mind, but he couldn't be positive.

"I'm not sure, either. We can explore." She tugged on his arm, leading him back down the hallway. Then she turned right down another long hallway that ended in a bank of windows looking out on a tropical atrium. "Maybe this way."

He didn't think so. The doors they passed looked like offices to him. At this time of night, no one was working in them. But maybe there was a rest room down here, and maybe that's really what Keely hoped to find.

As they neared the end of the hallway, he couldn't see any door marked Women. But he did notice the hallway widened at the end. Two private nooks on either side had been turned into conversation areas, and they each contained two armchairs, an end table and a potted palm. Probably a place for the office employees to take a short break.

His pulse quickened. Behind that chair. Up against the wall. It was the darkest corner he was likely to get. He doubted anyone came down this hallway at night. His mouth grew moist, his penis hard. No. This was insane.

He cleared his throat. "Nothing's here."

Keely eyed the two shadowy nooks. Then she glanced at Noah. "Pretty deserted spot, isn't it?"

"We need to get back," he said, his voice hoarse.

"We will." She tossed her purse on one of the chairs before turning to face him. Then she took the ends of his bow tie in her fingers. "In a little bit." Slowly she drew him closer until a bare inch was left between them.

He could feel the heat of her body and smell the scent of raspberries mixed with a more basic, musky aroma of excited woman. She'd been taunting him with this possibility all night. He'd never done something like this, never been driven to try. But then no woman had ever announced to him at the beginning of an evening that she wasn't wearing underwear.

Something within him snapped. With a groan he pushed her past the chair and into the corner of the tiny nook. With one hand he held her head while he plundered her mouth. With the other he found the slit in her skirt and reached inside. He encountered lace panties. He'd been had.

He gripped her lace-covered bottom and lifted his mouth from hers. "You're wearing panties," he said, breathing hard.

"Am I? I must have forgotten," she murmured.

"You were bluffing."

"I was teasing."

"I call it bluffing, and lady, I'm calling your bluff." He looked into her eyes as he reached down and grabbed a section of her skirt in each fist. Then he yanked it up over her hips and bunched it around her waist.

Her eyes burned with green fire. "Right here?"

"Right here." He held the skirt high while he used his free hand to pull down that underwear she'd promised she wasn't wearing. Then he slipped his hand between her legs and his mind reeled. She was drenched.

"Do you...have a condom?" she asked, her voice ragged.

"No," he whispered, allowing her skirt to ripple down around his wrist while he continued to caress her.

Her eyes fluttered closed and she began to pant. "We...need...one."

"Well, maybe you should have thought of that. You're the one who bought two boxes," he murmured before he claimed her mouth in another searing kiss.

12

NOT MUCH OF KEELY'S BRAIN was functioning, but she had to admit Noah was right. She *should* have thought of condoms. But she hadn't, and now…now he was driving her insane, using his fingers and thumb to create mind-altering pleasure. In a matter of seconds she'd lost all control of the situation.

Sensation rocketed through her, making her thighs quiver and her breasts tingle. Her nipples grew hard and thrust against the material of her dress. Oh. Yes. There.

She clutched his shoulders and arched toward him, craving more, craving deeper. If he chose to take her now, she wouldn't have the will to resist him. If he kept caressing her like this, she might beg him to take her, condom or no condom.

The birth control problem needed attention before it was too late. "Noah," she said, gasping. "We can't…" She couldn't think, let alone talk. "If we don't have a condom, then we can't…"

He lifted his mouth from hers while his fingers continued to work their magic. "I know we can't," he murmured. "So first you, then me. We'll take care of each other. Deal?"

"Deal," she said with a sigh as her legs turned to rubber.

And what a deal. He'd found the perfect rhythm to make her writhe in helpless abandon as her body throbbed and yearned for climax. He would give it to her fast, and that was fine. She wanted it fast.

Then, at the moment when she balanced on the very brink of ecstasy, he slowed the movement of his hand and gentled the pressure of his thumb. He slid his fingers out and teased her with a light, butterfly touch. Slipped slowly in again, then withdrew. Circled his thumb right where it would have the most effect, then stopped.

She whimpered against his mouth.

He lifted his lips a fraction from hers. His voice was rough and untamed. "I've decided I want more. Unhook your collar."

She trembled and fought for breath. She'd unleashed the wild man in Noah. "If I let go of you, I'll fall down."

He wrapped his arm more firmly around her waist. "Now you can let go." He nibbled at her lower lip. "I want that collar undone. And the way I feel right now, I might rip it."

Her hands shook as she reached back to unfasten the collar.

He brushed his mouth against hers. "I love it when you put your hands behind your head and push your breasts toward me like that." He continued to stroke her in a lazy way, just enough to keep her at a fevered pitch.

Oh, yes, Noah had made the transition from nice guy to rogue. She was quivering too much to manage the hooks. "I can't do it."

"I think you can."

"Then be still," she pleaded. He paused for a beat, and she unfastened the hooks. "There."

"Now pull the material down." He stroked her again with that easy rhythm, deceptively easy.

She was close. Very close. But it seemed he wanted her nearly naked when the moment arrived. Shaking with tension and the excitement of undressing in this barely concealed corner, she peeled away the top part of the dress and let it hang at her waist.

His breath was hot and sweet on her face. "Now put your hands behind your head again," he murmured.

She reached back and laced her fingers together, cradling her head in her hands. Her breasts lifted.

He leaned back slightly and looked down. A guttural sound of pure male satisfaction rumbled in his throat. Then his lust-filled gaze met hers. "Are you afraid?" he asked softly. "Afraid someone will see us? Hear us?"

"Sure." Her voice quivered. "That's part of the thrill."

His eyes darkened and his whole body began to shake. "Yeah," he said. "Yeah, it is. I didn't know. This is so good." With a soft moan he nuzzled her throat. "So good." He quickened the movement of his fingers, circled his thumb over her aching flashpoint.

"Yes. Oh, *yes*."

"You're going to come soon," he said hoarsely.

She began to pant. "I…am."

His hot mouth trailed down the slope of her breast. "If you make noise…."

"I won't," she whispered.

Slowing the rhythm of his fingers, he drew a moist circle around her nipple with his tongue. "You're sure?" he asked, his breath whispering over her breast. "It's going to be good."

"Yes, I'm sure." She moaned softly. "Make me come, Noah. Please make me come."

Lightly, ever so lightly, his tongue flicked against her taut nipple. Slowly at first, then more quickly. And his thumb, centered over her trigger point, mimicked the flicking motion. Faster, and faster still, connecting two charged points, arcing tension between them…tightening…vibrating… faster, faster, faster—*now*.

She clenched her jaw to keep from crying out as spasms shook her. Stroking rhythmically with his fingers, he closed his mouth over her breast and sucked in deeply, then released the pressure, sucked in and released. The liquid sound of his sucking followed the beat of her orgasm, and each tug on her breast became part of her climax as he drew on her again and again.

Her throat ached with silent moans of release—blissful, perfect release.

His hand movement slowed, then stopped, but his fingers were still buried deep. With one soft kiss on the very tip of her throbbing nipple, he straightened and eased his fingers free.

Gradually opening her eyes, she gazed into his—heavy-lidded with passion, and smoldering, still smoldering. She cupped his face in both hands. ''Thank you,'' she murmured.

''You're welcome.'' He lifted a damp finger and traced the outline of her lips. ''I want to taste your secrets,'' he whispered before covering her mouth with his.

He kissed her thoroughly, sharing the musky tang of her climax and stirring the embers of her desire. Unbelievably, she began to want again. But this time her needs had a different focus.

Reaching between them, she stroked his crotch and found the metal clasp of his zipper. As she pulled it down, he shuddered. She slid her hand inside, cupping the warm weight of him, tight and near to bursting, barely contained in the skimpy briefs she'd bought yesterday.

Such foresight. The soft cotton gave way easily to her quick tug, and in no time she had her hand around his big, beautiful penis.

He gasped in reaction, lifting his head to look into her eyes.

Meeting his darkened gaze, she closed her fingers around the base of his shaft. Then she stroked upward until she encountered his most vulnerable spot. Lingering there, she absorbed the tremors that shook him each time her fingers made contact. Then she stroked down again and eased back up to torture him some more.

His eyes burned hot and hungry and his voice rasped in the stillness. ''You're driving me crazy.''

''I hope so.'' She rubbed her thumb over the moisture-slick tip and he closed his eyes with a groan. She knew what he longed for, but she wanted him to ask. It was so much more exciting that way. "Tell me, Noah, what else can I do for you?"

His eyes opened, and unchecked passion flamed there. He stared at her, and his chest heaved with his struggle to breathe. "I want you on your knees," he whispered hoarsely. "I want your mouth on me."

She loved playing with fire, loved taunting him as he'd taunted her. "Will you make noise?"

He gasped again as she brushed a finger where she discovered he could feel it most. "No."

"You're sure?"

"Yes." His voice cracked. "Please, Keely."

Dizzy from the thrill of her own sexual power, she sank to her knees. At first she used her tongue to explore and caress him until he was trembling so violently that he braced both hands against the wall. As she anticipated the moment to come, as she imagined him anticipating it, desire spiraled tighter within her.

By the time she took his straining penis in her mouth, her frenzy matched his. His climax came quickly, and as she swallowed his warm, salty essence, she throbbed with unmet needs. She wanted everything this man had to offer. And she would get it. The night was young.

NOAH HAD NO IDEA how much time went by before he gathered the strength to put his clothes back together and help Keely with hers. He felt like the victim of a shipwreck. Probably resembled one, too.

He touched her cheek with a still-trembling hand. "Incredible," he said, gazing into her eyes.

"Yeah," she said softly. She was totally mussed and outrageously sexy-looking, all tousled and pink. Her hairdo had self-destructed and her lipstick was MIA. Just thinking about how her lipstick had gotten smeared was getting him worked up again, so he'd be better off not thinking about it.

A slow smile of satisfaction tilted those kiss-swollen lips of hers. "So you liked taking a little risk?"

He looked into her green, devilish eyes. She'd won. "Yes, I did."

"Want more?"

Yes, he wanted more. More of whatever she could dish out. "I think you know the answer to that."

"I do." She stroked a finger over his lower lip. "But it pleases me to hear you say it."

He caught her hand and licked the crevice between each finger. "Do you want me to tell you I'm your slave?"

"Are you?" She sounded a little breathless.

"Looks that way." And he wanted a chance to turn the tables.

"What about the luau? And your friends? Shouldn't we go back?"

He studied her and searched for some diplomatic way to describe her rumpled condition. "I guess we should. For a while longer. But you might need to do a little repair work first."

"Oh." She touched a hand to her hair. "Right."

"We never did find a bathroom."

"No, but the window should make a good enough mirror."

"Yeah." Reluctantly he stepped aside and let her out of their private corner. He felt like claiming a chunk of plaster or a section of carpet as a souvenir for one of the peak experiences of his life. "You weren't really looking for the bathroom, were you?"

She turned from pinning up her hair, and with her arms up like that, she was so inviting, so completely feminine. "No, I wasn't," she said.

"Didn't think so."

She looked in the window's reflection again and continued doing her hair. "You didn't believe for one minute I was looking for the bathroom, did you?"

"I was hoping you weren't," he admitted. "I was hoping you were looking for a dark corner, the same as me."

"It's so great to be on the same page for once."

Right now he wouldn't mind being on the same bed. But first they had to get back to the luau and put in an appearance. He glanced down to make sure his fly was completely zipped, and there, plain as could be on the dove-gray material, was a lipstick mark. "Damn," he mumbled, trying to scrape it off with his fingernail. It wasn't working.

"What's the matter?" She turned from the window, her lipstick tube in one hand. Then she began to giggle.

"I'm glad you think it's funny. Lipstick on my collar is one thing, but I don't really want to walk into the luau with lipstick on my fly."

"Stop rubbing it. You'll only make it worse." She grinned at him. "I have something to take care of your problem." She capped her lipstick tube and dropped it back inside her purse.

"Like what?" He had learned to be suspicious of a smiling Keely Branscom.

"This." She produced a small packet and ripped it open.

He was immediately aroused and ready to destroy the work she'd put into her hair and makeup. "You said you didn't have one."

"I usually tuck one in my purse." She pulled out a small, white square from the packet.

He imagined that she'd forgotten about it in the heat of the moment, but he was confused by the configuration of the condom in her hand. "They make them *square* and *white?* How does that work?"

"I'll show you." She sat in the chair. "Come on over here."

He couldn't believe she was being so nonchalant about it. Her casual attitude excited him even more. "While you're in the chair?" They would be way more visible in that chair than they had been in the corner. But if she was willing to try, he was more than willing.

"Sure. That puts me at the right level."

He'd heard about making love with the woman in a chair, her legs spread over the arms, and he'd always meant to try it. But he hadn't expected the chair to be at the end of an open hallway in a public building. He quivered with expectation as he walked toward her.

She gazed at his fly and glanced up, amusement in her eyes. "Looking forward to this, are we?"

"You'd better believe it."

"This should be very interesting." She used the white square to rub the spot where the lipstick was.

He jumped back. "What in hell are you doing?"

"Getting your stain out. What did you think I was going to do?"

"I thought that white thing was a condom!"

She looked at the moist square and began to laugh.

"Well, it comes in the same kind of package!"

"Yes," she said, grinning at him. "Yes, it does. But this is a laundry aid. You use it to take out stains when you aren't near a washing machine. I think it would be totally useless for birth control."

He stared at her, unable to process this practical streak in a woman who seemed focused only on sexual experiences. "So how come you remembered to bring that and not a condom?"

"Because I thought we'd be at the luau the whole time. I guess I was more concerned about ruining my dress than getting pregnant." Laughter danced in her eyes. "Do you want me to work on that lipstick mark or not?"

"You'd better give me that thing. If you do it, I'm liable to end up with more lipstick on here, not less."

"I can control myself."

"That may well be, but I think we've established that I can't."

"I see." Gazing at him, she rubbed the towelette lazily back and forth between her fingers. "Then I guess you'd better do it."

"Stop that."

"You don't really want me to stop," she said softly. "You love being sexually on edge. You thought we were going to make love in this chair and you were ready to try, even with the danger of someone coming down the hallway and catching us at it. You crave the adventure, don't you?"

"Maybe. But I crave chocolate cake, too. That doesn't mean it's good for me."

"Well, there are several differences between me and chocolate cake." She lowered her voice to a seductive murmur. "And some similarities. I'm smooth and creamy, but I won't clog your arteries. And if you think you crave chocolate cake, wait until you've tasted me."

Amazing how he could stand there, not ten minutes after an unbelievable orgasm, and feel as if he could do it all again. "Give me that towel thing," he said. "The sooner we get back to the luau, the sooner we can leave."

"Now there's a plan." She handed him the towelette. "But I should warn you that someone could still come along. Would you rather they caught you rubbing your crotch, or me doing it?"

"No one's going to see a thing." He walked over to the atrium window, keeping his back to the hallway. Then he started scrubbing at the spot on his fly.

She came to stand beside him and continued to fiddle with her hair as she looked at her reflection in the window. "I'll bet that doesn't feel as good as it might if I did it."

"Cut it out, Keely. I'm trying to clean this spot off without getting a major hard-on."

She lowered her voice again. "Looks like you're having difficulties with that. Have you ever allowed a woman to watch while you touched yourself?"

"No." Damn, but she had a way of thinking that turned him on. "And I'm not doing it now, either."

"We could save that for later. Did you like watching me in the hot tub?"

"Yes."

"I liked watching you, too. But you didn't know I was there. Next time, I want you to know."

He stopped rubbing the spot. If he kept it up while she was talking that way, he would lose control. "I guess that's good enough. Let's go back."

"Okay."

As they started back down the hall, he wadded up the towelette and tossed it in the planter on his way by. Then he took her hand, just to prove he could touch her without going crazy. It wasn't easy to keep the level down to hand-holding, but he would manage because he enjoyed the warmth of the connection.

"That was something," she said. "Really something."

"You've probably done stuff like that before." He shouldn't even ask, knowing he wouldn't like the answer.

"No, not really."

"You haven't?" He glanced at her in surprise.

"I only imagined doing it. I never did it for real."

"What do you know." As they continued down the hall, he smiled to himself. Without realizing it, he'd made one of Keely's sexual fantasies come true. That was pretty cool. "And no one saw anything," he said, feeling damn smug about that, too.

"Well, not for the first part, anyway."

He tensed. "What do you mean?"

"Nobody caught us when we were in the corner, at least."

"Nobody saw me sponging my fly, either!"

"Maybe not."

"What do you mean, *maybe not?*"

"The janitor standing on the other side of the atrium might not have been able to see what you were doing."

He came unglued. "There was a janitor standing on the other side of the atrium? Why didn't you say something?"

"Because you were almost done." She chuckled. "And I didn't think having you freak out and spin around would do anything to change his opinion of what you were up to. So I just smiled at him. He smiled back.''

Noah groaned. ''Great. First the gardener catches us making out in the bushes, and now there's a janitor who thinks I'm some sort of weirdo who stands around playing with himself. Just great.''

''Noah, if you're going to enjoy the weekend, you need to remember something.''

''What?''

''What other people think of you is none of your business.''

He sighed. She was right, of course, as long as they were here in the big city. But he had a lot of Saguaro Junction in him and, back home, such things mattered. And he was about to rejoin his buddies, people he would continue to see for years to come. He hoped that by the time they reached the party, his erection would be gone and the wet spot from the towelette would be dry. If not, he'd have to throw a cold drink on his lap to take care of both problems.

''How soon do you think we can leave?'' she asked as she walked beside him.

''We should stay until Jenny and Brandon head up to their honeymoon suite.'' His imagination filled with a picture of Keely lying naked in the middle of a pile of green pillows. ''I hope to God that's soon.''

13

KEELY HAD NO SOONER rejoined the party than Jenny, Tina, Sharon and Barb pounced on her and dragged her away from Noah.

"Something happened, didn't it?" Tina said, her dark Italian eyes sparkling. "You were gone a *very* long time."

"And that was the plan," Jenny said. "Brilliant of me to send you off together, if I do say so myself."

"After the way he pulled you down on his lap during the game, I knew things were progressing nicely." Sharon grinned. "So here's what I think. You two have known each other since you were kids, right?"

"That's right," Keely said.

"Then it's fate, you two meeting like this in Vegas," Sharon continued. "I've seen Noah with a lot of women, and I've never seen him so totally preoccupied with any of them. I'll bet he's been pining away for you all these years without realizing it."

"Oh, I doubt it." Didn't she just wish, but she'd be a fool to let herself believe that. Maybe she had a sexual hold on Noah right now, but that was the extent of it. "We're having fun being together this weekend, but that's all."

"I think there's more to it," Tina said. "You have that certain glow whenever you're with him, too. And—"

A roar of male laughter cut off whatever else Tina had meant to say. They all looked over at the crowd of guys standing by the bar. Noah held an empty glass in his hand, and from the looks of things, he'd spilled the contents of it down the front of his tux, including his pants.

Keely couldn't help smiling. She had a pretty good idea that he'd done it on purpose for camouflage. Apparently his friends thought so, too.

"Lame, totally lame!" Clint chortled. "Nobody thinks that was an accident, buddy."

Brandon clapped him on the shoulder. "Just give it up and admit there was frisky business going on while you and Keely were AWOL, and you came back with a little evidence on your clothes. It's happened to the best of us. Even me."

"Yeah," Greg said. "Shirts buttoned up wrong, underwear on inside out, suspicious wet spots—we've seen it all. Come on, 'fess up."

Keely didn't mind the good-natured teasing because it meant that Noah's friends had accepted her. But she wasn't sure how Noah would take it. He hadn't intended to include her in this event, yet she'd accepted Brandon's invitation, anyway. Then she'd become chummy with the women in the bridal party, and then she'd dressed for the wedding in an outfit to drive him wild. Now he was suffering the consequences of her actions.

To her surprise and relief, he grinned. "What are you guys, nooky narcs?"

"Hell, no," Greg said. "I hope you *did* do the nasty. We made bets on it, and I want my money."

"You should know better than to bet on an outcome you'll never learn," Noah said. He glanced in Keely's direction. "I don't intend to satisfy your curiosity or settle your bet. Unlike you morons, we have too much class, right, darlin'?"

"Right," she called over to him. Thank heavens he wasn't furious with her. She'd only meant to have some fun, not make him uncomfortable. Obviously he wasn't upset if he'd call her darlin' in front of everyone. She couldn't help feeling warm and special, and for one tender moment she imagined what it would be like to be his darlin' for more than a weekend. But she wouldn't be, and she needed to cool it around his friends so she wouldn't embarrass him any further.

"I was all set to claim my money on circumstantial evidence," Greg grumbled, "until you threw a piña colada all over Exhibit A."

"I'm willing to testify to what I saw before that suspicious event," Clint said.

"Yeah, me, too," Brandon added.

As the men started to wrangle about what they'd seen or hadn't seen, and the size and position of the spot, Jenny looked at her girlfriends and lowered her voice. "I think it's time to give those monkeys something else to think about before they mess up this budding relationship. They're starting to get a little crude."

"Agreed," Sharon said.

"It's not a budding relationship," Keely said.

Jenny smiled at her. "Sometimes the people in a budding relationship are the last ones to pick up on what's happening." Then she raised her voice. "Garter toss, guys! The bride has spoken!"

Brandon snapped to attention so quickly that Keely laughed. "That's impressive, Jenny."

Jenny grinned at her as Brandon started over toward them. "Oh, we came to an agreement. I get to be the boss during the ceremony and the reception. He gets to be the boss all during the wedding-night playtime. It works out."

"I'll bet it does." Keely saw the glow of love in Brandon's eyes as he took Jenny's hand.

They laughed and leaned against each other as they walked toward the center of the reception area where Greg had already placed a chair for Jenny to prop her foot on. During the removal of the garter, both Jenny and Brandon joked with the guests, but most of their teasing was directed at each other.

They'll have fun being married.

The thought zoomed through Keely's mind, startling her. She'd never considered that marriage and fun belonged in the same sentence. She hadn't had all that many examples to go by, but most of the marriages she'd known had seemed extremely boring and restrictive compared to the excitement of the single life. Both her father and Noah's father had been widowed fairly young, and neither of them had chosen to remarry, so she'd concluded that they must not have enjoyed matrimony all that much. From all reports, her mother hadn't, either.

In high school the parents of her friends had never seemed to have anything resembling fun. Mostly they'd spent time trying to spoil any fun their kids had wanted to have. A few of her high-school friends had acted interested in the concept of marriage and some had even gone through with it, but once she'd relocated to L.A., nobody in her city-girl circle had considered it an option until after they felt too old to party.

But Jenny and Brandon gave a new dimension to her concept of marriage. For that matter, so did the others—Tina and Greg, Clint and Sharon.

In Keely's world committed couples were unusual. In this gathering they were the norm. For the first time in years she felt out of step. That would be cured once she left this group and returned to her own life, of course, but she was strangely reluctant to do that. She'd been given a different perspective and she wasn't quite ready to shut the door on that.

But the door might be shut for her. She didn't fit into this cozy scene. She never had and she was foolish to think she ever would. These people accepted her as a childhood friend of Noah's because that's all they knew about her. True, she wasn't as wild and racy as Noah imagined, but she was definitely a bad girl compared to Jenny and her friends. She doubted that any of them had ever posed for a centerfold.

A cheer went up from the assembled guests as Brandon held the garter aloft. He started to throw it toward the small knot of bachelors clustered by the bar, a group that included

Noah, but Jenny caught his arm. Then she pulled him closer to whisper in his ear.

He straightened and turned toward the bar. "The bride wants to change the routine, and I'm sworn to give her absolute power during the ceremony and reception. If she wants the routine changed, then it'll be changed. There will be no throwing of the garter."

The bachelors looked relieved, even Noah, and here Keely had thought he was more than ready to catch a garter and be the next man in his group to walk down the aisle. But the married men weren't having any of it and they started complaining.

"Hold it." Brandon raised both hands. "I'm not going to *throw* the garter, but we can't let a perfectly good wedding garter go to waste. One of you single guys needs to end up with it. Jenny has asked that in this case I *bestow* the garter, so we don't leave the results to chance. It seems she has a particular person in mind."

Keely had a funny feeling in the pit of her stomach. Oh, well. It was only a silly superstition, anyway.

Brandon twirled the garter around his index finger as he walked toward the bachelors who were watching him nervously. Sure enough, Brandon stopped in front of Noah. "Sir Noah, you are hereby dubbed the keeper of the wedding garter. Cupid's got you in his sights, son."

Noah made some effort to protest, but in the end, with the not-so-gentle help of his friends, he was wearing the garter as an armband. He avoided Keely's gaze.

Of course, he wouldn't give her soulful looks, she thought. He wanted only one thing from her, and he didn't need a wedding ring to get it. That was fine, because she only wanted one thing from him, too. That was her story and she was sticking to it.

Greg turned on the microphone again and took charge of the proceedings. "And now for the throwing of the bridal bouquet," he announced.

That was her cue to duck out, Keely decided. No way

was she catching that thing, especially after Brandon had tagged Noah with the garter. Maybe it was only a superstition and meant nothing, but she didn't care to test it. If she ever did get married, it wouldn't be to a man like Noah who lived in Saguaro Junction. These friends of Noah's had made marriage look more attractive to her than it had in the past, but she was still a country mile away from the altar.

As she edged over to the sidelines, Tina caught her arm. "Where do you think you're going?"

"I, uh, need to go to the—"

"You can wait." Sharon grabbed her other arm.

"But—"

"Let's go, girl." Barb grabbed her waist from behind and pushed.

"Hey, wait a minute!" Keely tried to pull away from them as they tugged her over to an area where a small group of single women stood. A very small group. Four, besides her. Those were terrible odds.

"We have our instructions," Tina said. "Bride's orders."

Keely struggled in vain. "Look, I like all of you heaps and heaps, but you're about to be my new ex-best friends. I don't want to play this game."

"It's the hand of fate." Sharon gripped harder and kept pulling.

"Fate is a hell of a lot stronger than she used to be!" Keely tried her best to get away, but these were three determined women. "Have you girls been working out?"

"Oh, we rodeo from time to time," Tina said. "It's rough on the nails, but good for the ego."

"Rodeo? I thought you were all about Nordstrom's!"

"Those two interests aren't mutually exclusive, chick," Sharon said.

"Incoming!" Jenny yelled and sailed the bouquet in the air.

"We're on it!" called Sharon. "Excuse us, ladies," she said to the hopefuls standing nearby on the grass.

"What on earth are you doing?" She hadn't wrestled

with females like this since she was eight, and finally the episode became funny. She began to laugh as Tina, Sharon and Barb shoved her over to the spot where the bouquet was coming down.

It hit her on the head, and while she giggled helplessly, Tina and Sharon made sure the bouquet fell neatly into her arms. Then they released her, leaving her standing alone with a sweet-smelling bouquet clutched in both hands. She'd never held a bridal bouquet before, and damned if the experience wasn't turning her to mush. But she couldn't get all sentimental and let Noah in for even more teasing.

Jenny turned, a huge grin on her face. "That should do it." Then she walked over and exchanged high fives with her girlfriends before turning to the deejay. "Music, maestro, if you please. It's time for the owner of the garter and the owner of the bouquet to dance."

Keely knew she should refuse to do it, but instead she stood as if rooted in the grass while Noah slowly walked over to her and took her hand. "Sorry," she murmured as he led her to the circle of smooth concrete that served as a dance floor.

"About what?" He swung her into his arms as the deejay played a waltz.

"Catching the bouquet." She rested it on his shoulder and gazed at the cluster of orchids and roses so that she wouldn't have to look at Noah. He waltzed very well, which surprised her. There were many things she didn't know about him, apparently.

"It appears you didn't have much choice about catching it."

"I shouldn't be here in the first place. From the beginning, you didn't want me to be part of this wedding, but I had to be my usual obstinate self and accept the invitation from Brandon. Now here you are, dancing with me in front of all your friends."

"I don't mind."

She figured he was just being nice. She could tell from

the way he was dancing with her, keeping a good three inches' distance between them, that he didn't want to give anybody ideas about their relationship. "I know they're all trying to be matchmakers," she said, "but you don't have to worry. I told them this was a fun weekend, but that was all there was to it."

"You did, huh?"

"Yes," she said firmly. "So don't think I'm going to embarrass you out here by trying to snuggle closer or anything. I won't do that."

"I would love you to snuggle closer," he said. "But I have piña colada down the front of my tux and it's sticky stuff. I'd hate to get it all over that dress. I doubt if you have enough little white packets to take care of that."

She glanced up at him in surprise. "That's why you're keeping a space between us?"

"That's the only reason, darlin'." His brown eyes were warm as he looked down at her. "And that distance is killing me."

"Really?" Her heart lifted, and she couldn't help smiling. He wasn't embarrassed by being made a public spectacle with her. "Then to heck with the dress. I've never danced with you before, Noah. Let's make it count." She slid in tight.

Immediately cheers and catcalls erupted from the crowd.

"Maybe that was a mistake," she murmured, and started to back away.

Noah tightened his grip, holding her fast. "Uh-uh. I'm not giving up this sensation. Ignore them. Dance with me, Keely."

She took a deep breath. "All right." Meeting his gaze, she moved sensuously to the music, allowing her body to meld perfectly with his.

He sighed. "Yeah, like that. Sweet."

Oh, how they danced. The boisterous comments of their audience faded in the wonder of how perfectly they fit together and how easily they moved over the dance floor, as if they'd been practicing for years.

The corner of Noah's mouth tilted. "We should have tried this before."

"Who knew?"

"I think I did." His gaze heated. "I think I've always known how we'd fit."

Her breath caught. "They say that dancing like this is a lot like making love."

"Yes, they do." The flame burned brighter in his eyes. "And if this endless party ever winds down, I plan to test that theory. I wish we could leave right now."

Her blood pounded through her veins. "Me, too."

"Damn, that's the end of the song. With luck, the piña colada has glued us together and we'll be forced to leave the party to get unstuck."

Keely backed out of his embrace easily. "No such luck. Must be the material of this dress. I guess it repels everything."

Noah laughed. "Except me. I—"

"Miss November!" cried a hearty male voice near Keely's shoulder. "I finally figured it out!"

Horrified, she turned toward Brandon's father, Elmer. "Excuse me?"

"You're Miss November!" The festivities and a generous amount of liquor were prompting Elmer to speak much louder than usual. He beamed at her as if sharing the most wonderful news. "*Macho* magazine, right? I can't remember the exact year, but I sure remember how you looked, lying on that Thanksgiving table with all the food, and your—"

"You must have me confused with someone else." Keely glanced around and prayed nobody else had heard the exchange.

"Hey, Elmer." Noah hooked an arm around Elmer's shoulders. "Speaking of food, let's go get some of that wedding cake before it's all gone."

"No, thanks," Elmer said, ignoring him and focusing intently on Keely. "Listen, I'm sure it was you. I even remember the name Keely. I was going through a bit of a midlife crisis in those days, and so *Macho* was very appealing to me. I told my wife it beat running out and having an affair." He laughed and winked at her. "Good excuse, huh?"

"I'm flattered that you think I look like a centerfold," Keely said. "But you have the wrong girl." She glanced pleadingly at Noah, hoping he'd support her denial.

But for some reason he didn't. Instead, he turned his palms up as if to say he was out of ideas other than to continue distracting Elmer. Once again he tried to steer the older man gently away. "You look like a guy who could use another drink, Elmer," he said.

"Not yet," Elmer said. "First I want an autograph." He fumbled in his pocket. "I have one of the wedding napkins in here, which my wife insisted I take for a souvenir. Keely, would you sign it for me? And put *Miss November* on it, too? I still have that magazine in a box in the basement. Gosh, I wish I had it here right now so you could sign your picture!"

She wasn't going to talk him out of it. If she refused to go along with him, he might get louder and more insistent. At last she took the napkin and ballpoint pen he held out to her. "Okay, I'm Miss November," she said.

"I knew it! Here, use my back so you can write on that thing." He turned around.

"I try to maintain a low profile, Elmer, so I'd appreciate you keeping the information to yourself," she said as she braced the napkin on his back and signed her name. Considering how tipsy the guy was, she didn't think there was much chance of his keeping a secret, but at least she'd try.

"I think you should be proud of it!"

"Well, thank you, but not everyone agrees with you." She handed him the napkin. Too bad her father wasn't proud of her. But maybe Elmer wouldn't be, either, if she happened to be his daughter instead of a relative stranger he'd met at a wedding.

She didn't kid herself that everyone at the reception would be as thrilled as Brandon's father was to discover a centerfold in their midst. She'd found that out the hard way from her friends and neighbors in Saguaro Junction, and she didn't want to let herself in for the same kind of humiliation at this shindig.

Elmer gazed at the signature. "Keely Branscom. That's the name, all right." He looked up, and his gaze traveled over her from head to toe. "Yep, it's you, all right."

"Time for a drink, Elmer!" Noah grabbed him forcefully by the arm and propelled him toward the bar.

"Hey, is it true?" A young guy Keely hadn't met came over to her. "I heard him say you were in *Macho* magazine." He looked very hopeful.

Keely glanced toward the bar. Noah was trying desperately to keep Elmer under control, but the older man had still managed to sneak his napkin out of his pocket to let people look at it. In seconds she'd be the center of attention, taking the limelight away from the bride and causing herself and Noah all kinds of embarrassment.

She'd overstayed her welcome. How she'd looked forward to spending the night and the next day with Noah, but she'd be the subject of so much curiosity that she could only be an embarrassment to Noah now. Better for her to just disappear. A quick trip up to the suite to pick up her purse, and she could be gone.

The shock of such an abrupt ending to the weekend left her feeling numb. She hoped the numbness would last, acting as a painkiller at least until she made it out of the hotel.

"So, is it true?" the eager young man asked again.

"Yes," she said. "And if you'll stay right here, I'll run upstairs and get you an autographed picture."

"Just your face? Or…the rest?"

"The full monty."

"Cool!"

She looked in Noah's direction again, and luck was with her. He was so busy trying to keep Elmer corralled that he hadn't noticed she had more problems. He wouldn't see her leave.

"Stay here," she said to the guy. "I'll be right back." Then she hurried away toward the lobby to catch the elevator that would take her to the top floor.

14

NOAH NOTICED KEELY had attracted unwanted attention. He could tell from her harried expression that she wasn't happy dealing with the young stud who had cornered her. But it took him a minute to excuse himself from Elmer, and by the time he'd gone to her rescue, she'd disappeared. The young guy she'd been talking to was standing in the same spot, though, looking expectant.

Noah went over to him. "The woman in the silver dress. Where did she go?"

The kid glanced around and lowered his voice. "I don't know if I should say. She might not want me to."

Noah gripped his shoulder, exerting firm pressure. "I suggest you tell me, and tell me now."

"Hey! Who are you, her boyfriend?"

"Yes." The answer slipped right out, and he discovered he liked the sound of it. "Yes, I am."

The kid looked him over, as if measuring a rival. "I'd like to hear that from her."

Noah felt a stab of compassion for the kid, who was obviously awestruck by Keely. And the boy had no chance with her, first of all because Noah wouldn't give him one, and second because Keely hadn't looked enthralled with the guy, either.

He lightened his grip on the kid's shoulder. "Look, I think she was upset when she left, so I need to find her. I'd appreciate your help."

"She wasn't upset. She went upstairs to get me an autographed picture."

"I'm sorry to have to tell you, but there aren't any autographed pictures." At least Noah hoped there weren't.

"Oh, *man*. Then why did she say she was going to get one?"

"So she could cut out," Noah said.

"Why would she do that?"

"I think she was a little uncomfortable about being recognized."

"No kidding?" The kid thought that over. "I guess it could be a bummer." He shrugged. "Personally I think it would be cool to be famous, but I guess everybody's different."

"Yep, everybody is. And thanks for the info. I'll go see if I can smooth things over with her." He left the kid and looked around for Jenny and Brandon to let them know he was ducking out.

Maybe Keely had gone up to the suite and would wait for him there, but then again maybe she wouldn't. She'd looked pretty upset about being identified as Miss November, and he'd been caught flat-footed, not sure how to respond, so she might be upset with him, too.

She'd obviously wanted him to help her deny the whole thing, and the words had been on the tip of his tongue. But then he'd realized he couldn't win this one. If he helped her convince Elmer and everyone else that she wasn't a centerfold, it would be like denying that she'd ever done it, as if he was ashamed of her for posing.

And he'd never, ever been that. Frustrated, worried and confused—definitely. He hadn't known how to deal with the grown-up version of the little girl he'd been so close to, and so he'd only made things worse. But he'd never been ashamed of Keely Branscom.

He wasn't about to do anything that would give her that impression, either. But he could also understand why she wouldn't want the entire crowd at this reception to know her background, so he'd worked to keep Elmer toned down. It had been like trying to get shaving cream back in the can.

Well, now Keely was gone, and he felt a great urgency to follow her and find out her intentions. He didn't want her to disappear from his life and he was afraid that might be what she had in mind. Besides, nothing had been settled about her career, and she might go right back to dancing in topless bars, or worse. That possibility was no longer acceptable.

Locating Brandon and Jenny, he walked quickly over to them. "Listen, I need to—"

"Was Keely a centerfold for *Macho?*" Brandon asked. "My dad got her signature, and he swears—"

"She was, a long time ago," Noah said quietly.

"Get outta here!" Brandon said. "That's outrageous."

"She really was?" Jenny said. "Wow. A celebrity guest. That's cool."

"The thing is, I'm afraid she's a little embarrassed that your dad recognized her," Noah said.

"Oh, she shouldn't be!" Jenny looked concerned. "I think it's fabulous. I'm not surprised, either. Anyone could look at her and know she has the body for it." She glanced around. "Where did she go? I need to tell her that she has nothing to be embarrassed about."

"I think she left and went up to the suite," Noah said.

"You mean because of being recognized?" Jenny asked.

"I think so."

Jenny picked up her skirts. "I'm going straight to a house phone so I can call her and tell her to get her butt back down here. Leaving the party like she's in disgrace or something is plain ridiculous."

Brandon put a restraining hand on her arm. "Maybe not so ridiculous, Jen. I can't guarantee that every single person here will be open-minded about it. Can you?"

Jenny paused, a frown on her face. "I really hate to think that any of our guests would cause her a problem."

"But they might," Noah said, reluctantly agreeing with Brandon. "She's dealt with small-mindedness before, when the magazine hit the stands in Saguaro Junction ten years ago. I'm sure she doesn't want to put up with more of the same tonight, and I can't blame her."

"Okay." Jenny sighed. "You may have a point, and I'd feel terrible if somebody insulted her. So I'll call her and tell her that everyone in the bridal party is thrilled to have met Miss November. I know I can speak for all of us on that score. We've loved getting to know her. She's a kick."

"Go ahead and call if you want," Noah said, "but I'll bet she won't answer the phone. Listen, I was planning to stay here at the reception until you two headed up to your honeymoon suite, but I think I should check on Keely. If I know her, she might have decided to get out of Dodge."

"Oh!" Jenny's eyes widened. "You mean leave the hotel?"

"It's possible."

"Then go! Right now!"

Noah hesitated. "I don't know if I'll be back down before you leave, and tomorrow morning you have that early flight to Hawaii, so I might not see you again this weekend."

"Don't give that another thought." Jenny's eyes sparkled. "Your job right now is to convince Keely to stay. And I know you have what it takes."

Brandon clutched his chest in pretended shock. "You *do?* How could you know that?"

"By talking to his girlfriends." Jenny smacked her new husband on the arm. "Now stop goofing around and let this man go. We're still at the reception part of this shindig, which means I'm fully in charge."

"Right." Brandon winked at Noah.

"I wish you both the best." Noah gave Jenny a hug. He stuck out his hand to Brandon, but ended up giving him a hug, too. "I'll be in touch."

"You bet," Brandon said. "I want to know how this turns out."

So did he, Noah thought as he sprinted toward the elevators.

Before he boarded the one that would take him to the top

floor, he quickly scanned the lobby in case she'd already made it back down and was on her way out. He didn't see her. She wouldn't have left without going back to the suite, he reasoned. Her cell phone was up there, for one thing.

When the elevator opened, he half expected to see her in it. But the glass-and-brass cubicle was empty. All the way to the top floor he tried to decide what to say to her. He was beginning to realize that his original impulse to save her from herself had developed into something much more complicated. Now he was trying to figure out how to save her and also keep her in his life.

And that was plain crazy. They were from two different worlds now, and they certainly had different outlooks. She was a city girl who was glad to have escaped small-town life. He planned to spend the rest of his days on the Twin Boulders Ranch. His father had handed him the sacred trust of running the place, and he intended to pass the land on to his children one day.

Although Keely didn't think much of the institution of marriage, he wanted a wife and babies, and he wasn't getting any younger. Brandon's wedding made him sharply aware of that.

So he had no business chasing after Keely, who didn't fit in with his plans at all. Oh, but she fit perfectly when he was holding her. And the fit wasn't only sexual, either. Whenever he thought about Keely, he felt a sense of connection so strong that he couldn't imagine letting her disappear again.

Yet he had no clue what form a relationship might take at this point, or if she'd even agree that a relationship was a good idea, considering their differences. That's why they needed more time together, to work on those problems. And if they were destined to part, then he wanted to make love to her in that good old-fashioned, horizontal way at least once before they said goodbye. He thought they both owed themselves that much.

He had to convince her to stay, and if words wouldn't do

it, then he'd try the physical approach. Of course, there was always the chance she hadn't planned to leave at all. As he walked down the hall toward the suite's double doors, he remembered the scene she'd prepared for him the night before—the hot tub, the skimpy bathing suit, skin flicks on the big-screen TV, champagne in the ice bucket.

Maybe she'd had a setup like that in mind when she'd left the party. Heart pounding, he slid his key into the lock and opened the suite door. "Keely?" he called, loud enough to be heard over the sound of the fountain in the entryway.

No answer.

She might be lying seductively on the pillows in the living room…naked. His body surged with desire as he walked into the empty living room, lit only with soft indirect fixtures. "Keely?"

Still no answer.

She wasn't in the hot tub or on the balcony, but a light glowed from the bedroom. Maybe she was waiting for him in that big, white bed. The image quickened his step and his pulse. He called her name again as he crossed the footbridge.

She wasn't in the bed, either, and he had a bad feeling when he noticed a neat stack of twenty-dollar bills lying on the white sheets. He didn't stop to count the money, but he guessed it was the same amount he'd given her the day before to buy clothes.

When he didn't find her in the bathroom, he could think of only one other place she might be hiding to surprise him. She might be lying in the closet as a joke, mimicking the way she'd tucked herself in there yesterday when his buddies had visited the suite.

But the closet was empty, too.

"Keely!" He knew in his heart she wasn't anywhere in the suite. He could feel her absence, had felt it from the minute he'd stepped inside the door. The electric excitement she carried with her everywhere was missing from these rooms. But he shouted her name, anyway, in a hopeless attempt to vent some of his frustration.

The only response was the gurgling of the stream in the living room.

Damn it! Where the hell had she gone?

She couldn't be far away, he decided, hurrying back over the footbridge and through the living room. He hoped that she hadn't caught a cab somewhere, that she'd be on foot. The Saturday-night crowds would be heavy, but she wouldn't be hard to spot in that silver dress. A woman like her wouldn't be hard to spot no matter what she had on, but if she'd made it up here and back down to the lobby before he left the party, then she hadn't taken time to change.

He would find her. Damn it all, he would find her.

KEELY HAD GUESSED Noah would come after her once he noticed she was gone. After all, they'd had a pretty good time in that hallway, and once a gal had whistled a tune on a guy's piccolo, he usually wanted an encore. She wished she could give him one, because she'd truly enjoyed that first performance.

But it wasn't in the cards, as they said in Sin City. And if her heart was aching worse than she'd ever remembered, well, she'd have to get over it. Noah wasn't the right guy for her. Never had been and never would be.

Even he knew that, but chances were he wouldn't let her run away, so if she wanted to escape, she'd have to be smart about it. Consequently, when Noah hurried past the hotel's tropical garden on his way to the street, she watched him from behind the large lava boulder where they'd kissed the day before.

God, he was gorgeous. His mussed hair and rumpled tux only made him more adorable. And he was coming after her. Well, that was a picture to carry with her—Noah Garfield trying to chase her down. Years from now she'd probably still get a thrill thinking of this tall, broad-shouldered cowboy combing the streets of Vegas looking for her.

But it would be better for all concerned if he didn't find her.

Surrounded by dense foliage and night shadows, she crouched behind the boulder and waited for him to pass. Instead, he paused to stare at the lava rock. He couldn't possibly see her. The shadows were too deep. Yet her heart pounded frantically as she wondered if he'd somehow sensed she was there.

They'd played a lot of hide-and-seek as kids, and in those days she'd secretly wanted him to find her. Even at the tender age of seven, she'd felt a curl of excitement in her stomach when Noah was hunting for her. As he'd drawn near, she used to let him know her position with a slight rustle or faint cough. She'd squealed whenever he found her, as if she hadn't been hoping for that to happen all along.

Maybe she wanted him to find her now, too. Maybe she'd chosen the boulder hoping that he'd look there. She held her breath and waited.

He gazed in her direction for another tension-filled moment. Then, with a shake of his head, he continued down the walkway toward the street.

She let out her breath with a sigh of disappointment. She'd outsmarted him. Damn it. So now that she had, it was time to continue with her plan.

Creeping out from behind the boulder, she ignored the puzzled glances from other pedestrians and focused on Noah walking ahead of her. Fortunately, his height and his gray tux made him easy to see. She kept him in sight all the way to the busy street.

He hesitated, looking right and left, studying the crowds. Finally he chose to turn left. Which way he went didn't matter to Keely, but she had to know so that she could head in the opposite direction. Once she had about four blocks between them, she hailed a cab and gave the driver the address of her hotel downtown.

The route took them along the Strip in the same direction Noah was walking, and soon she spotted him striding down the street and scanning the crowds on both sides. She pressed her lips together, determined that she wouldn't ask the cabdriver to let her out.

Although she longed to be with Noah again, she'd only be buying a little more time and a little more loving. The ending would be the same. Better to deal with the pain when it was manageable than to take a chance on getting hurt worse than she'd bargained for.

Blinking back tears, she settled deeper into the back seat of the cab as the driver maneuvered through the heavy traffic. Once they'd passed the point where she'd seen Noah moving along the sidewalk, she turned to look through the back window, but she couldn't pick him out of the crowd. Their little sexual adventure had come to an end.

Noah walked to the point of exhaustion before he finally dragged himself back to the Tahitian. He believed Keely was still in Vegas, but he finally admitted to himself that finding her would be tougher than he'd first thought. And he was sick of walking the streets in a tux that smelled like overripe piña coladas.

Once back in the suite he went quickly into the bedroom and stripped down to the briefs Keely had bought him the day before. He thought about that first night and her open, generous invitation to make love. He'd been the noble fool who'd resisted her with no concept of what he was throwing away. He'd wasted hours trying to prove his superior morality, while he was living in the same suite with a goddess.

What a dope he was. If he hadn't been such a stiff-necked jerk in the beginning, he might have established a bond between them by now, one she wouldn't feel so free to break. He couldn't let her slip through his fingers, and he wouldn't.

But first he needed a few minutes of rest. Just a few. He stretched out on the big empty bed and figured on staying there a maximum of thirty minutes. Then he'd go back out and look some more.

Many hours later he awoke with a start to find sunlight streaming into the room. He glanced at his watch and groaned. Nearly noon.

Leaping out of bed, he showered and shaved in record time. While he dressed in jeans and one of Clint's denim shirts, he figured out where he had to start his search, where he would have gone the night before if he'd taken time to think about it.

Not long afterward he walked into the Pussycat Lounge. "I'm looking for Keely Branscom," he told the thin guy who offered to show him to a table.

"Keely? I don't think she's coming by today, but I can check with Suzanne after her number's over, if you'd like to have a seat."

Bingo. Anxiety and anticipation churned in his stomach. She wasn't coming by today, the guy had said. That didn't sound as if she'd landed a job here. He hoped to hell it didn't mean she picked up clients at the Pussycat.

But at least he'd found a link to her. That was the main thing. And once they'd connected again, she wasn't going back to whatever it was she was doing. He'd be better off if he didn't think too much about what that might be.

Rock music from a faulty sound system blared and crackled as a brunette with large breasts shimmied topless for half a dozen customers scattered throughout the bar. She must be Suzanne, he decided. No doubt the dance was supposed to be arousing, but he was so eager to find out about Keely that he just wanted it to be over.

Finally it was, and the brunette sauntered backstage while the men in the bar whistled and called for her to come back for an encore. Noah hoped she wouldn't decide to perform one.

Fortunately she didn't. Moments later she walked toward Noah's table wearing an oversize T-shirt to cover what passed as a costume. When she sat down across from him, her gaze and manner were direct. "Brad said you were looking for Keely. What for?"

He'd expected that. "We grew up together," he said. "I heard she was in town, so I'd like a chance to see her."

Suzanne didn't seem totally convinced. "So where's home?"

"Saguaro Junction, Arizona. Her dad's the foreman on the ranch I own with my brother, Jonas."

Her expression softened a little. "She mentioned Saguaro Junction to me, so I guess you could be legit. You look pretty honest to me."

"Thanks. I don't mean her any harm."

"Probably not. But women like Keely and me have to be careful, you know? Guys can become, like, obsessed with us."

His gut clenched as he thought of the nutcases Keely might attract if she continued on her present course. "I'm sure that's true."

"I guess there's no harm in telling you where she's staying, though." She gave him the name of a midpriced hotel downtown.

"Oh," he said, unable to hide his surprise. The hotel wasn't the best Las Vegas had to offer but it wasn't the worst, either. He'd braced himself for some sleazy dive in a bad part of town.

Suzanne smiled. "I know. I was surprised, too. You'd think *Attitude!* magazine would put out the bucks for someplace a little glitzier, huh?"

"*Attitude!* magazine?" Noah's thoughts scrambled. The only magazine he'd ever connected to Keely was *Macho.* He'd vaguely heard of the other one, and thought it was for twenty-something women, although he wasn't absolutely sure about that.

"Wait a minute." Suzanne's eyes narrowed. "You sound surprised, like you didn't even know she's working for them. If you're such a good friend, how could you not know that?"

The information hit him like a microblast, and he struggled to come up with an answer. "We've been out of touch." *She worked for a magazine. She'd let him believe that she was a call girl, and she was a reporter for a women's magazine. She hadn't needed saving at all, and she'd played him for a fool.*

Suzanne stood. "In that case, she might not want to see you. What did you say your name was?"

"Noah. Noah Garfield." *Noah "the idiot" Garfield.*

"Noah." She backed away from the table. "I'm going to call her and warn her you're on your way. I shouldn't have told you where she is, but at least they have good security at that hotel."

"You don't have to warn her." He felt completely betrayed. Sure, at first he'd thought this weekend would be an isolated event, but then…then he'd started to care about her. He'd thought they were building something between them, and all the while she'd been laughing at him. "She has nothing to fear from me."

"So you say. I'm going to call her, anyway. I should have done that in the first place." Suzanne hurried away.

Noah left the bar and stood in the sunlit street trying to get his bearings. As the shock began to wear off, anger moved in. She'd been toying with him, amused with his white-knight routine, determined to corrupt the man who was trying to save her.

And she'd succeeded beyond her wildest dreams. He would dare anything now. He wondered if she could handle that. Maybe it was time to find out. As long as Suzanne was going to announce his visit, he might as well make it. He wouldn't want to disappoint a lady.

But he might make her wait a while, wait and wonder what he planned to do. He'd grab some breakfast. Something told him he was going to need his strength.

15

CAUGHT.

Keely thanked Suzanne for calling and slowly hung up the phone. Then she began to pace her small hotel room while her stomach did flip-flops. Childhood lessons kicked in, telling her that being found out this way, with Noah learning the truth from a stranger, was much worse than if she'd confessed, herself. If she'd told him the truth when her cell phone had rung while they were in the suite's bathroom, then he might have been able to laugh about the situation…eventually.

But when he'd assumed the worst—that she used the phone to turn tricks—she'd let him believe that, figuring it served him right for leaping to conclusions.

She'd still been into revenge at that stage. The sixteen-year-old who'd been rejected that night in the barn had wanted her payback. But now, after a sleepless night of missing Noah, she realized what she'd done to herself. The game had turned serious, and she'd fallen in love with him. Or, to be brutally honest with herself, she'd never fallen *out* of love with him. He'd been the only man she'd wanted for so long, and apparently he still was.

Ever since she'd left the Tahitian, she'd tried to talk herself out of being in love with him. When she couldn't sleep, she'd switched on her laptop and started her article, hoping that work would keep her from aching so badly. The laptop was still on, and she'd typed and retyped the first paragraph, but mostly she'd sat staring at the screen and thinking about Noah.

Perhaps most irritating of all was the stupid X-rated screensaver that flashed on automatically whenever she stopped typing for a while. Talk about rubbing salt in her wounds. If only she had aquarium fish swimming on that screen.

But she didn't have fish. Instead, a little naked cartoon woman chased a naked cartoon man, shoved him down and hopped on top of him. After some vigorous movement she jumped off, the man leaped to his feet and chased her down for more of the same. The cycle continued endlessly. A girlfriend who was into computers had created it for her as a joke.

This morning she wasn't laughing.

What a bummer of a weekend. For a few sweet hours she'd had Noah wrapped around her little finger. But that was history. Suzanne had said he looked stunned by the news that she was a reporter. Keely could just imagine. But once he recovered, he would be furious. He might leave Vegas without trying to see her, but she doubted it. No, he'd come to her hotel to give her a piece of his mind, and then he would leave, cussing her all the way back to Saguaro Junction.

She wondered if he'd tell her father, B.J. or Jonas about this. Probably not, considering the sexual nature of their encounter. But if she'd secretly been considering going home for B.J.'s wedding, she could kiss that idea goodbye. Even if Noah didn't say anything to the others, the tension she'd create on the ranch by reappearing would ruin B.J.'s wedding day, and Keely wasn't about to do that.

As she continued to pace she wondered how best to handle the confrontation with Noah. She could avoid it altogether by checking out of the hotel and moving to another one. She could even head for the airport and try to snag a flight to Reno this afternoon instead of going in the morning.

But that seemed cowardly. At nineteen she hadn't had the guts to face the music after her centerfold had appeared in *Macho* and she'd run away to L.A. Ten years later, she liked to believe she had more courage. Besides, what difference did it make if Noah yelled at her? It wasn't as if they had a future together or anything.

So she'd stay and wait for him to arrive. Because of the scene she anticipated, she'd better invite him up to the room. Dealing with his fury would be difficult enough without also putting on a show for every person in the lobby or the hotel coffee shop.

If he'd taken a cab downtown, he could be here any minute. Her room was trashed, the bed unmade and the covers tossed aside during her hopeless attempt to sleep. A couple of towels lay on the floor from a long shower that had done nothing to relax her. She thought of making the bed and picking up the area, but that seemed way too anal.

Then she glanced down at her outfit—her favorite knit tank top, the old white one she wore for writing because it was soft as a baby's bottom, and yellow gingham stretch capris, also a writing favorite because, for some reason, she always felt more creative wearing them.

Her clothes hadn't helped her write so far this morning. Neither had a big pot of room-service coffee. With Noah on the way, she might as well give up.

She thought about changing clothes now that she didn't intend to work on her article anymore. But she had no idea what to wear for a fight. And she was sure that's what they were about to have.

Maybe she should put on makeup, too, except that she didn't want to look as if she was coming on to him and make him even angrier. He couldn't very well think she was being seductive if she met him looking like this—barefoot, no makeup and her hair pulled into a ponytail. Maybe that was exactly the look she needed for a fight. In this outfit, she felt stripped to the basic, with her gloves off. Lean and mean, ready for anything.

She'd done an article on fair fighting for couples and the suggestions had sounded perfectly reasonable at the time. Now, as adrenaline poured through her system, the suggestions sounded ridiculous. To heck with fair fighting. Time to line up her defense. This whole thing wouldn't have happened if he hadn't assumed she was looking for a job dancing topless and pompously tried to save her. Just who did he think he was, anyway?

Yeah, no wonder she'd decided to teach him a thing or two. He'd been asking for it, behaving as if he had the corner on right living. Who made him in charge of the world? Suppose she had been a topless dancer and had loved her job? What right did he have passing judgment on her choice of career?

Okay, she was geared up for this donnybrook now. Let him come. And speaking of that, where the hell was he? Traffic wouldn't be that heavy right now, and if he'd come straight to her hotel from the Pussycat Lounge, he'd be here.

So he hadn't come straight to her hotel. That was a depressing thought. The only thing worse than having this fight with Noah would be not having it. She couldn't believe he'd go back to Arizona without telling her what he thought of her behavior. He'd want to have the last word. Wouldn't he?

When another half hour passed and her phone hadn't rung, she was nearly ready to stomp over to the Tahitian and find out what was keeping him. Damn it, he'd stirred her up and then left her to wear a path in the carpet. Surely he wouldn't track her down and then drop the whole matter. That would be so diabolical, so unlike Noah's direct approach to things.

She was ready to scream with frustration by the time the phone finally rang. She snatched it up and uttered a curt greeting.

"Keely, darlin'," Noah drawled, "you sound upset."

"Where have you been?"

He chuckled. "Not far away. Just having a bite to eat in the coffee shop of your hotel."

She couldn't figure it out. He should be yelling, and he

was *chuckling*. She was the one yelling. "How can you sit down there and *eat* at a time like this?"

"I was hungry." He sounded lazy and content...almost. But there was a subtle thread of tension underneath that casual tone.

Her heartbeat slid into a faster tempo. The years had made a few changes in Noah's behavior, apparently, because he wasn't reacting the way she'd thought he would. She had to believe he was full out furious, and yet he sounded loose and in control. All she had to go on was that hint of tension, which she might be imagining because she expected it to be there. "I guess...I guess you should come up so we can talk about this."

"That would be fine. But I don't want to interrupt your work."

His voice tickled up and down her spine, making her shiver. "I'm not working."

"Then maybe you're doing research."

"No." Maybe it was his location holding him back. He didn't want to yell at her while he was using the house phone in the lobby. Made sense.

"Then maybe you're testing the suggestions you made in your latest article," he said smoothly.

"Excuse me?" She was so nervous about this coming fight that she could barely remember her name, let alone what she'd written for the last issue.

"I picked up one of your magazines in the gift shop and, sure enough, there was an article by you. I read it while I was eating. Learned quite a bit about multiple orgasms."

She swallowed. "Oh."

"The way I understand it, self-gratification is a big part of women learning how to have them." He might have been discussing cattle prices, from the nonchalant way he said it. "I thought you might be practicing."

If she didn't know better, she'd think he was sexually teasing her the way she'd teased him earlier in the weekend. But that didn't seem like Noah, especially now, when he was so angry. She wished he'd start yelling at her, because then she'd know what to do. She'd figured out her side of the argument. But he wasn't playing this according to her script and she was having trouble keeping her balance with the conversation.

She cleared her throat. "Noah, what's your point?"

"It seems I underestimated you, Keely. You have a lot more talents than I was giving you credit for. I'm here to apologize for reading you so wrong."

"You *are?*" Now she was thrown completely off-kilter.

"Absolutely. I'd like to make that apology in person, if you'll give me your room number."

Maybe they were going to discuss this like two mature adults. No passion. Damn it, that didn't feel right, but if that was his approach, she had to go along. You couldn't fight with someone if they wouldn't fight back, and it was up to him to strike the first verbal blow.

She cleared her throat, determined to take the high road, too. "Noah, I should apologize, too, for leading you astray."

He laughed. "You certainly did lead me astray, darlin'."

Her skin flushed hot. And that sexy laugh rolled through her, doing all kinds of mischief. If only he didn't have a sexy laugh. And a sexy voice. And a sexy mouth. "Actually, I meant for *misleading* you about my occupation."

"No apology necessary. There was a certain thrill involved, thinking that you were a bad girl. You taught me a lot about fantasies, Keely. I'm grateful for that."

"Oh." She rubbed her temple, which was beginning to throb with the promise of a headache. She'd introduced him to fantasy and now he'd probably use that knowledge to enrich his life with somebody else. She'd been *useful*. Triple bummer. "I see," she said. "That's very…nice."

"Give me your room number. I think it would be better to say these things to each other face-to-face."

If they were going to have a civilized discussion, she

could just as easily meet him in the lobby, but she wasn't really dressed for that. She gave him her room number.

"Thanks. I'll be right there."

She hung up the phone, totally confused. She'd expected him to blow sky-high on the phone, then demand her room number so he could yell at her some more in person. Instead, he was apologizing. Thanking her for introducing him to some fantasy concepts. *Getting ready for a kiss-off speech.*

Oh, Lord, that was it. Thanks for the memories. It's been a lot of fun. Bye.

She felt sick to her stomach. This was the speech she'd been trying to avoid ever since they'd met in front of the Pussycat and he'd indicated he wanted to save her. She'd figured if she called the shots, she could make the speech instead of him and protect her heart at least a little.

Even leaving the Tahitian hadn't been all bad, because she'd been the one saying a silent goodbye. If Noah had stormed up to her room and raged at her before stomping out, that wouldn't have been all bad either. Passion was never bad. Instead, he planned to deliver a calm, rational kiss-off speech. He sure knew how to hurt a girl.

When he knocked on the door, she jumped and her heart began to pound. Well, she'd grown up in the years they'd been apart, too. She would simply beat him to the punch. Somewhere, she'd dredge up a few chuckles of her own as she told him what a fun and frivolous time she'd had this weekend. Years from now she'd be able to look back and laugh at how crazy they'd been, she'd tell him.

She opened the door with a smile. Forced, yes, but a smile, damn it. The smile wavered.

He stood there looking better than any man had a right to look, especially after the weekend they'd had. "Hello, Keely," he said quietly.

She glanced away. She'd never pull this off if she spent any time staring into those warm brown eyes. "Well, we certainly did it up this weekend, didn't we?" She stepped aside to let him in. "I also need to thank you for sharing that suite with me. As you can see, I don't have much in the way of fountains and hot tubs in here.''

Noah walked into the room and glanced around. "It'll do.''

She closed the door and leaned against it while she contemplated his choice of words. She watched as he took off his Stetson and laid it brim-side up on the table where her computer sat, still switched on. "Do for what?'' she asked warily.

Without answering, he glanced at the computer, pulled out the chair she'd been sitting in and settled into it. He gazed at the screen for several seconds. "Some screensaver you have here,'' he said. "Puts my shooting stars all to shame.''

"Why don't I turn that thing off?'' She shouldn't be surprised that he used a computer at the ranch. Saguaro Junction was small and conservative, but that didn't mean the town was filled with hicks.

He leaned back in the chair and glanced at her. "Why turn it off? I'm not embarrassed, and you certainly shouldn't be, considering how daring you are.''

She shrugged, not willing to admit that the stupid little screensaver reminded her of what she'd never experience with Noah. "Well, I'm not embarrassed, but for the record, I don't use that screensaver on my office computer. It's strictly for private use on my laptop.''

He gazed at her. "You're really destroying my image of you, Keely. First I find out you're not a call girl, not even a topless dancer, and now you tell me you don't have X-rated screensavers on your office computer. Next you'll be telling me that you've never had a multiple orgasm, despite writing a whole article about it.''

She drew in a quick breath and her pulse hammered. Man, she'd never expected that comment, and what was worse, he was dead-on. After writing the article, she'd meant to experiment a little, but then she just…hadn't. There were many sexual adventures she'd written about, fantasized about and ultimately retreated from. It was one of her well-kept secrets.

Her weekend with Noah had seemed like the perfect time to be brave. Here was a man who thought she would dare anything, and she'd felt the thrill of living up to her reputation for once. It had been liberating and wonderful, and…safe. Maybe that was why she'd cut loose. She could be as wild as she wanted to be with Noah because she'd trusted him to keep her safe.

Pushing back the chair, he stood. "Did I touch a nerve, Keely?"

She laughed, hoping she sounded amused and not nervous. "Are you kidding? You know what kind of woman I am, Noah. I have no rules, no limits. A free spirit, that's me."

"I thought so, too." He came closer, a gleam of purpose in his eyes. "But I'm beginning to wonder if I know you at all."

She backed up. He looked more intimidating now and a muscle twitched in his jaw. This was what she'd expected from him in the first place. She dredged up her carefully conceived arguments. "I'm sorry I tricked you, Noah, but it's your own fault."

"Is that right?" He advanced another step.

"I told you I was going into the Pussycat for an interview. You're the one who jumped to the conclusion that it was a job interview." She had nowhere to go. Her butt was pressed against the top drawer of a low-slung dresser and she gripped the edge for balance. Lifting her chin, she tried to stare him down. She wasn't afraid that he'd physically attack her, but by deliberately invading her space he was making her very uncomfortable and…yes…aroused.

She didn't want him to know that.

"When you realized what I was thinking, you could have corrected me," he said easily. But there was nothing easy about the look in his eyes.

"And I might have, if you hadn't offered to help me

mend my wicked ways! Do you have any concept of how
arrogant that offer was?''

He gazed at her, his eyes dark and intense. "You know,
I think I do."

She blinked. Just when she was getting up to speed, he
threw marbles under her feet. "You do?"

"Yeah. And maybe I deserved everything you dished
out."

"Really?" She scrambled to regroup. "Right! You sure
did!" She tried to breathe normally, but he was so very
close, almost touching her. Her nostrils flared as she caught
the scent of him. That alone was enough to get her juices
flowing. "There you were, acting so high and mighty, like
you were above it all, some sort of Eliot Ness of the sex
world. I had to knock you off your perch and show you that
you were corruptible like everybody else."

"You did a good job." He paused and the light of challenge sparkled in his eyes. "For an amateur."

"Amateur?" she yelped. Then she realized he was trying
to undermine her credibility, which would give him more
power. She couldn't let him get away with that. "Amateur,
my G-string. You're talking to Miss November, buster. And
what about all the articles on sex I've written in the past six
years? When it comes to erotic fantasies, I know what I'm
talking about!"

"Oh, I believe you." He'd closed the small gap between
them and now he braced a hand on either side of her and
leaned down until his face was inches from hers. His tone
remained conversational. "I just wonder how much practical
experience you've had—other than this weekend, that is."

Her heart thundered. She wanted him to think she was
five times more experienced than he was so she could keep
control of the situation. But she didn't feel in control. She
wanted him to make wild, crazy love to her, and that wasn't
good, because she figured he had a different plan.

Too late she realized she stood braced against the dresser
with her legs slightly apart. She was too open, too vulner-

able. And, oh, God, too wet. Yet if she moved to close her legs, that would tip him off that she was falling prey to his sexual game.

"Have you ever had a multiple orgasm, Keely?" he asked softly.

She could barely breathe. "None of your beeswax."

His lips twitched in amusement. "What did you say?"

"I said none of your business."

"No, you didn't." He grinned. "You said 'none of your beeswax,' just like you used to say when you were nine years old and I caught you trying to sneak sugar cubes to the horses."

"I'm not nine years old anymore."

His grin faded and heat blazed in his eyes. "I'm well aware of that." He stepped neatly between her legs and settled his erection against her crotch. "Painfully aware of that."

She swallowed a gasp. He felt way too good there. "I know where you're going with this," she said.

He pressed forward slightly and his gaze held hers. "Do you?"

She tried to keep the tremble from her voice, tried not to get lost in those dark eyes. "You want to get me worked up, and then you're going to walk out of here without doing anything, to punish me for fooling you."

"That's not a bad idea. There's only one flaw in it. Walking out of here without doing anything would punish me, too. On the way over I decided that I've suffered enough this weekend trying to hold back and be noble. I intend to leave here a very satisfied man."

She was light-headed with desire, but she fought the urge to give in. She might be in love with him, but he obviously didn't feel that way about her. In the end, he still planned to leave. "I won't let you use me for sex and then discard me."

His tone was low and intimate, and his eyes burned with

an unholy fire. "Why not? Isn't that what you had in mind
for me?" He nudged her with the ridge of his fly.

Sensation zinged from that tender spot between her legs
to the tips of her toes and fingers. "No, I—"

"I think the big-city girl wanted some fun with the small-
town boy." He nudged her again. "I think you wanted to
play at being a really hot babe, a sex-driven bad girl, with
a guy from back home who didn't know any different. Yeah,
I think you wanted to use me for sex and then discard me.
I think that's exactly what you wanted. I think you might
even have been hoping for some of those multiple orgasms
you've never had. Only, the plan got interrupted because
somebody recognized you."

"You don't know anything about it! For your information, I—" She stopped speaking abruptly when she realized
the trap she was in. The only way she could convince him
that she wasn't a sexual predator was to admit she'd been
in love with him for most of her life, and her weakness for
him had motivated her more than anything else. She'd
wanted one weekend to remember. But she wasn't about to
give him that information and be hurt even worse than she
had been at sixteen.

"Cat got your tongue?" he murmured, rubbing his fly
back and forth, coaxing a response from her.

"Okay, you're right!" She was beginning to quiver all
over, so she talked fast to hide it. "When you were determined to save me, I decided to turn the tables and have
some fun with you for the weekend. Only the weekend.
Then it would be over between us." *Because that's what
you would want.* "If that qualifies as using you for sex, then
I'm guilty. So shoot me."

"I had something else in mind. Did you get enough this
weekend?"

She knew what he meant, but she just tightened her jaw
and stared at him, refusing to answer.

"Let me put it another way. You're a liberated, fantasy-minded gal who likes good sex with no strings attached, right?''

She gripped the edge of the dresser so hard her fingers ached. ''Yes.''

''Then, darlin', you're going to love what happens next.''

16

NOAH HAD FOUND OUT the truth and it wasn't pretty. If he'd been entertaining the faint hope that Keely had some deeper emotion going on, that she had more than sex on her mind and would like to continue their relationship somehow, that hope had been crushed. She obviously saw this weekend as a one-time experience.

Okay, if that's the way things were, he'd make it a hell of an experience. He'd stuffed more condoms in his pocket than he imagined ever needing, but as he stood there breathing in the scent of raspberries, he wondered if he'd brought enough. Time to get that first urgent need taken care of. Then he'd be able to experiment a little. Or a lot.

Maybe in the back of his mind he hoped he could love her so hard and long that he would break through that protective shell of hers and make her care about him. He might be kidding himself about that, but even if he didn't succeed, he'd have a terrific time trying.

He looked into her green eyes and found desire mixed with uneasiness. Good. He wanted her to be uneasy. He was planning to turn her inside out once he took the edge off his own needs.

"We'll start with the basics and work up from there." He hooked his thumbs inside the waistband of her pants and before she could react, he'd dragged them, along with her underwear, down past her knees.

She drew in a sharp breath, but whether she was shocked or delighted, he wasn't sure.

"Kick them off," he said as he unbuckled his belt.

Her eyes sparked green fire. "You seem so determined to run this show. Let's see if you can make me."

"Love to." Using the strength and sure-handedness that had won him ribbons on the rodeo circuit, he lifted her to the glossy surface of the dresser. As he'd calculated, it was the perfect height. Holding her there with the fingers of one hand splayed over her firm bottom, he slid two fingers of his other hand deep inside her. His penis throbbed as he probed her slick heat.

She moaned and squeezed her eyes shut.

"Are you going to kick them off?" he asked softly as he stroked her.

"Oooh, yes," she whispered, keeping her eyes closed.

"Glad to hear it." He eased his fingers free and unfastened his jeans.

Opening her eyes, she held his gaze as she braced her hands behind her on the dresser and kicked the pants and underwear to the floor. "Done."

"I'm nearly there." He was shaking, but he managed to rip the condom package open, shove down his briefs and roll the latex over his rigid penis.

He even made small talk. "In case you're wondering, this is the ribbed kind." His heart pounded like a jackhammer as he cupped her bottom in both hands and pulled her to the edge of the dresser. "I hope you like it." Then he entered her in one smooth stroke. He nearly passed out from the relief of finally being inside her.

Her gasp this time was all about pleasure. He could see it reflected in her eyes and the delicate wild-raspberry flush of her skin. Without mascara darkening her eyelashes, and her hair in that ponytail, she looked young, almost too young to have a man planted firmly between her thighs.

"Ribs...are good," she said.

"I'll...I'll make a...note of it." His breath hissed out between clenched teeth as he fought to keep from coming instantly. She wasn't too young, he reminded himself. She might not be as sophisticated as she'd led him to believe, but she was old enough to know exactly what she was doing.

And she felt so damn good. He should have known that he and Keely would be a perfect fit. He should have known that once he'd connected to her in this basic way he'd feel a surge of possessiveness so strong that he doubted he'd be able to leave his heart out of the equation.

Too late to reconsider. It was done. He was deep inside her, and very soon he would seek the release he had to have or go crazy. But first he wanted to burn this moment into his memory. Standing very still so he wouldn't climax while he looked at her, he let his gaze drift to her mouth.

He'd thought nothing could be sexier than the sheen of freshly applied lipstick on her sensuous mouth, but he'd been wrong. Her bare lips, naturally rosy and parted with desire, tempted him beyond belief. He remembered what that mouth could do, had done in the hallway of the hotel. Just thinking about that would take him past the point of no return. And he didn't want to go there yet.

Instead, he was going to look. His gaze traveled over the golden skin of her throat as he listened to the sexy, liquid sound as she swallowed in air. More memories rose, memories of losing control and listening to that same sweet sound as she'd taken all he had to give.

His climax hovered ever nearer as he savored the view of her breasts, plump as honeydews beneath her tank top. It pleased him to leave them covered this time and watch the snug white cotton pucker over her erect nipples. Then his glance dipped lower, past the hem of her tank top to red-gold curls surrounding the spot where his penis was buried to the hilt.

He tested his control by easing slowly out and sinking deep again, all the while absorbing the sight of that perfect connection. And he nearly came apart from the visual high that gave him.

Balanced on the knife's edge of release, he looked into her eyes. "This one's for me."

She sucked in a breath. "Go for it."

Tightening his grip, he felt the muscles of her buttocks contract beneath his fingers. With a groan of anticipation, he began to thrust. Oh, yes. Deeper and faster.

Her breasts jiggled from the impact. His excitement ratcheted up a notch, watching them shake faster and faster the quicker he pumped. Oh, damn, this was good.

Panting, she wrapped her legs around his hips and threw her head back.

He listened to her soft but urgent moans and knew she was close, but he couldn't wait, couldn't make sure she'd take off with him. Not this time. She'd have lots of turns later.

But now…now…the world tipped and he plunged forward with a moan wrenched from deep in his chest. Spasms ripped through him as he poured himself into her tight warmth. Fireworks exploded in his head and his knees began to buckle.

"Noah! Please!"

Her desperation broke through the song of joy bubbling through his body. He'd meant to be selfish this time, but he couldn't leave her writhing in frustration. Trembling with the aftershocks of his own climax, he sank to his knees, rested her thighs on his shoulders and pressed his open mouth right where he knew she needed him to be.

In no time she arched away from the dresser with a wild cry. And as he listened to her breathless words of gratitude, he decided to settle in.

But she seemed to have other ideas as she struggled weakly, as if to get away. "You…were right." She gasped for breath. "I've never…I don't think I can.…"

He ignored her and kept going.

"Noah…you don't have to prove any—" She gasped and her thighs began to quiver.

A fierce sense of pride surged through him. Ah, she tasted so good, and he was going to give her something no man ever had.

She moaned. "Oh…my. I've never… I think maybe…
oh…oh…*my!*" Words became unintelligible whimpers as
she arched like a bow once again.

He thought he had the combination now, was pretty sure
he'd found the right rhythm and the right pressure, but he
needed one more run to lock it in. Loving every second, he
took her up a third time as she laughed and shrieked and
called him a genius.

At last he stood, lifted her quaking body from the dresser
and carried her to the unmade bed. Considerate of her not
to have had the maid come in yet. Keely was limp as a wet
mop when he settled her on the bed. While he shucked his
clothes and tossed his remaining condoms on the bedside
table, he enjoyed basking in her satisfied expression. As for
him, he was already erect, already wanted her again. But he
could wait.

KEELY WONDERED how many women had made the mistake
of thinking that sex this good must mean that Noah was in
love with them. She *felt* loved, even though she kept reminding herself that all he wanted was one action-packed
weekend with her, and then it was *adiós, muchachas.*

Still, he sure made her feel cherished when he looked at
her like that, his brown eyes warm and appreciative.

She was pretty darned appreciative, herself. She glanced
at his stiff penis. "I'd be happy to return the favor."

"Maybe later. Considering the difference between guys
and gals, I want to pace myself." He walked to the bedside
telephone and picked up the receiver.

"What are you doing?"

"Ordering up some food."

"Food?" It was the last thing she'd expected him to suggest, considering he'd just had breakfast. She, on the other
hand, was starving.

"Yeah, food." He grinned at her. "I tried to eat before
I came up here but I didn't get much down. I'm willing to

bet you haven't had anything either. And, right now, I'm damn hungry. How about you?''

"I could eat."

"Good." He punched in the number for room service and looked over at her. "How about a couple of club sandwiches and some fresh fruit?"

"Sure." Anything sounded good. And suddenly she realized that this was what a honeymoon would be like—making love and ordering room service afterward. But she had no honeymoon in her immediate future and she'd do well to remember that.

Noah placed the order and hung up the phone. Then he sat down on the bed beside her. "One of us has more clothes on than the other." He reached for the hem of her tank top.

"Wait." She placed her hands over his. "Won't we have to be dressed when the food arrives?"

"Will we?" His eyes sparkled.

"Yes. Taking a chance in a deserted hallway at night is one thing. Stripping down and inviting the room-service waiter in is beyond where I want to go."

"Okay. We'll put on clothes again. But I'll bet they won't show up for at least twenty minutes, and I want to see your breasts. Kiss your breasts. I'm crazy about your breasts. And look at that. They're crazy about me, too." He leaned down and gently bit one of the nipples that had stiffened under his gaze.

She sighed with pleasure.

"They want out," he murmured, moving to catch the other nipple between his teeth.

"Maybe so." She offered no resistance as he pushed her top up. She wanted to feel his hot mouth against her skin.

He licked and nibbled until, despite the satisfaction he'd given her not long ago, she began to ache for him again.

"Tell me a secret fantasy." He covered her breasts with tiny kisses. "Something you've never done. Something we could do in this room."

She didn't have to think very long about it, especially

considering the sensual daze he'd put her in by stroking and lapping at her breasts. "To be tied up," she murmured. "Gently and considerately, of course. And then teased to distraction."

"You wouldn't be scared of me doing that?"

"Not with you." Her blood heated just thinking about it. "I'd be safe with you."

"Yeah, you'd be safe." He rolled her nipple against his tongue. "Let's do it."

"After room service."

"Before."

"Before?"

"Now." In a split second he'd pinned her to the mattress with his body and skimmed her tank top over her head, bringing her arms up with it.

Her wrists seemed tangled in the material and she tried to free them. "I'm stuck."

He raised up on one elbow and looked down at her with a satisfied smile. "I know."

Then she realized he was holding her wrists with his free hand. "Wait a minute! You can't just do it! I have to let you!"

He shook his head. "Way too tame for a woman like you."

"Tame was what I had in mind!" She tried to wiggle out from under him.

"Sorry." He held her still with the weight of his body while he twisted the material of her top and looped one armhole over the bedpost. Then he slipped the scrunchie from her ponytail and wound that around her wrists for good measure.

That was about the time she remembered she'd just invited a cowboy who bull-dogged cattle for a living to play bondage games with her. She might be in over her head. "Noah, seriously, room service will be here any minute. Let me go."

"Nope. This is fun." As he slid downward he grasped one ankle.

"Stop it!" She tried kicking with her free foot, but with both hands tied above her head and one ankle in his grasp, she couldn't get any leverage. "Noah! I'll scream!"

"I imagine the folks in the neighboring rooms will only think you're having another amazing orgasm, which, eventually, is what will happen if you're a good girl." Holding her ankle firmly in one hand, he picked up a corner of the sheet, put it between his teeth and ripped away a strip of it.

"You're destroying hotel property!"

"I'll pay them for the sheet." He moved to the other side of the bed to repeat the process and there she was, neatly tied, hand and foot, naked on the bed. He surveyed his work. "Nice. Very, very nice. Are you comfy?"

"Well, you didn't hurt me or anything, if that's what you mean, but I didn't mean for you to do it like this." She was panting, both from the struggle and—she had to admit it— from excitement. He'd tied her up while promising her an amazing orgasm. And he'd been quick, but gentle. None of her muscles were stretched too tight and, God, she felt sexy. A fantasy didn't get much better than that.

And yet she still felt honor-bound to complain. "I was picturing velvet ropes or silk scarves."

"You got any velvet ropes or silk scarves?"

"Well, no. Even so, you could have led up to it and taken it slower."

"You don't lead up to a stunt like this. That's boring." His smile was positively wicked as his gaze traveled over her. "And, don't worry, we'll take it slow. Now."

A shiver of anticipation ran down her spine. "My, how you've changed since Friday afternoon."

"That's where you're wrong. I've had my fantasies, the same as you." He walked slowly around the bed, eyeing her from every angle. "This is one we share."

She didn't dare ask him if she was the woman he'd fantasized about. If she hadn't been, she didn't want to know.

Besides, if she hadn't been his fantasy woman before this weekend, she would be after this.

Taking his gaze from her briefly, he reached down and picked up his briefs. They didn't fit very well over his erection.

"I didn't hear anybody at the door," she said.

"Nobody's there yet."

"Then why—"

"I want to be ready." He stepped into his jeans and winced as he zipped them. "Talk about bondage." Then he walked casually over to the bed and sat on the edge of the mattress.

Her pulse raced at the look in his eyes. An involuntary shudder of excitement ran through her as the fact of her vulnerability finally penetrated. She was totally at his mercy. Did she trust him that much? Yes and no. Yes, that he wouldn't hurt her. No, that he wouldn't drive her beyond all her limits and strip away all her defenses. And that was where the thrill of danger came in.

"Cold?"

She shook her head.

"I didn't think so." Reaching down to her ankle, he trailed a finger along the inside of her calf, then continued up the tender skin of her inner thigh, drawing closer, closer, closer...and stopping. Holding her gaze, he brushed his knuckles lightly over her damp curls and she discovered how incredibly sensitive she was as she responded with a rush of moisture.

"You smell so good," he murmured. Boldly he slid a finger in deep, drew it out and licked it. "And you taste even better."

She wanted more...much more. But he'd promised to take it slow. She wondered if she'd survive the wait.

"Remember finger paints?" he asked.

Her chest was tight with anticipation, her answer breathy. "Yes."

"Let's pretend this is a jar of finger paint." He slipped

two fingers back into her. "And I'm going to paint a beautiful picture on your soft body. You're so wet I should be able to create quite a masterpiece."

Delicious heat poured through her, flushing her skin and making her entire body tingle. "You're going to torture me, aren't you?"

He circled her breast with his damp fingers. "Yes, darlin', I am. And you're going to love it."

As an erotic tease, it was world-class. He stroked every part of her body with the musky liquid of her passion, always returning to the wellspring to caress her into panting readiness again. Yet he'd only stay long enough to make her whimper, never long enough to give her the climax that soon became her entire focus.

And just as she was ready to offer him anything if he'd only give her that precious release, a knock at the door announced room service had arrived.

Noah leaned down and brushed his lips over hers. "Our food's here."

She gasped for breath. "Who cares? Noah, I need—"

"Soon." He climbed from the bed. "Be right there!" he called to the bellman.

"What do you mean, you'll *be right there?* Noah, don't open that door!"

"Don't panic," he murmured. Then he reached for the quilted bedspread that had fallen to the floor and pulled it carefully up to her chin.

"What—what are you doing?"

"Completing your fantasy." He propped two pillows under her head and arranged two more to disguise the fact that her hands were bound. "I've been paying attention, Keely. I'm going to turn us both on like we've never been turned on in our lives."

"H-how?"

"The waiter's going to come in and leave our food while you're lying there totally naked and aroused under that bedspread, unable to move, and by the time he's left the tray and I've paid the bill and he's gone, you're going to be hotter than you've ever been in your life, because it's so risky. Better than the hallway."

"Oh, Noah." She thought her heart would pound out of her chest. But in a secret, hidden part of her mind she suspected he was right.

"Trust me?"

"O-okay."

He walked over and opened the door.

The waiter came in, and after one quick look at Keely in the bed, he bustled about his task of setting down the tray. Noah pretended to ignore her, too, as he took his time paying the bellman and walking him to the door.

It was the wildest feeling she'd ever had, knowing that the minute the bellman was gone Noah would whip off the bedspread and make love to her.

Her body throbbed with unreleased tension as she watched Noah open the door, let the guy walk out, close the door again and carefully lock it.

Then he turned and nearly tore off his jeans and briefs. The condom went on in record time. Then he yanked off the bedspread and released Keely's restraints before moving between her thighs and plunging deep. Her orgasm came instantly, rocking her with the most powerful contractions she'd ever felt. She clung to Noah as his frenzied cries of release blended with hers.

Gradually the world stopped spinning as they lay sweaty and entwined, gasping for breath.

Noah chuckled. Keely started to smile. And before they knew it, they were clutching each other and howling with laughter.

"Can you believe we did that?" Noah asked.

"No! You are really crazy!"

"You started the whole thing." He propped himself up on an elbow and looked down at her, a grin on his face.

"You mean the hallway?"

"No, I mean behind that lava rock! My imagination has been in overdrive ever since."

"I was trying to corrupt you."

"It worked. Man, did it ever work. I am never going to forget this weekend."

She felt a pain in the general region of her heart. If only he'd said he would never forget her. She managed a smile. "Me neither."

17

NOAH WAS GLAD he'd ordered the fruit to go along with the sandwiches. With a willing woman like Keely, a guy could find all kinds of interesting things to do with fruit. He'd turned her into quite a fruit cocktail before he'd finished. And in the process she'd become a real fan of multiple orgasms.

Then she'd become creative with the mayo she'd scraped off her club sandwich and he'd gladly served as her private bedroom deli. He might not have been able to do the multiple-orgasm thing like she could, but the climax she'd given him had almost killed him.

All in all, it was the most excellent meal he'd ever had— best food, best atmosphere, best company.

He wondered why he'd never tried eating naked with a woman before. You could save a bundle on napkins. If either of you happened to drip, the other gladly licked it off. Personally he'd made an effort to be messy and he figured she had, too.

With all the interruptions, their lunch had taken quite a while. He realized just how long when he had to switch on a light to see Keely better. At the same time he glanced at the numbers on the digital bedside clock. Damn. His plane left in two short hours.

"Why the frown?" she asked, snuggling into the pillows. "Indigestion?"

"No." He settled down next to her and cupped her breast, rubbing her nipple to erectness with his thumb. "It's just that I can't stay much longer."

Her green eyes flashed with alarm. "Really?"

"My plane leaves tonight."

"Miss it."

"Can't."

She reached down and circled his penis with her hand. "Are you quite sure about that?"

He closed his eyes as she stroked and tickled him into aching readiness in no time at all. In the past forty-eight hours he'd become like his bulls when they were in the same pen with a heifer in heat. He couldn't get enough.

But he'd promised Jonas he'd be home tonight. Because of his promise, Jonas and B.J. had left the ranch that afternoon bound for Phoenix to check out wedding decorations. They'd planned to stay in Phoenix a couple of days and Noah needed to be at the ranch to take care of business while they were gone. Several matters demanded his attention, and he intended to keep his word to be back on time.

Keely scooted down and placed a kiss on the tip of his penis. "I'm sure you could get a plane in the morning." Then she used her tongue to add more fuel to her argument.

His breathing roughened and his voice grew husky with a passion that seemed to have no end. "Keep that up and I'll be able to fly there without a plane."

"I want you to stay with me tonight," she murmured as she nibbled her way from base to tip.

"There's nothing I want more. But I can't. I—" He drew in a sharp breath as she took him fully into her mouth and applied gentle suction. "But you have amazing powers of persuasion." By all rights he shouldn't be getting hard again, but damned if he wasn't. If he didn't stop her, she'd make him come, and he didn't want to spend the last orgasm he would share with her in that way.

Ah, but she gave him such pleasure. Reluctantly he combed his fingers through her hair and cradled her head, drawing her slowly away, bringing her tender mouth up to meet his. "Time for one of those little raincoats," he murmured between light kisses. "I want to be inside you this time."

"Okay," she said in a breathy, excited voice as she met his teasing kisses with ones of her own. "We can try a new position."

"I had in mind something boring. Hang on a sec." He turned over and grabbed a condom packet from the bedside table.

"Boring?" She smiled at him. "Here, let me put that on."

"I thought you'd never ask." He gave her the condom and she made a big production of unrolling it over his totally recharged penis. He loved her careful attention and tried not to think about this being the last time he'd feel her hands on him.

"I don't see how anything we do in this bed could be boring." She gave one last little tug on the latex. Then she cupped his balls and massaged them gently as she glanced up at him. "Not considering what we have to work with."

He couldn't believe he was so hot for her again, but she seemed to know instinctively how to touch him to turn him into a raging maniac. "Then you wouldn't mind the plain old missionary position?"

She gazed into his eyes. "You mean no props, no unique location, no thrill of discovery?"

"That's right." He searched her eyes for the emotion he wanted to find. "Just you and me."

"Scary."

"I know. Think you can handle it?" There. He thought he saw the visual clue he was seeking, but then it was gone again.

"I don't know." She looked nervous.

"Let's try it." He eased her to her back and braced his hands beside her shoulders as he moved between her thighs.

She ran her hands lightly down his back and paused as her fingers encountered the ridge of a small scar. "How did

I miss this?'' she asked softly. Slowly she traced the ridge with her forefinger.

''You couldn't have discovered everything. It's only been a weekend.''

Regret flashed in her eyes. ''That's right.''

He gazed down at her, memorizing what he saw. This was his last chance to awaken real emotion in her. If he failed, he would never see her this way again.

Her tousled hair fanned out against the white pillow in waves of dark red, the color of desire. His glance raked over her, from her flushed cheeks to her passion-darkened nipples, from her flat belly to the red-gold curls between her thighs. A shell-pink treasure beckoned to him, peeking out from beneath those soft curls.

He focused on her face again—full lips parted, nostrils flared, green eyes dark with secrets. He held her gaze and moved his hips forward, easing partway in, adjusting to her heat so he could build his control.

''That feels so good,'' she murmured.

''Nothing like it.'' And he wasn't talking about sex in general, either. He'd never experienced anything to compare with making love to Keely. He was beginning to understand how rare this connection was…for him. But he didn't know how rare it was for her. Not yet.

Taking a deep breath, he pushed home. Slowly a flame grew in her eyes, a flame that warmed his soul. Maybe they had a chance. But he wasn't putting anything on the line by speaking about it. Instead, he'd talk around the problem. ''Just so you know, I'm not going for the multiples this time.''

''Okay.'' She swallowed and tried another smile, but it faltered. ''Back to basics?''

''Yeah.''

''You're leaving after this, aren't you?''

''Yeah.''

Her grip tightened on his back and she closed her eyes. ''I thought so,'' she whispered, her voice choked.

"Keely, open your eyes."

She shook her head.

"Please."

Her lashes fluttered upward, and her eyes glistened with tears.

Those tears hit him like a fist in the gut. "You're crying," he said, his throat raw.

Her voice was tight. "I think I have something in my eye."

"Bull. You don't want this to end any more than I do."

"It has to end." Her voice quivered. "I can't go back."

His heart sank. "To the ranch?"

"To the ranch, to my family, to my old life, to anything."

She didn't think he was worth the sacrifice. He could beg her to change her mind. And then what? Convince her to live a life she didn't want because he couldn't imagine giving her up? No.

"I guess this is it, then," he said.

"Yes, this is it."

"Well, you'd better hang on, sweetheart, because it's gonna be one hell of a goodbye." He began slowly, making each stroke count, and even her tears couldn't put out the flame in her eyes. "You know this is about more than sex," he murmured.

She didn't reply, but the flame burned brighter.

"It's about more than games and thrills." He increased the pace, building that flame. She cared about him, damn it. He could see that she did. "It's about more than orgasms."

Tears dribbled from the corners of her eyes, and her gasps sounded almost like sobs, but she kept her eyes open and her gaze locked with his.

"But if I can't give you anything else, at least I can give you that." Shifting his angle slightly, he came in high and tight, stroking relentlessly now, drawing broken cries of pleasure from her lips. "Good, isn't it?"

"Yes!" she cried, helpless in her need.

"The best, right?"

"Yes, oh...*yes.*" She met him thrust for thrust.

"Even just the basics."

Her fingers dug into his back. "I love...the basics," she said, panting.

His heart wept. She'd nearly said it. "I love...the basics, too," he murmured.

"Oh, Noah...Noah...now!"

As she tightened around him and pushed upward, he spiraled out of control with a groan of surrender—to his passion, to Keely, to a future that would not include this flame-haired woman. Shuddering, he held her close and gulped back a sob of frustration. It was over.

KEELY STAYED IN BED, cocooned in the covers while Noah dressed. Part of the time she watched him and part of the time she closed her eyes and battled tears. The gutsy move would be to get up and put her clothes on, too, but she couldn't bear to leave the haven they'd shared for so many hours. She wanted to stay here for as long as his scent remained in the sheets.

They'd had lots of sex in this room, but they'd only made love once, this last time. That cataclysmic event had nearly destroyed her. Their love, unspoken but real, was incredibly beautiful and absolutely hopeless.

Oh, if they could live their days in this room, if they never had to put on the clothes that branded each of them with the roles they'd chosen, then they might be able to make a go of their relationship. He'd just proved to her that they'd crossed into a whole other realm, one in which the mating of bodies was overshadowed by the joining of souls.

But they couldn't live in this room, and he was already dressed in the clothes of his chosen profession. Buckling his belt, he went in search of his hat. He was headed back to his ranch, and she had a story to finish for the magazine. In the real world they'd make each other miserable. She had to let him go.

He might think he wanted her around, but good sex had

muddled his brain. Maybe, in the hot flush of desire, he'd
imagined that he could mold her into the kind of rural
woman he needed by his side. She, on the other hand, had
never even considered asking Noah to become a city man.

As if he ever could. He stood in the middle of the hotel
room smoothing the brim of his black hat, his long legs
tucked into denim, his broad shoulders covered in soft
chambray. He might own a computer and understand the
principles of investing in the stock market, but in his heart
he was a cowboy.

And she loved him that way. She wouldn't urbanize Noah
even if she had the power.

He looked at her for a long moment. "I'll stop by the
desk and settle up with them about the sheet."

She propped herself up against the headboard while holding the bedspread over her breasts. They'd dared everything
with each other, and yet nudity seemed inappropriate now.
"What are you going to say?"

A faint smile touched his mouth, the mouth she would
never kiss again. "I'll tell them we each took a strip of it
for a souvenir."

"That's an idea."

He pulled a rolled strip of white material out of his back
pocket and showed it to her. "I thought so."

She stared at the piece of sheet he'd carefully preserved
and meant to take home with him. For some reason, that
sentimental gesture got to her more than anything else, and
she swallowed several times, praying she wouldn't break
down.

"I have to go," he said softly.

She nodded, not trusting herself to speak.

"I'd better not kiss you goodbye, or I'll never leave."

She cleared her throat. "Okay." She clutched the bedspread and tried to breathe normally.

He walked toward the door.

In that moment she imagined how a condemned person

must feel in the last few seconds of life. She'd known heaven today. In less than a minute she'd know hell.

Perhaps she could make things easier for herself if she looked away while he twisted open the dead bolt and reached for the doorknob. But instead, she watched every move, cherishing each second that he remained.

He turned the knob and opened the door. She braced herself. Then, slowly, he closed the door again and faced her. Her heart thundered with new hope, even though she couldn't imagine that he'd found a solution.

"At least come to B.J. and Jonas's wedding," he said.

Her heart twisted with agony. The wedding. Of course. What had she expected, that he'd fall to his knees and declare he couldn't live without her? That only happened in the movies. Somehow she managed to speak around the lump in her throat. "I'd only cause problems."

He shook his head. "I really think B.J. would love to have you there, and so would Arch."

She didn't know where she found the reserves to discuss this with him, but she dug deep and came up with a reasonably coherent response. "I haven't spoken to either of them for ten years. I can't just waltz in there in the middle of B.J.'s big day. That wouldn't be fair to anyone." And loving Noah as she did, she'd want to touch him, hold him, make love to him. Knowing that she couldn't would be torture.

"All right," he said quietly. "What if I mentioned to them that I ran into you and—"

She started. "Noah, you can't be planning to tell them what we—"

"No. I wouldn't do that, Keely. What we've done this weekend is our own private business."

"Thank you." The panic quieted in her chest. Noah had been a safe choice for adventure because he would never endanger her, physically or mentally. She knew that, but he'd given her a scare for a moment.

"Would you like to be at the wedding?" he asked.

Such a complicated question. But in the end, when she considered that her baby sister was getting married, that it was a day that could never be repeated, there was only one answer. "Yes."

"Then let me mention that I saw you. I'm sure they'll want you there, but I can drop you a line and let you know for sure, so there's no doubt that they're expecting you."

"There's another issue." She held his gaze, her heart thumping. "We both agree there's no future for us, right?"

His expression was guarded. "That's what you said."

"It's what I believe." She ran a tongue over her dry lips. "So how will that be, if I come back to the ranch for a couple of days? Can we handle that?"

His glance settled briefly on her mouth and heat flickered in his eyes. Then he looked away and cleared his throat. "Looks like we'll have to, for B.J. and Jonas's sake. Like you said, we don't want to take the focus off their big day." He faced her again and his chest heaved. "If you can deal with it, then I can."

She had no idea if she could or not. "Like you said, we'll have to. For the sake of the people we love." And she included him in that category.

"Right."

"Thank you for suggesting that I go," she said, meaning every word. "Assuming B.J. and Dad want me, it's the right thing to do. After all, B.J. and Jonas will probably have kids someday."

"Yeah, they probably will." His response was rich with longing.

Of course, he wanted children, she thought with a pang of regret. She hadn't ever considered kids, but if she could have one who called Noah daddy, that would be…special. Talk about a daydream. "I'll want to see my nieces and nephews," she said, "so I need to get past this awkwardness with B.J. and Dad, and the sooner I do that, the better."

He nodded. Then he stood there gazing at her until the air seemed to crackle between them.

She wondered what he'd do if she flung back the covers and opened her arms. From the look in his eyes, he'd miss his plane. But he didn't really want to do that.

So she would help him. "You need to go," she murmured.

He closed his eyes. "Keely—"

"Go, damn it! I can only be noble for so long!"

Without another word he left, closing the door carefully behind him. The automatic lock clicked into place.

She lost track of time as she sat staring at the closed door, willing him to knock and ask to be let back in. She stayed rigid and motionless until her head pounded and her eyes stung. But no knock came. He'd accepted her decision to end this amazingly beautiful connection between them.

The words she'd never spoken aloud rose in her throat, demanding to be free. "I love you, Noah," she whispered hoarsely into the silence.

KEELY DIDN'T WANT his love. Noah struggled with that knowledge as the plane left Las Vegas. In spite of everything, he'd been about to tell her that he loved her, but she'd cut him off, as if she didn't want him to make the mistake of declaring his feelings and saying things he couldn't take back.

Maybe she even loved him a little bit, too. He would have sworn that was love he'd seen in her eyes toward the end of their precious time together. But loving a guy like him would only tie her down, so she'd do her best to get over it. He wondered how well she'd succeed. As for him, there was a hole in his heart big enough to drive a truck through.

Suggesting that she come to the wedding had been a desperate attempt to maintain a tie with her. He suspected that B.J. and Arch would be thrilled to have her come home for the big day, and Jonas would be happy about it, too. Noah was more than willing to do them a favor, but his motives were purely selfish. Keely might not want his love, but the closer he came to Arizona, the less he was prepared to accept that as a final decision.

Still, he knew there were rough times ahead, and he was glad he'd arranged to get Keely back on Twin Boulders soil, where he was thoroughly grounded. In order to perform a miracle and coax Keely into his life, he needed all his strength, and he drew that strength from the land where he was born.

Yet he had to be careful that he didn't overpower her and force her into a life she didn't want. He was counting on the fact that she might not know what she wanted, or more precisely, what she needed. She'd convinced herself that she couldn't possibly fit in at the ranch, but he wanted to see that for himself.

Maybe she was right. Maybe when he looked at her and visualized her surrounded by their children, he was experiencing hallucinations brought on by the greatest sex he'd ever known. But after making love to Keely the way he had that last time, he couldn't imagine anyone else as his mate or the mother of his kids. A few other times in his life when he'd been sexually involved with a woman, even thought himself in love, he'd tried to picture that woman pregnant with his baby. The image had never come into focus.

But now...now it was clear as a bell. He could feel himself thrusting deep inside Keely and spilling his seed. Then, in a few weeks, they'd share the joy of knowing that she'd conceived. He could picture her eyes lighting up at the moment they knew for sure. Her body would grow round and ripe, sensuous in a new way. The image brought a rush of anticipation. Then the hour would come when she would give birth, and he would hold the child they'd created, the baby who was a visible sign of their passion....

He must be going crazy. Only a crazy man would fantasize about making a woman pregnant when she didn't want to admit that she loved him and certainly didn't want him to tell her of his love. Only a crazy man would think he had enough imagination, enough moves, enough love to satisfy a wild child like Keely Branscom.

But Noah would give ten years of his life for a chance to prove that he was the only man fit for the job.

18

"I'VE DECIDED we need a piece on cyber-infidelity. The angle I had in mind was 'Are you cheating with an online lover?'" Carolyn clicked her ballpoint pen repetitively as she glanced at her editorial staff seated around the conference table. "Keely, why don't you see what you can do with that?"

Keely nodded automatically. She didn't want the assignment, but she'd take that up with Carolyn later. One of the younger writers might really get into the topic, but it didn't do a thing for Keely.

Although five days had gone by since she'd made love to Noah, her body still hummed with memories. After being touched like that, she had zero interest in the subject of cybersex. The idea of screen-to-screen hanky-panky paled next to being in the same bed with a man like Noah, skin-to-skin.

As the meeting droned on, she evaluated the other story assignments Carolyn handed out in case one of them would work as a potential trade. Unfortunately, they all sounded like a major yawn. She probably needed more caffeine.

Or more sleep. Sleep would be a good thing. Sleep had not been her friend since leaving Vegas. She gazed out the office window. Maybe the air quality was dragging her down. L.A. had been suffering through a major inversion the last couple of days and the air was the color and odor of dirty gym socks.

A day at the beach catching those California rays and

she'd be right as rain. Sure she would. Like hell she would. She missed the guy, missed him like crazy.

She wondered how long she'd feel the effects of her weekend with Noah. Anyone would think she'd broken off a five-year relationship the way she was moping around the office and her apartment. Nothing interested her, with the exception of one brief shopping trip when she'd bought a dress to wear to B.J.'s wedding. She might have been premature in that purchase, because for some reason Noah's letter giving her the all-clear signal hadn't arrived yet. The absence of that letter nagged at her constantly.

She'd realized several hours after he'd left that she hadn't given him her home address, so she'd begun worrying that he wouldn't think to send the letter to her office. If he'd thought of doing that, she wondered if he'd know to look inside the magazine's cover for the address. Not everyone realized that the publisher could be reached at—

"Keely? Yo, Keely!"

She glanced up with a start and discovered everyone at the conference table smirking at her, including Carolyn.

"We've all taken bets," Carolyn said, "and most of us, myself included, think you met some hunk in either Vegas or Reno, which explains why you've been so whacked since you came back. Care to enlighten us?"

"No."

"I was right!" said Andrea, a cute blonde of twenty-two with a bright future in journalism. She'd be perfect for the cybersex story. "I said if she refuses to dish, then it was more than a fling."

Keely pushed back her chair. She really didn't need this. "It's flu, is what it is, and if you guys aren't careful I'll plant a big kiss full of icky germs on each one of you."

Denise, the outer-office receptionist, poked her head in the conference-room door. "Excuse me, but I have a guy out here who needs to deliver his singing telegram, and he's late for his next gig. Can you spare Keely for a minute?"

Keely groaned. "You guys didn't have to do this. I promise to cheer up. Just don't make me face a singing telegram.''

Carolyn looked around the room, her eyebrows raised. "Well, *I* didn't order the singing telegram. Did one of you?''

Their chorus of denials didn't convince Keely. She leveled a stern look at all of them, but nobody cracked. She sighed. "Okay, I might as well get this over with." She stood and headed for the door. "Note to self—stay perky on the job or you'll be sent a singing telegram and be embarrassed like you wouldn't believe."

Her cohorts trailed out after her, the better to view her humiliation, she assumed. She'd never received a singing telegram before, so she didn't know exactly what to expect, but definitely not a black guy who looked as if he played pro football. He wore a baseball cap backward, a T-shirt and rapper shorts. He held a boom box on one broad shoulder.

"Miz Keely Branscom?" he asked.

Keely grimaced. "I'm afraid so."

The man nodded and punched a button on his boom box. As a steady rap beat filled the office, he gyrated to the rhythm and began to chant.

"Well, you gotta come home, 'cause your sister's gettin' hitched.
	Girl, the knot will be tied and the rice will be pitched.
	So we just wanna know if you're comin' or you're not,
	'Cause to give it to you straight, we been missin' you a lot."

Keely's first reaction was shock, because a singing telegram was so not what she'd expected from her family, but as the significance of the message sank in, tears pushed at the back of her eyes. "Th-thank you," she told the guy as she blinked to clear her vision.

"No problem." With a little bow, the man turned and sauntered out of the office.

"Wow," Carolyn said as she walked over to Keely's desk. "You have a sister who's getting married?"

Keely nodded, not trusting herself to speak. *We been missin' you a lot.* Oh, God, why had she let ten years go by?

Carolyn took a closer look at Keely's face. "I think you have an RSVP call to make."

"Yep." Keely sniffed.

Carolyn tilted her head toward the door of her private office. "Why don't you use my phone?"

Keely gave her a shaky smile of gratitude. "I'd appreciate that," she said, her voice thick with emotion. Swiping at her eyes, she walked quickly into Carolyn's office and closed the door. Then she pressed both hands against her stomach. Ten years. She'd missed ten years of her father's voice and B.J.'s laughter. Ten years of birthdays, Christmas mornings, hugs and memories.

She couldn't imagine how they could ever forgive her. And yet they'd sent a singing telegram with a corny, touching, homemade rap verse just for her.

With trembling hands she picked up the receiver of Carolyn's telephone and dialed an outside line. Then she punched in the number that came to her as easily as a favorite nursery rhyme, even though she hadn't used it in ten years.

B.J. answered, sounding older. Of course she was older. She'd been only seventeen the last time Keely had seen her.

"B.J., it's Keely." Tears poured down her cheeks.

"Keely? Is it really you?"

"Oh, God, yes. I'm so sorry, B.J." Her words tumbled out between choked little sobs. "I've missed you so much. So much. Can I really come to your wedding?"

B.J. started crying, too. "You'd better! You'd better come or I'll send another singing-telegram guy, and this one will be armed!'' Laughter mixed in with her jerky sobs. "You hear me, Keely Marie?''

"I hear you,'' Keely said, smiling despite the tears that didn't seem to want to stop. She fumbled for the box of tissues on Carolyn's desk. "I'll be there. So, was the singing telegram your idea?''

"Nope.''

"Dad's?'' Keely had a hard time picturing that.

"No, but he was all for it.''

"Okay, I know. Jonas was behind it. He's just the type.''

B.J. laughed. "You're right, he is, but Noah's actually the one who thought it up. He said we couldn't just send a letter because it would be too boring.''

"Noah?'' Keely's heart squeezed. Lord, how she loved that man. "Well, tell him I wasn't bored.'' *Tell him I'm crazy about him.* "Who made up the rap thing?''

"Oh, we all worked on that. Pretty cool, huh?''

"Very cool.'' Her throat tightened with a fresh surge of emotion. "I loved it.''

"Dad wanted to make it country instead, but we thought rap fit L.A. better, and maybe it wouldn't be *quite* so embarrassing for you at the office.''

"Oh, it was plenty embarrassing, but I don't care a bit.''

"Good. I was hoping that would be the way you'd react. Listen, Dad's out in the west pasture, but if you want to call back tonight—''

"You know what? When I talk to Dad, I'd like to be standing right in front of him. I think I'll wait until I get there.''

B.J.'s voice was gentle. "His bark is worse than his bite, Keely. He's missed you something awful. We all have. Noah told us about your job. I can't believe I've never seen your name in that magazine, but you know me, I mostly read State Line Tack catalogs for fun.'' She paused and chuckled. "Or I did. Lately my tastes run more toward *Playgirl.*''

"B.J.!" Keely wasn't sure what she thought about her little sister ogling naked men.

B.J. laughed. "I'm not the same uptight woman I was when you left, Keely."

"Well, I guess not!"

"In fact, I think we're overdue for a long, sisterly talk."

Keely gulped back a fresh onslaught of tears. "We sure are," she said.

"When can you get here?"

Keely had been eyeing her schedule ever since she'd returned from her trip. It was packed with work. "Coming in the day before is the best I can do. I know that sucks, but this was unexpected. I'll have to juggle a few things to even take that Friday off, but I'm determined to do it."

"Then Friday it is. Want me to pick you up at the airport?"

"Absolutely not. You're the bride and you have things to do."

"I'll bet Noah could."

Not on your life, babe. "You know what? Let me rent a car." A convertible, she was thinking. The prodigal daughter needed to make a splash when she arrived back in Saguaro Junction after a ten-year absence.

"Renting a car seems silly," B.J. said. "I'm sure that Noah—"

"I want to rent the car," Keely said. "Think red Mustang convertible. Think top down, radio blaring, going down Main Street past the feed store, past the café, past the bench in front of the post office…"

"Okay." There was a grin in B.J.'s voice. "I get it. God, it's gonna be great to see you again. Set those tongues to waggin', Keely. It's been duller than dust around here without you."

Keely had a sudden moment of uncertainty. "Maybe I shouldn't do the convertible thing. I don't want to upstage the bride."

That really made B.J. laugh. "There was a time I would

have been worried about that. But I have Jonas right where I want him, and that's all I care about. Come back in full sail, Keely. This girl can take it."

"I can hardly wait."

"Me neither. See you soon."

Keely couldn't stop grinning as she hung up the phone. She was dying to see what sort of transformation had taken place with B.J., who'd been the quintessential tomboy the whole time they'd been growing up. Keely had always thought that B.J. took that role in self-defense because Keely had grabbed the sex-symbol image so early on and B.J. hadn't wanted to compete.

But maybe Keely's long absence had been a good thing for B.J. Without Keely around, she might have felt more free to try her sexual wings. It was majorly weird to think about that, but it was comforting to imagine that the separation might have produced something positive. And Keely was thrilled to be forewarned, so she wouldn't head to the ranch expecting her sister to be an Annie Oakley look-alike.

Then Keely's mind circled back to the topic it couldn't seem to leave alone. Noah. She still couldn't believe he'd instigated the rapper stunt. The guy was full of surprises, and she was a sucker for surprises. Leaving him strictly alone next weekend was not going to be easy.

NOAH GOT HOME after dark to find Jonas and B.J. cozied up on the front-porch swing. "Okay, keep it clean," he said as he walked up the steps. "I want all your hands out where I can see them."

Jonas flashed him a dry smile. "You're just jealous because you don't have a babe like B.J. to make out with."

"Keely called," B.J. said. "She loved the rapper telegram and she's definitely coming to the wedding. You must have stayed well out of sight, because obviously she didn't have a clue you were there."

"That's good." Noah leaned against the porch railing. In a way, he'd been disappointed that she hadn't seen him just outside the door of the office. He wasn't sure what he'd have done if she'd caught him standing there, but he'd had a tough time being so close and not making contact. Damn, but she'd looked incredible in her silk blouse and tight little skirt.

"Was the office nice?" B.J. asked.

"I guess." He'd barely noticed the office once Keely had walked out of that conference room looking so efficient, with her hair scooped up on top of her head and a pencil stuck through her red curls. The spiral notebook in her hand had reminded him of teenage fantasies in which a full-breasted secretary invited him to have sex on the top of a wide executive desk. Come to think of it, he had a desk like that in his office at the ranch....

"How was L.A.?" Jonas asked.

"Smoggy." He wondered if Keely noticed the smog, or if she was so caught up in all that a big city had to offer that she didn't care what the air was like or how bad the traffic was. After seeing her in the bright, bustling office he was beginning to doubt himself again. But he'd needed to see her in that environment so that he had a better idea of what he was up against. She probably liked that hectic pace. She must like it if she'd stayed there for ten years.

"Dad's excited that she's coming home," B.J. said. "You know him, he doesn't want to let on that he's excited, but he's over at our place cleaning like I've never seen him clean. I offered to help, but he wouldn't let me. He still thinks he does it better than anybody, and he wants the house to be perfect."

Noah nodded. He understood the urge. He'd left the inside of the ranch house to their housekeeper, Lupita, but he'd spent his spare time trimming the mesquite trees that surrounded the house and raking up the beans. Jonas had talked him out of slapping a new coat of paint on the front door, but he still might get around to that.

Jonas chuckled. "I wish I could've been there to see her face when the guy started his routine. Now that it's over,

I'm glad you decided to fly over and supervise, so we could be sure it was done right.''

"If I'd been able to locate somebody I had confidence would do the job the way we wanted it done, I wouldn't have," he said.

"Uh-huh," Jonas said. "I think you wanted to go over and check things out, is what I think. I know you better than you realize, big brother."

Noah thought of all the things Jonas didn't know about him. But Keely knew. She was the only person who had tapped into his deepest fantasies, the only person he trusted with them. She'd shown him a whole new world, and he'd fallen in love with her vision and with her. He needed her by his side so they could continue to explore that world together. If only he could be sure that she needed him just as much.

KEELY'S ONE-WOMAN PARADE through Saguaro Junction the following Friday turned heads exactly as she'd hoped. What she hadn't expected were the shouts of greeting and the enthusiastic waves of welcome. She'd had to stop the car four different times to talk with folks, or risk running them over as they hurried toward her car.

Not a single person had insulted her. Quite the contrary. They'd made her feel like a celebrity. Apparently the good people of Saguaro Junction had mellowed toward her. More likely her little sister, and maybe even her father, had spread the word that she was published nationwide in *Attitude!* magazine. From every indication, her earlier transgression of posing nude had been forgiven.

Of course, they didn't know that she was still a sexual risk-taker, a fact she'd proven to herself and Noah in Vegas. She didn't really fit in here any better than she had before.

And yet she couldn't stop the rush of nostalgia when she drove past the small park and swimming pool where she'd hung out with her friends back in high school. High-school kids clustered there now, their shouts and laughter carrying to the road on the clear desert air.

She remembered what a hot August day was like for a teenager in Saguaro Junction, and she felt a stab of envy for their uncomplicated existence. At the time she'd thought her world was terminally boring, but now she sort of missed the simplicity of a life where the Roadrunner Theater had only one screen and the Cactus Café was your only choice if you wanted to eat out.

Yes, she'd stirred things up nicely, she thought as she drove on out of town past the gas station and the Elks Lodge. She'd forgotten what it was like to cause a commotion on a major thoroughfare, and she rather enjoyed it. In L.A. you could find auburn-haired, well-endowed women in convertibles at every intersection. She fit in there, all right. Yessir, fit right in. She might be wild by Saguaro Junction standards, but in L.A. she was like everybody else.

If she lived here she'd be unique again. Not that she would really consider such a thing, but there was a certain appeal. Of course, her father had never wanted her to be unique.

As she continued down the two-lane highway and glimpsed the arched iron gate over the entrance to the Twin Boulders Ranch, the bravado that had taken her through town with a flourish began to disappear. In a few minutes she'd have to face Arch Branscom, and she was scared to death.

Even the prospect of dealing with Noah again didn't worry her as much as this meeting with her father after all these years. Their parting words had been bitter. He'd flung a copy of *Macho* in the fire and said that she had way too much of her mother in her for her own good. Then he'd as much as told her to leave his house.

She'd planned to use the money she'd earned from the photo session to get out of town, anyway. But she'd counted on it being her idea, not his. Packing a bag, she'd bought a bus ticket for L.A. She'd said goodbye to B.J., Jonas and

Jonas's father. Noah had been out of town at the time, which
had been just as well.

But she'd left without telling her own father goodbye.
These would be the first words she'd spoken to him since
he'd declared her a disgrace to the family ten long, lonely
years ago.

And she had been lonely, she finally admitted to herself
as she drove toward the ranch. Her car kicked up a rooster
tail of dust on the dirt road as she passed the two large
boulders on the left that gave the ranch its name. She'd
made friends and had lovers in L.A., but nobody had filled
the empty place where her family used to be. She wanted
her family back, but not at the expense of her self-esteem.
If her father showed any signs of disapproval, she'd leave
right after the wedding Saturday night and never come back.

Passing the ranch house, she wondered if Noah was inside
and if he might be watching for her. As she drove around
the main house toward the smaller cabin where her father
lived, she noticed a man on horseback cantering over a cac-
tus-studded hill on his way toward the ranch. Even from
this distance she recognized Noah.

Her already stressed heart kicked into an even faster
rhythm. But she could only deal with one of these men at
a time, and her father was first on her list. She parked beside
a battered pickup that she assumed belonged to him. He'd
bought different trucks through the years, but Arch Branscom's transportation always looked about the same—a
light-colored paint job so it wouldn't show the dust and an
assortment of dings and scratches where he'd taken it
through the brush in pursuit of cattle, horses and even a few
lost dogs.

She left her suitcase in the back seat of the Mustang and
took only her purse with her. If her reception was too chilly,
she could always stay in Saguaro Junction's only motel. As
she walked up to the small covered porch, she noticed that
the bushes were trimmed and the porch had been swept

recently. The woven straw mat in front of the door looked new.

Maybe her dad had spruced up the place for the wedding. She could hardly believe he'd done it for her. Heart pounding, she stood in front of the door and couldn't decide whether to go in or knock. Although she'd sailed in and out of this door with complete ease for the first nineteen years of her life, she didn't live here anymore.

But knocking at the door of her father's house seemed ridiculous. She reached for the knob then pulled her hand back. Then she raised her fist to knock and couldn't make herself do that, either.

Finally the door opened and her father stood there staring at her.

She stared back. Although logic should have told her he'd look older, she hadn't expected him to. His hair and mustache used to be dark red sprinkled with gray. Now they were nearly white. His face was more weathered and he seemed...shorter. She'd always imagined him towering over her, but in her three-inch heels she could look him straight in the eye.

Those piercing blue eyes of his hadn't changed at all. They still seemed to look clear into her heart. She wondered if he could tell how scared she was. Probably.

"Hello, Keely," he said in his deep, gruff voice.

"Hello, Dad."

"Figured I'd better open the door for you. You seemed to have forgotten how to do it."

"I...couldn't decide if I should knock."

And just like that, the fierceness left his expression. "No," he said softly. "You should never knock." His voice shook. "You're always welcome here."

A dam broke inside her as she flung herself into his arms. "I'm sorry," she sobbed, pressing her face against his shirt. He smelled so achingly familiar, a mixture of sunshine, soap and pipe tobacco.

He held her close and patted her back. "I'm the one

who's sorry," he said, his voice even gruffer than before. "I didn't really mean for you to go away, Keely-girl. I was…hasty."

"You were just being a dad," she said, her voice muffled against his shirt. "I couldn't expect you to be overjoyed with what I did."

"I'll admit you did test my patience."

She smiled against his shirt. "You tested mine, too." She lifted her head and gazed at his beloved face with watery eyes. "But maybe we can start over."

He shook his head. "That would mean throwing out all the good things along with the bad. You gave me plenty of joy, too. So we aren't starting over. We're just going on from here."

"Okay." She took a deep breath and felt her body fill with a kind of peace she hadn't known in years. "Where's B.J.?"

"Right here."

Keely disengaged herself from her father and turned to see her sister standing there with tears in her eyes. Keely barely recognized B.J. She was actually wearing *makeup*, and she'd cut her hair. No more single braid down the back. Instead, her hair curled softly around her face. She hadn't given up her jeans, but she'd replaced her usual faded denim shirt with a sexy halter top.

With a squeal of delight, Keely ran over to grab her. "My God, look at you!" She hugged her sister, held her away to admire her some more, then hugged her again. "Jonas is *so* lucky."

"I think so," B.J. said.

"I definitely think so," Jonas said from the doorway. "How're you doing, Keely?"

"Fabulous." Her heart full, she walked over and gave Jonas a hug, too. He'd always been a little too handsome for his own good, with his thick brown hair and laughing hazel eyes. In the ten years since she'd last seen him he'd become even more attractive. He and B.J. were a stunning couple.

"Now that Jonas has shown up, I'm gonna go find us some beers," her father announced as he started toward the kitchen.

"Need help?" B.J. asked.

Keely wished she had the nerve to offer, but the truce was too new and fragile to risk being alone again with her father.

"I'll take care of it," her father said. "You kids go on out to the porch and catch up on your news."

"He sounds so happy," Keely said as they trooped outside the way they used to when her dad had promised them a Popsicle.

"He is happy," B.J. said. "All he's been talking about for the past week is you coming home."

"Oh, he's added a few comments on the wedding," Jonas said with a chuckle as he pulled B.J. down next to him on the swing. "Especially about how much we're spending on it." He glanced up at Keely and patted the swing. "Come on. There's plenty of room, and I've never been opposed to having a babe on each side of me."

"Thanks, anyway." Keely leaned up against the porch railing. "I just want to stand here and get used to the sight of you two together."

"Amazing, isn't it?" Jonas said with a grin. "Who'd have thought I'd end up with such a goddess?"

"Not me, that's for sure," said a deep male voice behind Keely.

She turned to see Noah coming up the walk. Immediately her heart began to pound. "Hi, there," she said, trying to sound all breezy and big-city.

"Hi, yourself." He gave her an easy smile. "I might have known you'd roll up in a red Mustang convertible. I'll bet you had the top down and the RPMs up all the way through town."

It sounded like a perfectly innocent comment, but when

she glanced into his eyes, she knew there was sexual in-
nuendo written all over it. And her body heated, right on
schedule. So that was how he intended to play it.

Well, she knew how to play that game, too. She might
even be better at it than he was. "Of course," she said,
smiling back at him. "And if you're a good boy maybe I'll
give you a ride before I leave."

Noah gulped and Keely mentally chalked up one for her
side.

"Woo-hoo!" Jonas yelled. "Keely's back!"

19

AT FOUR THE NEXT AFTERNOON Noah stood next to his brother at the altar of the Saguaro Junction Community Church. All eyes were supposed to be on the bride coming down the aisle on her father's arm, but Noah's attention kept straying to the woman sitting in the left front pew.

He wondered if she stood out in this crowd as much as he imagined, or if his agitated state of mind only made it seem that way. No, it wasn't his imagination. She really did look like an orchid plopped in the middle of a field of daisies and sunflowers. Her color-of-sin hair was one reason. That deep, foxy red wasn't common in these parts. Add in her traffic-stopping figure wrapped in a leaf-green halter dress and gold hoop earrings that nearly touched the golden skin of her shoulders, and you had a spectacular sight.

If he'd expected her to melt into the landscape so he could kid himself that she belonged here, he could forget that fantasy right now. The minute he'd seen that cherry-red car, he'd realized his mistake. That red car had flashed like a stoplight, warning him to back off.

Of course, he hadn't been able to do that, obsessed as he was with her. So instead he'd needled her every chance he could get, and she'd fired right back at him with that smart mouth of hers. He was pretty well disgusted with himself. His tactics for getting her attention weren't much more sophisticated than they had been at sixteen when he'd put a frog down her blouse.

Still, he couldn't seem to stop his sophomoric attempts to get her riled, and none of them seemed to be working worth a damn. So here they were at his brother's wedding, Keely sitting in that wooden pew looking totally together and ravishing, and him turning into a heat-seeking missile counting down to launch. His need to make love to her was making him irrational about their relationship, or lack of one, and he vaguely realized that just enough to know that a hot babe like Keely was not interested in settling down on the ranch to play erotic games with him for the rest of her life. So now with that dream in the toilet, all he could think was that she'd leave tomorrow and return to her big-city job, and he would never, ever touch her naked body again.

Oh, sure, she'd come back once in a while for a visit, but by then the gulf between them would be like the Grand Canyon. His last opportunity was tonight, when they only had to cross a little irrigation ditch.

He thought he could talk her into an encore performance if he could get her alone. She'd been avoiding being alone with him, but avoidance had been easy with all the wedding stuff going on. The wedding would be over soon. Maybe sometime during the reception he'd get his chance. They had already set a precedent for wedding-reception hanky-panky. She might still be tuned to that channel.

If he got lucky—and for the first time in his life that phrase really meant something to him—then he only had to remember one thing: He must not, under any circumstances, no matter how fantastic the experience, let it slip that he loved her.

KEELY HAD FORGOTTEN how hot an Arizona summer could be, even at nine o'clock at night. Noah, Jonas and Arch had installed a misting system under the canopy they'd erected for the reception, but it didn't affect the temperature much. Still, having the reception at the ranch in an outdoor setting had allowed more people to come, and the whole town had turned out. Apparently everyone was perfectly willing to sweat in order to be here.

To be fair, part of her discomfort was her own fault. She would have stayed *mucho* cooler if she hadn't insisted on dancing every blessed number the band played. But that wouldn't have been her style.

Besides, she needed to stay busy in order to forget that look she'd seen today on Noah's face. He'd spent a fair amount of time glancing her way during the ceremony, and his speculative, worried frown told her more clearly than any words could have that he'd figured out she really didn't belong here.

The rebel in her had decided to underline that opinion and put about five exclamation points after it. The woman in her was trying to hold her heart together. Just about the time Noah had formed his opinion that she had no business staying in Saguaro Junction, she'd begun to think maybe she wanted to, after all. Murphy's Law.

She'd enjoyed being home more than she ever would have imagined and had begun to think of what it would be like to live here again. Yes, she would stand out, but while that had seemed terrible at nineteen, it sounded like fun at twenty-nine. She seemed to have outgrown the need to blend in.

Nor would she have to give up her career. She could use the move to reposition herself at a different type of magazine, maybe one that ran exotic-travel features. Two publications she was thinking of were based in New York, but now that she had a decent résumé, she wouldn't necessarily have to spend much time at the office. In fact, she could live anywhere there was Internet access. Twin Boulders had Internet access.

But she'd figured out from Noah's expression during the wedding that he didn't share any part of her reworked vision for the future. And so at the reception she'd flirted and laughed and completely ignored the only man she cared to build a future with. Outrageous behavior had always been her protection and it would serve her well again.

Inevitably the band took a break. Thanking her latest conquest, she slipped away from him and headed over toward her sister. In her effort to forget Noah, she didn't want to miss spending time with B.J. On the way over, she grabbed a glass of champagne and a paper napkin from a table. She wiped the napkin over the cool moisture on the flute and dabbed it against her throat.

B.J. motioned her to a couple of folding chairs. "Whew," she said, sinking down to the chair and arranging the full skirt of her wedding dress. "Maybe we should have waited until November for this shindig."

"Jonas wouldn't have stood for it," Keely said with a grin. "That man wants you bad."

"Yeah, he does." B.J.'s gaze wandered over to where Jonas stood talking with Noah. "But I had to get around his preconceptions before he realized he was crazy about me."

"Now that you've brought it up, I'm dying to know how you managed that."

B.J. turned to her, looking virginal and pure in her white dress and lacy veil. "Anonymous sex."

Keely nearly dropped her champagne flute. "Excuse me?"

"In a bad rainstorm I dodged into one of those caves we used to play in when we were kids. My horse had run away, so when Jonas ducked into the same dark cave, he didn't know anyone was in there."

Keely laughed. "You must have scared the living daylights out of him."

"I did, but when I realized he didn't know it was me, I pretended to be someone else and seduced him."

"No way!"

"Yep. I did."

Keely stared at her sister in admiration. "Way to go, sis!"

B.J. grinned. "It gets better. Before he left the cave, we agreed to meet secretly, and each time I made him wear a blindfold so he wouldn't know who I was."

"Get outta town!" Keely shook her head in amazement.

"You had total control of the situation. Now, that sounds like something I'd do."

"I know." B.J. looked smug. "In fact, many times along the way I asked myself what you would do, and I did that. I had a blast."

"Cool." She smiled at her sister. "I'm so glad you made it happen. You're perfect for each other."

"So it seems." B.J. gazed at Keely. "Listen, you can tell me to mind my own business if you want, but...what's up with you and Noah? I keep picking up on all kinds of tension between you two."

Keely swallowed, thinking how much she longed for a confidante. And after all, her sister had confessed her secret. "We, um, sort of got involved in Vegas."

"You *did?*" B.J.'s blue eyes glowed with eagerness. "That sure explains a lot about his weird mood lately, and the singing telegram."

"Yeah, you told me he was the one who thought of that."

"He not only thought of it, he was there."

Keely was sure she must have misunderstood. "What do you mean?"

"I mean that he flew to L.A. and supervised the whole stunt, to make sure it went the way we'd planned. He stood just outside the door of your office where he could see you, but I guess you never noticed him."

Keely was stunned. "No. No, I sure didn't."

"He pretended his being there was necessary, and we went along with it because we could tell from the beginning that he wanted to go over there and see you. I wondered at the time if something had happened in Vegas."

"Yeah, something happened in Vegas." Keely sighed. "But we don't belong together. He doesn't want a wild child like me."

"Oh, you're dead wrong there."

"Trust me, I'm not. His expression when he looks at me tells it all."

"Mmm." B.J. glanced over to where Jonas and Noah stood. "By the way, can I have a sip of your champagne?"

"Sure, but I can get you a whole glass. I—"

"Don't want a whole glass. I plan to treat Jonas to some fun and games tonight, and I don't want to be fuzzy headed for that." She winked as she handed the flute back to Keely. "Which brings me back to your comment. I don't know what you're reading into Noah's expression, but it's my opinion every man wants a wild child. Jonas sure does, and I'm having a great time turning into one."

"But that's just it—on the outside you don't seem wild at all. You know that old saying about being a naughty girl in the bedroom and a lady in the parlor. That's what a man wants in a wife."

"Did Noah tell you that?"

"No, but—"

"Excuse me for saying so, Keely, but for a big sister and a city girl, you have some ideas that are seriously out of date. From what I've seen, Noah would take you any way he could get you."

"Then you're not looking close enough," Keely said. "Haven't you noticed how standoffish and stuffy he's been tonight?"

"Well, duh!" B.J. said. "That's *exactly* how he acted after that incident in the barn when you were sixteen and, according to Jonas, Noah wanted you so bad that summer he finally went rodeoing to try and get you out of his system. That's how he gets when he wants something he thinks he can't have—stuffy."

Keely stared at her sister. "He wanted me? But he was so awful to me!"

"You were sixteen," B.J. said gently. "A guy with principles as strong as Noah's couldn't have taken you up on your offer. But turning you down nearly killed him, which he disguised by being standoffish."

"Wow." Keely thought of how she'd tortured herself with that rejection. Then she'd tortured Noah for revenge.

"I guess I was so wrapped up in my own pain I didn't even think he might be suffering, too."

"Feel better now?" B.J. asked.

"You have no idea." Her self-esteem felt healthier by the minute.

"Oh, I think I do. I needed to know Jonas had suffered a little, too, after all he'd put me through."

"I understand." Keely cast a sideways glance at Noah. Was it really possible that he not only wanted her, but that he loved her?

"Listen, I have to warn you that Noah's superglued to this place," B.J. said. "So the question is, could you come back?"

"Maybe." Keely desperately wanted to believe B.J. was right about Noah's feelings, but if she acted on the information and her sister was wrong, life wouldn't be worth living. "I mean, I might come back, if it wouldn't freak everybody out."

"I would dearly love it and so would Dad. And this town could use some freaking out, if you know what I mean."

Keely took a sip of champagne. "Are you sure? From what I've heard, Mom was kinda flamboyant, and I don't think she was all that well received."

"The town's grown up a lot," B.J. said. "Besides, you've already done the ultimate with that centerfold," she added with a grin. "Whatever else you come up with will be anticlimactic."

"Well, shoot, that's no fun."

B.J. chuckled. "Or maybe not anticlimactic. What do I know? Anyway, here's the deal—you have to take a chance and come on to Noah, instead of ignoring him like you've been doing. That won't work."

Keely opened her mouth to object on the grounds that she might not survive the crash if Noah rejected her again.

B.J. held up her hand to stave off her comment. "You don't have to say it. Believe me, I know what it could cost you if the plan turns sour. I had to gamble, too, with no guarantee of winning.'' She reached for Keely's hand and gave it a squeeze. ''Can a little sister offer a big sister some advice?''

Keely managed a smile, although her chest was tight with anxiety. ''Sure.''

''That stuff we were told when we were teenagers is wrong. The way to a man's heart is not through his stomach. You have to aim a little lower.''

Keely looked at B.J. and they both began to giggle. It felt like old times.

NOAH HAD BEEN LOOKING for an opportunity to get Keely alone all night, but she seemed determined to dance with every man at the reception except him, and when she wasn't doing that she was hanging out with B.J. or talking with Arch. Apparently she was still trying to avoid him.

As he was wondering how to work around that, lo and behold, she walked in his direction. He knew he'd better act fast before she veered off to ask some other cowboy to dance, or one of them trotted over to ask her. Striding forward, he caught her arm.

Sensation zinged straight to his crotch. It was the first time he'd touched her since Vegas, and his body certainly remembered what to do with the information transmitted by her warm skin.

He looked into her eyes and was encouraged by the glow he saw there. ''Could we go somewhere to talk?''

''We could.'' Her voice was low and seductive. ''But let's not start any gossip like we did at the last reception.''

That had to mean her mind was on the same track as his. His blood heated.

''Let me leave first,'' she murmured. ''Give me five minutes or so before you leave. I'll tell people I'm going back over to Dad's to freshen up. I'll meet you there.''

''In your dad's house?'' He wasn't so sure about that. He'd feel damn uncomfortable doing what he had in mind in her father's little cabin.

"Of course not, silly. I'll meet you by my car."

Her car. Now, that had possibilities. "Okay."

"See you in a few." Then she walked away from him with that little swing to her hips that always drove him around the bend.

Noah had never spent a longer five minutes in his life. He had no idea what he said to the people he talked to during those five minutes, and he hoped nobody noticed how often he glanced at his watch. He checked his pocket at least twenty times to make sure the condom he'd stashed there earlier hadn't somehow disappeared. Once again he was wearing rented clothes, and rented pockets could have holes.

Finally he figured he could start after her. His excuse for leaving was to go find a bottle of aspirin. Consequently he walked in the front door of the ranch house and then slipped out the back. On the short trek over to her dad's, he recited instructions to himself. *Enjoy the moment. Remember the condom. Don't tell her you love her.*

He didn't see her beside the car, but he sure as heck saw a pair of black lace panties dangling from the radio antenna. His heart beat like crazy. Softly he called her name.

"Back here," she said in a low voice.

He could barely breathe as he peered into the back seat of the Mustang. The light wasn't very good, but good enough that he could see that she lay there naked, her dress rolled neatly and tucked under her head for a pillow, her knees bent delicately so that she'd fit on the seat.

Smiling at him, she cupped her breasts in both hands. "It's so hot. I could hardly wait to get out of those clothes."

His tongue didn't seem to want to work.

"Is this what you had in mind when you said we needed to talk?" she asked.

Still unable to speak, he nodded.

"I thought so." Then she slid one hand between her thighs and caressed herself. "This weather just makes you want to be bad, doesn't it?"

With a soft moan, he reached for the car's door handle.

"Wait."

"Wait?" Now, there was a terrible word if he'd ever heard one.

"Not yet," she whispered.

Not yet. Two more words that should be wiped right out of the language. He gripped the handle and his voice was a harsh croak. "What do you mean, not yet?"

"What's the password?"

He felt like someone was trying to strangle him. "Password?"

"Tell me the password and you can come in. I'll give you a hint. It has four letters." Her hand fluttered between her thighs. "Mmm, that feels good."

"*Keely.*"

"*Four* letters, Noah."

He gripped the door handle so hard his fingers hurt. And all the while he was drawn to the indistinct but riveting sight of her fingers gliding into the place that he'd had wet dreams about. "I'm thinking of a four-letter word, all right," he ground out, struggling for breath. "What is this game, Keely?"

"It's a shakedown, Noah. Here's a big hint. The word rhymes with the name of a bird."

His jaw clenched. "A duck."

Her soft, musical laughter rode the night breeze. "Now, there's a man for you. Not a duck. A different bird."

"Damn it, I don't know anything about birds. And I—"

"A dove."

"A *dove?*" His brain stalled. Only one four-letter word rhymed with dove. And last he knew, she hadn't been interested in hearing that word. Hope surged in his chest. "Okay, a dove it is." He opened the door.

"What are you doing?" she said. "You didn't say the password."

"I will," he said fervently. "Trust me, I will." He nudged off his shoes, grateful that he wasn't wearing boots.

Then he took off the rest of his clothes, heaving them piece by piece into the front seat of the car. At the last minute he remembered to take the condom out of his pants pocket.

"But that's the rule," she said. "No password, no nooky."

"That's what you think." He put on the condom and climbed into the car, hoping she wasn't serious enough about this rule business to kick him in the balls. "I'm the kind of guy who breaks rules." Kneeling on the edge of the seat, he braced one hand against the convertible's boot as he leaned over her. "And I happen to think that's the kind of guy who turns you on."

"Is that right?" She gazed up at him, seeming disinclined to kick him. In fact, she seemed quite glad to have him there.

"Yeah, that's right." If only he could see her face better. He tried to plan his next move, but he couldn't see much of her at all. His body was casting a shadow over the very spot he was aiming for. He drew back. "Put your foot down."

"I was trying to put my foot down by making you say the password, but you're not playing by the rules, so—"

"I mean your actual foot. Put it on the floor."

"Oh." She followed his directions.

Okay. He had clearance. It was cramped quarters, yet worth every charley horse he might get in the process. But as he leaned toward her, his shadow fell on her willing body once again and he fumbled a bit.

And then, wonder of wonders, she took his sheathed penis in her hand and guided him toward paradise. But right before he reached heaven, she stopped.

"What's the password?" she whispered. "You promised to say it."

"Love," he murmured, rolling the word on his tongue, tasting its sweetness. "I love you, Keely."

"That's the password," she said, guiding him forward. "Now you can come in."

He slid home with a sigh. Nothing was equal to the feeling of being right here. Nothing. But a million questions buzzed in his brain. "Now what?"

She stroked his back. "I thought we had that part down. In, out, in, out. It works very well with us."

In spite of the enormous significance of the moment, he couldn't keep from grinning. "I mean, now what do we do about us? You don't want to live here."

"Yes, I do."

He leaned down, trying to see her face better. "You do? Just like that? Why?"

"Because I love *you,* you big dope."

"You love me?" Incredible. She'd said it. He decided to ignore the *big dope* part and focus on the *I love you* part. Besides, she was right. He was a big dope for not tracking her down years ago.

"Yes, I really, really love you," she said. "And I know I stick out like a sore thumb in this town, but if you can deal with that, I sure can."

"You love me." He couldn't believe that a man could be this happy. What a perfect night. He began gently to rock. "If you love me, I can deal with anything. Besides, you're not a sore thumb. You're a Ferrari in a world of Fords. This town needs you in it. And I need to be in you. It all works out."

"That sounds nice."

"I'll think up more nice things to say when I'm not so busy. Oh, God, but you feel good. Let's have a small wedding."

She picked up his rhythm and tightened around him in that special way of hers. "Let's have a big one. A blowout."

"Fine." He was through being chatty. He just wanted to revel in the sensation of pushing into the warmest place on earth while a cool breeze tickled his butt. "A big wedding it is."

"That was easy."

"You keep letting me do this and you can have anything you want."

"Then stop right this minute."

He froze in mid-thrust. "Stop?"

"Pull out a minute. Then I promise you can come back, and you'll have oh so much more fun. Please, Noah. If you love me."

He did love her, so he pulled out.

Before he realized what she meant to do, she'd reached between them and slid the condom right off, slick as a whistle. Then she tossed it out of the car.

"Hey!" he said. "That was my only one! I thought you liked the ribbed kind."

"Well, I did, but you said I could have whatever I wanted, right?"

"Yeah, but—"

"I want babies, Noah. Now come to momma, big boy."

With a groan of pure bliss, he did exactly that.

Epilogue

"*YES!*" Keely grinned in triumph as she read an e-mail from her editor, Jim Stevens, at *Prime Destinations* magazine.

"That sounds like my cue." Noah appeared in the doorway of the ranch-house bedroom he'd converted into an office for Keely. "Have you been downloading from that Kama Sutra site again?"

"Nope. This is better." She glanced up as he leaned casually against the door frame and wondered how she'd ever imagined life on this ranch could be boring. She'd enjoyed more innovative sex and pure bliss in the past six months with Noah than in all her years of being single.

What she hadn't thought of he had. They'd made love in every room inside and most of the secluded areas outside. A major bathroom remodel had resulted in a large whirlpool bath plus a huge shower with nozzles at interesting levels and bench seats at an appropriate height for fun and games. Mirrored closet doors in the bedroom reflected a four-poster bed dressed in satin sheets.

They'd also enjoyed some spectacular, sensual episodes when he'd gone along on some of her travel assignments. But he'd never encountered an assignment like the one she'd landed this time. She smiled and hit the print command on her computer.

"Better, huh?" His gaze warmed as it slid over her. "Am I going to need props for this one?"

"Only a suitcase."

His eyebrows lifted. "If I'm going to make love to you on top of a suitcase, we'd better look around and see if I have any hard-sided ones left. Those soft-sided jobs will cave in for sure.''

With a laugh she reached for the hard copy of the e-mail. ''I don't know what benefit we could get from making love on a suitcase, but I'm willing to give it some thought. In the meantime, take a look at this.'' She handed him the piece of paper.

He scanned it before meeting her gaze. ''A nude beach resort?''

''I've always been curious about those places, so I proposed the idea to Jim. I just got clearance.'' She challenged him with a bold glance.

''And I suppose as the writer covering this you will have to be...''

''Naked. Yes. But that's okay. Then I won't have to buy any maternity beachwear.'' She paused. ''Wanna come along, cowboy?''

She watched him struggle with the concept of a nude vacation destination. No doubt he would always approach unusual sexual ideas with some hesitation. That made him Noah, after all, and made his eventual capitulation even more exciting. She'd also learned that once he embraced a new idea, he gave it all he had.

''I double dare you,'' she said softly.

His eyes sparkled in response to her taunt, yet still he hesitated. ''I don't know, Keely. I mean, walking around without any—''

''Don't think of it as walking around. Think of it as lying on a towel on soft, warm sand, rubbing oil all over my body, me rubbing oil all over yours.'' She stood and moved toward him.

''I'd have to spend the whole vacation on my stomach. I'd have to dig a little hole in the sand for my—''

''A private stretch of warm sand.'' She began unbuttoning her blouse. When they weren't expecting visitors, like this afternoon, she skipped wearing a bra. ''I checked out the site online, and they have all sorts of intimate spots where couples can be alone."

"They do?" His attention drifted to her unbuttoned blouse. "You're not playing fair, Keely. You know I can't think when you do that."

"Don't think. Use your imagination. Picture a secluded little cove, soft sand, thick towels, each of us warm and slick with oil…everywhere…." She pulled her blouse from the waistband of her jeans. Lately she'd had to leave the top button of her jeans unfastened to accommodate the baby growing inside her. Noah liked that, because then she was even more accessible to him. He loved to pull the zipper of her jeans down and stroke her round belly whenever he had a chance.

With a gusty sigh he reached for her, slipping his hands inside the lapels of her blouse and caressing her breasts. "Okay, you win. I'm going."

"Good." She tingled with anticipation of pleasures to come, both long range and more immediate ones. He would make love to her now, because he was surely thinking about that nude beach and getting hot. She closed her eyes the better to enjoy his touch. "I promise you won't be sorry."

"Easy for you to say." He pulled her close and leaned down to nuzzle her neck. "I'll probably sunburn my ass and won't be able to ride for a week."

His mouth could make her crazy, no matter where on her body he chose to place it. "And that would be bad because…?"

"Because then I wouldn't be able to work. I'd have to let Jonas do everything while I hung around here, and—" He paused and began to laugh. "I see your point."

"I thought you might." She drew him toward her desk. "Now let me emphasize it."

"On the desk?" His voice vibrated with excitement.

"On your big, old executive desk." With a sweep of her hand she sent pages flying. "After all, it's on the list."

He unzipped his jeans. "I love that list," he said in a

voice roughened with desire. "Think we'll ever get through it?"

She shoved her jeans and panties down and stepped out of them. "Not if we keep adding to it like we've been doing."

He lifted her to the polished surface of the desk. "Think the baby will slow us down?"

"Nope."

"Me neither. Now open your legs for me, woman. Time to cross this one off the list." As she complied, he cupped her bottom in both hands and held her gaze as he slid deep. "Ahhh...that is so sweet, Keely. Every time. Every blessed time."

"I know."

He settled in tighter. "Think we'll be this crazy when we're eighty?"

"Crazier," she murmured. "Now love me, you wild man. Love me good."

And he did.